My Cousin the Writer

First published in the UK in 2002 by
Dewi Lewis Publishing
8 Broomfield Road
Heaton Moor
Stockport SK4 4ND
+44 (0)161 442 9450

www.dewilewispublishing.com

ISBN: 1-899235-09-4

Design & artwork production: Dewi Lewis Publishing
Printed and bound in Great Britain by
Biddles Ltd, Guildford and King's Lynn

9   8   7   6   5   4   3   2   1

My Cousin the Writer

Paul Binding

DEWI LEWIS
PUBLISHING

PART ONE

Documents

They sat confronting me, my cousin and my old friend, a kangaroo court in a land of elk, bear and lynx. They'd both of them, they told me, wanted for so long to make me realise what I was (or, at any rate, had been) – devious, selfish, stuck up. I'd been so ignorant too, even about *The Parkers* itself... Beyond the windows the continuing snow came between us and the sombre mountains that walled in the valley.

Ian Armitage and Neil Micklewright from the past.

'Ian,' I said, 'there were times when we got on together. You'd refer to me as "my cousin the writer".'

The hard, mocking laughter from the two of them which greeted this remark is responsible, more than any other one factor, I now think, for my decision, once I was home, to recreate (as a writer would) that period of my life. Cousin and friend were cooperative, I have to admit, lending me letters and other documents. Each assured me, however, that he would take no interest at all in what I produced.

Perhaps I don't blame them for that.

At the top of the pile as I work now is an old English Composition exercise-book. On its purple cover in Gothic lettering (below an ersatz crest and motto) are the words TANBURY GRAMMAR SCHOOL, and underneath these, in thick-nibbed italic, my younger cousin's name and form – I. J. ARMITAGE 3A, AUTUMN TERM 1957. During that term Ian was asked to write an essay on 'A Favourite Programme'.

5

A favourite radio programme of mine is *The Parkers* which comes on the BBC Home Service from 4.30 to 4.45 every weekday. I hardly ever miss an episode. This is really because my Mum likes the programme so much. When I come home from school each afternoon, she's got tea ready, and we have it in our sitting-room so we can listen to it together. *(Teacher's comment in margin: What does this second 'it' refer to? Not to the tea presumably?)* There are times when I think my Mum is a bit Parker-mad, but that's understandable when you think how interesting this serial always is.

The Parkers is about a vicar and his family who live in a suburb of London called Greenfield End. The announcer always says after telling us it's half-past four: "And now it's time for *The Parkers*, a chronicle of everyday life in a vicar's family." It really does seem like everyday life too, even though there is a multitude of excitements and often highly mysterious happenings. After the signature tune (which, *Radio Times* said recently, is a country dance tune called 'Sellinger's Round') Mrs Parker – Elizabeth – tells us a few things *(Comment: What meaning does 'things' ever really have? Avoid!)* about what's been going on since she last spoke to us, and then we're ready to move into the drama.

Her husband, the Rev. Derek Parker of St. Luke's, is the sort of vicar everybody would like to have. I wish there was someone as good-humoured and kind in Tanbury. Of course he has his faults. He is extremely forgetful. There was one very funny episode in which he posted his gloves instead of an important letter, and sometimes he lets his wife do too much work, at least that's what my Mum thinks. Quite often she has to rescue him *(Comment: is 'she' your mother or the vicar's wife?)* from the muddles he's made, but she's never really angry with him because nobody could be. At times he seems almost a saint, as in the matter of the old woman and the stolen money.

The Parkers have a daughter, Gillian, who has just got married and a son, Davey, who qualified last year as a vet. and has just joined a practice guess where? Greenfield End itself! Davey hasn't married; he says he's never going to, but he goes out with many girls. A new character in the programme whom we all like very much is Tom Cavan who has come to finish off his training as a vet with Davey. Davey gives him lots of advice, and not only about animal matters!!

Here are some of the Parkers' friends; the local doctor, Hector Macdonald, who is Scottish and a terrible pessimist, and his daughter, Minty, whom he brought up himself; a Welshman called Glyn Pritchard who runs a private hotel, The Elms, though he really prefers cats to people; and a famous writer, Kevin O'Flynn (uncle of Tom Cavan, by the way). There's also the curate, James Hedley, who is far too shy for his own good, and the church-worker, Miss Venables, who's dreadfully bossy and nosy. And we mustn't forget the Parkers' cleaning-lady, Mrs Bobbington, who's always going on about her health, especially her corns, and their gardener, Verges, who is almost always grumpy but is greatly valued for his green fingers and earthy wisdom.

The people in *The Parkers* all speak most characteristically, which is something I like a lot about this programme. You can recognise them all very easily from their favourite expressions, and this makes you feel at home with them. For instance Glyn Pritchard is always saying 'Look you!' and 'There's nice!' and 'A cat, boyo, has got more sense in one of its whiskers than a human being in the whole of his body!' And Kevin O'Flynn often remarks: 'It's melancholy I'm feeling today, with so many memories from my boyhood in Limerick *pressing* so hard upon me!'

The programme, as you can see, is exceedingly amusing, and it never fails to leave you wondering what's going to happen next, so I can get quite cross when the signature tune comes on at the end and I know I'll be learning nothing else that day.

Every Friday, when it's all over, the announcer reads out the cast-list: 'The part of Elizabeth Parker was played by Enid Berridge; that of the Rev. Derek Parker by Derek Parker,' (that's a weird coincidence, isn't it?) 'that of Tom Cavan by Neil Micklewright' and so on and so on. But I never feel they are actors, I think they're all real people who could be my friends and relatives. The chief script-writer, who also devised the programme, is someone called Verity Orchard. I think Verity Orchard has a very fine imagination and great abilities, and she has given pleasure to many thousands, nay, millions, including my mother and myself.

[The Ian who wrote this – round, rosy-cheeked, snub-nosed face

7

offset by short-cut darkish curly hair, and neat body that served him well for running, swimming, cycling – can he still be found inside today's Ian, as in one of those Russian dolls you go on lifting up to find the inner one? I suppose he's asking the same sort of question about me, and answering himself sadly: 'Yes!'

About three weeks after the above-quoted, Ian was given another essay-topic, 'A Person I Admire'. And can you credit it (in the light of his later judgements)? He chose me for his subject.]

(ii)

Though there are a number of people who command my admiration, including several I have never met, like Albert Schweitzer and Yehudi Menuhin, the person I admire most of all is my cousin, Bruno Armitage. He's six years older than me, and though I've known him all my life, I've never really had much to do with him. But ever since the last week in September he has been living with us here in Tanbury, for reasons I will shortly give. I can honestly say that the more I see him, the more I admire him.

I'd like to say something about what he was like before, otherwise you won't be able to appreciate the changes that have come over him, and understand why I feel about him as I do.

Bruno is the son of my dead father's older brother, Uncle Raymond, an Industrial Consultant who runs his business from London and lives near Primrose Hill. He divorced his wife, Cynthia, Bruno's mother, when I myself was only a baby. (She emigrated to America; Mum once said it was a case of good riddance to bad rubbish.) Bruno has had rather a lonely life, with Uncle Raymond off on business such a lot, and housekeepers more like dragons than human beings (at least so Bruno himself says). Bruno was sent away when he was very young to a posh preparatory school *(Comment: There is no place for the word 'posh' in a serious essay!)* and after that to a swank public school called Riverbury, over in Northamptonshire. Riverbury consists principally of an enormous mansion built in Palladian style and set in a big park, with woods and lakes and even mock-temples. Sometimes my mother

8

and I would go and visit him there on a Sunday, as Riverbury (as you probably know) is not so very far from here. But Bruno never seemed particularly pleased to see us, at least that's what I thought, I don't think my Mum noticed.

Bruno didn't do well at school, and there was a lot of bother when he was caught cheating in an exam. Later they said *(Comment: Who are 'they'? How can the reader be expected to know?)* that it wasn't a good idea for him to take 'A' Levels, he just wasn't academic enough, but take them he did, at Uncle Raymond's insistence, and he failed them, though Bruno himself thinks there was probably a mix-up, and the markers got his papers confused with someone else's. Bruno appeared on the stage in several of Riverbury's school productions, and I thought he was pretty good, but other people said he wasn't as good as he obviously thought he was, and that every time he walked on, you could see he wanted to steal the thunder.

In the holidays Uncle Raymond would send Bruno to camps and on courses and exchanges, but he never appeared to enjoy any of these very much, though he can dance and ski and play tennis with the best of them. Many people find Bruno good-looking. He is of average height and rather thin, but he has, as he says himself, an admirably supple and muscular body. His hair, like mine, is curly, but it's red in colour; he has greeny-brown eyes, and an extremely freckled skin. Apparently his teeth are just about perfect, and a dentist he went to was so impressed he made a cast of them. Bruno mentions this quite often. He is very fond indeed of clothes. He got his father to give him a generous allowance for them, though my Mum says that the reason Uncle Raymond agreed to this so readily was that he was quite a 'masher' himself in the past, just as my own dad was. One funny thing about Bruno is his great liking for photographs of himself; he'll stick them all round his room. He has never collected things like me so he has little interest in the stamps, Roman coins, fossils, shells etc. in which I myself delight.

The big change in my cousin's life came the day he received the letter telling him to register for National Service. Mum had said: Surely Bruno'll defer this as so many boys are doing now. But Bruno said, no, he really fancied a spell in the Navy. He had no doubts about the Senior Service being of all the forces the right one for him. He knew he'd look good in uniform, and he'd probably get sent to the Mediterranean where there'd be both sun and action. Uncle Raymond said, well, it would perhaps give him time to decide what he really did want to do, he was certainly clueless enough at the moment. Two weeks afterwards Bruno was told to present himself for a Medical, and here it was that he – and all the family – received a tremendous shock.

He was found to have a tubercular patch on his lung, and they said *(Comment: 'They, they', who can these overworked 'they' be now?)* that not only was he unfit for National Service, he would have to undergo a further medical examination. So he was sent to the best specialist who prescribed a course of deep-ray treatment, accompanied by exercises and rest.

Uncle Raymond was so worried he spent hours talking to my Mum on the telephone about the matter. That would surprise you if you knew them both, as my uncle obviously considers himself a higher class sort of person, and has always been distinctly snooty to my mother. Then came another surprise. Uncle Raymond asked if Bruno could come and live with us in Tanbury for the duration of his treatment. He said he thought it was essential that Bruno had a family background at this stage, you never knew what he might get up to otherwise, and he could have his treatment just as well at the Tanbury Royal as at any London hospital. He could re-take his 'A' Levels through correspondence courses with the Metropolitan College of St Albans and part-time attendance at Tanbury Tech. Mum agreed to this proposal straightaway.

I don't mind confessing I was really excited when I heard this news. My father died when I was five years old (I don't remember him very well, though I try hard – Mum said he never got used to the War being over). Since then there's just been my mother and myself in our house in Church Terrace. All these years I've been longing for a companion, for someone a little nearer my age to be around the place. But then I remembered how Bruno had behaved when we visited him at Riverbury, and I felt very unsure how him coming to live with us would work out.

Well, I needn't have worried. Bruno never tires of telling us how delighted he is to be here. Mum says it's a real pleasure having him about; he lights the house up. Of course there were things he had to get used to; he still doesn't like laying out the dessert fork and spoon *above* the table mats, as Mum always does, or calling a certain room the 'toilet'. But not once has he complained about what has befallen him, though now and again he will refer to his disappointment at not being in Her Majesty's Navy, or to the 'gigantic bore' of having to go thrice weekly to the hospital. Then you realise what he's going through. But mostly his spirits are very cheerful. He has – naturally! – a room to himself, and he's decorated it with masses of photos of himself, more even than I'd seen before. He whistles when using the bathroom or helping Mum in the kitchen, and his favourite tunes are 'Last Train to San Fernando', 'All Shook Up', and 'Whole Lotta Shakin' Goin' On'. He's rather picky about his food – he doesn't like cheese or tomato, and declares that the very sight of ham or bacon makes him physically sick – but he eats what things *(Comment: Please, NO!!)* he does like very eagerly, and is always paying my Mum compliments, especially on her puddings and cakes: 'This apple-pie is utterly ambrosial, Auntie Eileen!' or 'I could spend eternity putting pieces of this exquisite chocolate-cake into my mouth!'

But as far as my Mum is concerned, the really good thing about Bruno is that he shares her love of *The Parkers*. When he first came to live with us, I have to confess I was a bit embarrassed by our 4.30 date with the Vicar of Greenfield End and his family. I was even a little ashamed of my own fondness for the programme. But Bruno has turned out to be almost the greatest fan of us all. At the beginning he asked Mum to put him in the picture about the characters and what was happening to them, but he soon got to know them all and to have strong ideas about them. He and Mum love to discuss the episode when it's finished and speculate about what should happen next. Bruno's favourite characters are undoubtedly Kevin O'Flynn, the romantic Irish writer, and Kevin's nephew, Tom Cavan, whom I believe I remarked on in an earlier composition of mine as a new character to the serial, a young man who has come to Greenfield End as an apprentice vet. *(Comment: You mustn't refer back to your own essays like this. You're hardly Charles Lamb or William Hazlitt – at least not yet.)*

It certainly makes a difference to our tea-times having Bruno in the room. Three times a week tea-time coincides with him returning from the hospital. He looks dreadfully tired, and you can tell he's also horribly sore because every now and again he touches his chest and flinches with pain. But he never says anything, and Mum says she's rather surprised at this because when he was a little boy Bruno made an inordinate fuss if he so much as cut himself on brambles or got stung by nettles. But he has grown up now!

My Mum says that Bruno's room is sacrosanct, a place he and we must think of as entirely private to him. Of course I never would have dreamed of going in without knocking first, and I always try to ration the times I do even this. Mostly he seems pleased to see me. He likes showing me photographs of himself and telling me the stories behind them – skiing trips to Wengen and Chamonix, and performances on the Riverbury stage in *The Winslow Boy* and *The Tempest* and *Arms and the Man*. He's a very good story-teller in my view. Sometimes, I have to confess, I feel quite shy with him, but then there's always *The Parkers* to talk about; he has so many ideas about them and what they could be up to next.

My Mum says that Bruno is still not interested in the work he's supposed to be doing, and daydreams instead of concentrating on his reading or writing. Sometimes when you think he's poring over a book, he's doodling in the margin or even scribbbling lines of poetry. I couldn't help reading some of the latter one time I went into the room, and, because I thought them so strange, I committed them to memory immediately:

> *NINA, you whose beauty wraps*
> *My heart, as ivy doth*
> *The sap-nourished branch,*
> *I prithee, in your inestimable sweetness,*
> *Do not let your great gifts*
> *Strangle my life, my need for light!*

Bruno does seem to enjoy, however, the evening class in Spoken French that he attends twice a week at the Adult Education Centre. Mum says that she knows the reason for this, and smiles to herself, but I don't know it.

What I do know is that I am exceedingly glad that Bruno is living with us, and seems so happy in our Tanbury house, and that I hope *I* can be as brave and cheerful in the face of adversity as him if and when my time to face trials comes. I don't know how long his hospital treatment will continue, but – selfishly – I'd like it to last a long time, because it is good having a cousin in the house. In the summer holidays, when his health will surely be back to normal, I'd like the two of us to go cycling together. We could go out to Foxton Woods and the Reedrush Valley, because by then I'll surely have a new bicycle – a Raleigh Lenten Sports – that I've already dropped strong hints I want to have for my birthday in late May. And who knows what will have happened in *The Parkers* by then?

[*The other documents I have decided to include in Part One of this memoir speak for themselves.*]

(iii)
Excerpt from *The Parkers*, (Thursday, October 10, 1957)

ELIZABETH PARKER: We're all becoming very fond of young Tom Cavan, and already it's hard to imagine Greenfield End without him. He is so pleasant and cheery to everybody, even to such 'old-uns' as Derek and myself. He is doing extremely good work down at the Kennels, and his Uncle Kevin is obviously getting more and more attached to him. Reminds him, I suppose, of his own boyhood back in Limerick, even though Tom, of course, grew up in Leicester, and doesn't have a trace of a brogue. Yesterday, though, I appreciated how Tom *is* only young after all, and is not – shall I say? – altogether uninterested in the opposite sex.

(Sound of doorbell ringing, and of door being opened.)
TOM: Good morning, Mrs Parker.
ELIZABETH: Why, Tom, how nice to see you!
TOM: I've brought you half-a-dozen eggs newly laid this morning by the chickens at the Practice.

13

ELIZABETH: What a *very* kind thought, Tom, to remember such old fogeys as the Vicar and his wife.

TOM: Noone could think you an old fogey, Mrs Parker.

ELIZABETH *(laughing gently)*: Now, Tom, flattery will get you nowhere. Have you time to come in for a quick cup of coffee?

TOM: That's awfully kind of you, Mrs Parker. I'd love a cup.

(Fade. Sound of coffee being poured into mugs.)

TOM: I must say, I did enjoy that 'do' at the Parish Hall the other evening. So many nice people to meet and talk to!

ELIZABETH: I'm so glad you liked it. I suppose you must be getting to know a good many people here in Greenfield End now.

TOM: Yes, and there are some that I......*(speaking all in a rush)* Mrs Parker, that's a very nice daughter that Dr Macdonald has.

ELIZABETH: Minty?

TOM *(shyly)*: Yes, I believe that's her name.

ELIZABETH: I'm so fond of Minty, we all are. I remember when she was born. And then her poor mother dying. And Hector's great excitement when she first started to speak.

TOM: She struck me as an exceptionally sensitive sort of person. She told me she's studying nursing. I can imagine her making a wonderful nurse.

ELIZABETH: Oh, so can I! And, you know, Tom, she's never too busy to give us a hand with parish activities. She even teaches Sunday School for us when she can.

TOM: The moment I saw her, I thought: there's a very kind, unselfish sort of girl.

ELIZABETH *(slyly)*: She's extremely pretty too.

TOM *(Confused, but trying to sound casual)*: Oh, pretty... Oh...!

ELIZABETH: Now, Tom, I can't believe you haven't noticed.

TOM *(mumbling, but more confused still)*:In a sort of way...

ELIZABETH *(in a sweet, motherly voice)*: Tom, dear, there's no need to blush like that. It's the most natural thing in the world for a boy like you to find Minty Macdonald attractive.

TOM *(suddenly finding words but unable to check the emotion behind them, so that they come tumbling out)*: Oh, Mrs Parker, it isn't just that I find her attractive, she seems to me the most perfect girl in the world – everything about her, her voice, her movements, the expresions on her face, the look in her eyes. Night and day she's in my thoughts. Every morning I ask myself: will I meet Minty Macdonald today?

ELIZABETH *(with a little laugh)*: But Tom, you only met her last Thursday!

TOM: Last Thursday, was it? It can't be possible. It seems a lifetime ago!... Mrs Parker, what should I do? I'm sure she has no idea how I feel.

ELIZABETH: Well, Tom, it might not be such a very bad thing if you plucked up enough courage and gave her some idea. For all you know she may be going about saying to herself: "I like that Tom Cavan, but I don't suppose he's ever given me a thought."

TOM: Oh, Mrs Parker, do you really think that's likely?

ELIZABETH: I can't say whether it's likely or not; I'm just saying that it's perfectly possible. So why don't you give her some indication that you'd like to know her better? But... *(changing her tone to a serious one)* think about pleasing her, not overwhelming her. Take things very gently, Tom!

(At this point, the signature tune 'Sellinger's Round' starts up)

(iv)
Friday, October 11, 1957

Dear Mr Compson,

I write to thank you for an evening of the profoundest interest. Never can Tanbury W.E.A. have arranged a more enthralling talk. Many of your words on the stage-sets needed for successful productions of Shakespeare have continued to resound in my head. I firmly agree with you that the richness of Shakespeare's language has to be matched by a richness of scenery.

It was a great pleasure to be able to address a few remarks to you after your talk. Lest you have forgotten – for I know what a busy man you are, in demand everywhere – I told you of a production of *The Tempest* at my public school, Riverbury, in which I took the part of

Ferdinand. I drew many compliments. *The Northamptonshire Herald* wrote: 'We found the Ferdinand of B. Armitage most engaging – and how well he looked the part! – and, this being the case, it did not seriously matter that he once or twice muffed his cues.' During the rehearsals I gave much thought to the question of sets truly appropriate for the play, wanting as lush and marvellous an island as possible, and I even found photographs and paintings (Douanier Rousseau, for instance) to back up my ideas, (or dare I write *our* ideas?) but the producer was, I'm sorry to say, too set in conventional ways to appreciate them.

I noticed you looking at me many times during your visit to the Tanbury Municipal Rooms, and felt that you were aware of a sort of affinity between us. Perhaps I remind you of your younger self before you ascended to the heights you so rightly enjoy as Shakespearean designer.

I would greatly like to meet you again, and discuss your talk with you. For my part I feel that I have something to give to the world of culture. Of late I've suffered a sad reversal of fortune where my health is concerned, but feel confident that all will be well again ere long.

Yours in gratitude, and eagerly awaiting a reply,

Bruno Armitage

(v)

Article in *Everywoman* (week ending October 19, 1957)

Few programmes are followed with greater keenness than *The Parkers* which keeps people all over Britain captives of the radio-set while the cups that cheer but don't inebriate pleasantly rattle. But what do they know of its creator and chief script-writer, Verity Orchard? For most listeners she is nothing but a name in *Radio Times*. *Everywoman* decided to put an end to the mystery that surrounds Miss Orchard. We tracked her down to her charming house in Dorset to talk to her about her life, her work, her achievements and her hopes.

EVERYWOMAN: What gave you the idea for *The Parkers*?

V.O.: I was a vicar's daughter myself, do you see? So what was more appropriate for me, when I'd established myself as a writer, than to be recreating for millions of listeners a vicar's household, with all its ups-and-downs? Though I think you'll agree that in the long run they're mostly 'ups'.

EVERYWOMAN: Certainly! Indeed, one of the things we admire most about *The Parkers* is its wholesome and encouraging view of life. In the end –

V.O.: People triumph, they rise splendidly above adversity. That's what we British did as a nation during the War. Yes, in those dark days we understood what kind of life we cherished and wanted to continue, and *The Parkers*, I like to think, carries that spirit forward... I learned a lot then from the writer I think of as my great predecessor, Anthony Trollope. Do you remember those brilliant adaptations of his inimitable Barset novels that lightened our darkness so regularly in the War years?

EVERYWOMAN: How could we forget them? We take it then that, like that great predecessor, you think of your characters as real people?

V.O.: Oh, but entirely! I think about them, I care about them, I even find myself worrying about them.

EVERYWOMAN: And this explains why we all feel for the programme as we do – its truthfulness to life, its concern for others. Would you like to say something about how you decide on what is to happen to the Parkers and their circle? Do outside factors have any part to play here?

V.O.: First of all, I should tell you that, after many years of single-handedly writing the programme I invented, I am building up a team of script-writers. We get together for a formal meeting once a week (in addition to informal conversations beyond counting) – and at these we pool ideas about what should – or could – take place in Greenfield End. Maybe as yet... *Miss Orchard pauses as if in wistful thought, and then continues*: We also receive a vast quantity of mail, and no letters give me personally more pleasure than those which assume that the characters are actual individuals I happen to know. I should add that these please the actors also. And some of these letters obviously suggest future developments. Listeners will remark, for instance, that in their view this person should not really be going out with that, and we say to ourselves: 'Well, really, you know, they're right.'

EVERYWOMAN: Are there any kind of listeners you're particularly influenced by?

V.O.: Yes, and no! On the one hand, every but every opinion is taken seriously by us; all our listeners are equal in our view. On the other hand, I have to say that I have a very special interest in the younger listeners. After all they're *The Parkers* followers not only of the present but of the future......And I haven't yet mentioned my husband – for I have one – who, mostly without knowing that he's doing so, gives me ideas, deriving from his vast experience of the theatre, and of the greatest theatre of all, the theatre that is Life. God has written and is writing a script greater than any writer can hope to do justice to.

(vi)
Saturday, October 19, 1957

Dear Mr Armitage,

Tanbury W.E.A. forwarded your letter to me. I suppose I should be too old to be flattered, but I am. How gratifying to know that one's talks can be received in the way you describe! I am often under the gloomy impression that the young and clever nowadays want Shakespeare tragedies set in a Nazi concentration-camp, or else on some bare stage graced (!) by the odd dustbin-lid or scrap of twisted metal – and the comedies located on a Soviet collective farm. So I was more than delighted when I saw from your letter that there are just a few of tender years who believe in richness and colour and fancy and joy, those enduring human attributes which we are so in danger of forgetting about today.

I do indeed remember your telling me about the Riverbury production of *The Tempest*. What a pity that the powers-that-be did not heed your imaginative suggestions! I would have loved to have seen you as Ferdinand – I'm sure you were as charming as *The Northamptonshire Herald* said you were – and of course occasionally forgetting a cue doesn't matter a hoot.

I hope that your health is on the mend now. It sounds as if it's been a worrying matter. You are rather mysterious about it; I trust it wasn't what's so strangely called a 'social' disease that has caused this setback. Anyway modern medicine is pretty wonderful in that respect, I gather.

Yes, I too would like it very much if we could meet again. I gather the train service between Tanbury and London Paddington is a good one. Having as I do an 'interest' in a little antique shop in Fulham (the 'hat' of theatre designer is not the only one I wear, you note!), I am quite frequently in London. Can I suggest Tuesday October 29 as a suitable day on which I could stand you lunch? Just drop me a card at the above address (itself unsuitable for entertaining anybody) and tell me yes or no. If yes, we can meet at my club, the Kemble, at 12.45. They do you very nicely there, as they say.

Yours,

Charles Compson

(vii)
Saturday, October 26, 1957

Dear Miss Orchard,

I was most interested to read in my aunt's copy of *Everywoman* that very informative interview with you. You sounded so friendly and sympathetic that I have not found my decision to write to you difficult to act on. I was especially impressed by the emphasis you put on *younger* listeners, and how you hoped to hear from them, particularly about what they thought ought to happen in Greenfield End. Well, I am young (not yet nineteen), and I have some rather strong ideas about future situations in *The Parkers*, and I'm hoping that you'll be glad to hear from me.

First, though, I want to tell you something about myself. I have to confess that I did not listen to *The Parkers* at all until after I'd left my public school earlier this year. (Riverbury; you've probably heard of it, in Northamptonshire, it's rather famous!) Boarding establishments are not conducive to much afternoon radio, and then at home, I don't live with my mother, so in the holidays there was no-one listening to your programme in the household. Then, this September I came to live with my aunt and cousin in Tanbury, Oxfordshire, and I'd like to tell you that your wonderful contribution to English life has become part and parcel of my own, and that it has had the greatest – and truly beneficial – effect on me.

Why have I come to live in Tanbury, you may ask? I wanted to do my National Service, to join Her Majesty's Navy. How moved I was by your references in that interview to our War Spirit. We still live in troubled times, the Communist menace ever with us, and naturally I've been asking myself how I could best do my bit to make them a little less troubled. I was really looking forward to serious naval engagement, so imagine my distress when – when I learned that I had a tubercular patch and so was not eligible, but had instead to submit to rigid hospital treatment and a kind of rest-cure. Instead of the excitement and challenge of the Med., an aunt's house in the dull Midlands town where my father was born. I have known much pain as well as disappointment. But what has sustained me during this dark period? *THE PARKERS!* Thank you, Miss Orchard, from the depths of my heart!

Alas, physical pain is not the only kind I have known of late! I fell in love, Miss Orchard, just like your Tom Cavan, and, like him, with a doctor's beautiful daughter. There the similarity ends. Tom appears all set for happiness; I have suffered deeply, nor can I pretend that my sufferings are over. Tom has an uncle who cares for him greatly, whereas I have no understanding older man in my life. Please don't think that I am blaming you in any way, but naturally, at the height of my love, I compared my position with that of Tom Cavan and sought to learn from instalments featuring him. Elizabeth Parker told Tom to make Minty Macdonald aware of his feelings. Then I will do the same, I said to myself. I walked this girl home after one of the evening classes in Spoken French that we both attend, and, after paying her gentle compliments, invited her to go to a folk-music concert in a pub, Tanbury's celebrated *Pig and Whistle*, to be given by a local group famous in the skiffle world, The Strummers. So delighted was I by her saying yes that I sat down that same evening and wrote her a letter, hymning her charms and what they already meant to me. She was far less friendly the next time we met than she had been before. In truth she tried to extricate herself from my invitation. But when I told her that I had already bought the tickets and had informed a member of The Strummers that we were coming to the concert (untrue, I'm afraid, but that's love for you!), she – a bit reluctantly – agreed to keep the date.

Miss Orchard, I could hardly concentrate on anything for the next two days. Even the tedious time under the sunray lamp at the hospital went by in a flash, so preoccupied was I with my day-dreams about Saturday night, October 19. I thought of Tom Cavan taking Minty Macdonald to the Robinsons' party, and became hopeful as a young man my age should be!

Pride, they say, comes before a fall. I will not dwell too much on details. Suffice it to relate that Nina (the name of my loved one) looked particularly stunning as she stepped forth from her father's house, and that she was markedly cool to me all the way to *The Pig and Whistle*. Though to someone of a sophisticated metropolitan background like myself Tanbury frequently seems hopelessly provincial, it is justly proud of itself as an English market-town of historic significance. *The Pig and Whistle*, it is said, was once visited by Shakespeare and his players, and it is in truth a fine place with dark oak-beams and flag-floors and a copper-hooded inglenook fireplace, plus a largish modern annexe for dancing etc. Did Nina Cardew show any sign of appreciating the venue for the concert? She did not. 'Didn't you like the letter I wrote you?' I asked eventually. '*Must* we talk about that?' she replied.

The band didn't play so very well, I have to admit, and Nina was pleased to remark on this, though it was hardly my fault. I tried to pretend the musician I'd said was looking forward to seeing us hadn't turned up, but this didn't wash with her. After a while everyone started to dance to rockabilly numbers, but I had practically to force Nina on to her feet (very different from Tom and Minty, you'll agree!) and – I don't know what came over me – but once we were on the floor and hemmed in by other folk, I pulled her as close to me as I dared and told her that I thought myself in love with her. Her face changed as I'd never seen one do before; it was as though ice had suddenly been injected into her bloodstream. While the folk-group, who got better as the evening proceeded, played one of my favourite numbers, 'Teddy Bear', Nina was saying to me in a devastatingly frigid and cutting voice: 'You didn't really suppose I could ever be in love with you, did you? I mean, it's one thing agreeing to invitations to coffee, specially if I've been pestered into accepting them, quite another having *feelings* for you.'

Can't you, Miss Orchard, as one of England's leading writers, imagine my emotion when she spoke thus? There's worse to come, I'm afraid. Please bear with me while I tell you about it. I hope you will not think the worse of me.

All of a sudden I felt wild, possessed – quite Bacchic as a classic might have put it. One reason for this was her extraordinarily close physical proximity to me (I had her closer to me than any girl has ever been before, to tell you the truth) and then the music was pounding away so arousingly. (Isn't that what rock'n'roll's all about?) I pulled Nina closer to me still, right against the contours of my body, and started kissing her. My kisses seemed to go everywhere, and not just on her face, though there was no grossness in my mind, only a need to express genuine desire. Then ensued a great fuss of a most unpleasant and embarrassing nature – ending with me being ordered to leave *The Pig and Whistle*. Nina insisted on going home in a taxi, and, the very next day, a letter came from Dr Cardew (Nina's father) for my own father. Dr Cardew said I'd behaved like a young brute who ought to be severely dealt with until he acquired some respect for the opposite sex. Daddy – to whom my aunt, of course, sent on the letter – has been, I have to say, more sad than angry, but sorrow can be pretty hard to handle too. What a week it has been for me!

My request for you with regard to *The Parkers* is to include more of the tribulations that young people inevitably go through when they fall in love. There is no reason, of course, why there should be episodes quite so horrible as these experiences of mine in *The Pig and Whistle* but I think many younger listeners – and probably older ones too – would like to have their own set-backs and difficulties mirrored in your otherwise so excellent and truthful programme. Could not Minty turn against Tom – if only for a while? Could not Davey suddenly become difficult with his charming Lizzie?

It would be wonderful if you could give these thoughts of mine your attention. I have had much opportunity of late, in this time of my illness, to think about what I most want to do in life. Artistic by nature and talent, I toyed with the idea of theatre design, being rather an ardent Shakespearean. But no! Give me something contemporary, I said to myself, something that reaches out to a really wide public. To write scripts for such programmes as *The Parkers* (indeed precisely FOR *The Parkers*) is at present (and will, I'm sure, remain) my dearest ambition. I could even write some scenes between Tom and Minty for you, which will be charged with my own emotions. I thought I detected, in that interview in *Everywoman*, behind those mysterious words 'Maybe as yet...', in reference to your team, a need for new assistance for your important and so widely loved literary endeavours.

I look forward to hearing from you, and meanwhile, many thanks again for what you have given me through your creations,

Cordially yours,

Bruno Armitage

(viii)
Wednesday, October 30, 1957

Dear Bruno,

I would be deeply grateful if I could be allowed to make amends to you. As I said at the time (rather clumsily and inadequately, I fear) one consequence of growing up (as, most gracefully, you are doing) is that you have to accept, on some level or other, the diverse and not always palatable ways of other people. This applies even – or maybe particularly – to those who wish you nothing but well. I had read the warm and increasingly more intimate atmosphere between us at The Kemble differently from how, I now see, I *should* have read it, and for this I, humbly, beseechingly, apologise.

I would like to take you – for a day, or, if it could be arranged, a weekend – to the house in Dorset where my wife and I make our home. I think you would like it down there; it has a very special beauty in autumn. My wife would make you extremely welcome, and we'll feed

23

you on country fare, and make you forget not only your regular ordeals at Tanbury Royal Hospital, but also the stupidity and insensitivity of Yours Truly. We have many animals – which I think may appeal to you! – and I can testify to there being excellent walks in the vicinity. My wife is also a most interesting person in her own right, and quite a famous one too, as she is the Verity Orchard who invented and writes (nowadays with some assistance) that British-institution-of-a-programme, *The Parkers*, which you may or may not have heard of.

Please say yes to this proposal, and I will then work out the hows and wheres and whens of it all. I have the weekend of Friday, November 15th in mind, and devoutly hope that you're free then. Believe me to be,

Your good friend,

Charles Compson

(ix)

All of us admit to a great attachment to the Vicarage kitchen, a large, old-fashioned, shabby sort of room, the windows of which look out on to our garden, so lovingly tended by dear old Verges. We often have supper there of an evening, and in summer this is particularly pleasant. At times it can seem almost too much like a clubroom or meeting-place, with members of the family – and a general assortment of parishioners – dropping in and talking to me all the time I'm trying to get the (usually expanding) supper ready. Miss Venables may have called to ferret out some piece of personal information; Kevin O'Flynn, tiring of the latest chapter of his novel, will have popped round from next door for a chat (or rather a long reminiscence about his 'beautiful boyhood' back in Limerick); son or son-in-law will be badgering me to listen to details of a latest scheme for raising money. But I have to say that I don't mind all this in the least, though some of my dishes occasionally suffer (!!), for what could be nicer than hearing all the latest news of Greenfield End while watching the sun go down on Verges' proudly patriotic 'Union Jack' flower-bed of red geraniums, white alyssum and blue lobelia?

The sense of peace and fellowship is not confined to humans only, I have to say. By Derek's chair, a little too close to his feet for comfort, Festus will be lying, occasionally thumping his white, stump-like tail. Further under the table you will come across Mutt, so black that you can sometimes not distinguish him from shadow. You often think Mutt's fast asleep, and hear snores that seem to confirm this, but a conversation will only have to include words like 'dog' or 'walk' or even an emphasized 'out' and 'outside', and he's reacting with sharp, very meaningful barks! And by the window, Marmalade, Jam and Honey, our three beloved cats, will be dozing in the sunshine, purring softly with sheer contentment at being alive.

From *Round and About Our Vicarage* by 'Elizabeth Parker' (birthday present October 31st, 1957 from Ian Armitage to his mother).

PART TWO

Bruno Writes

1

When I was a kid, I loved to sing to the hum of car engines, mostly stuff I'd learned in prep. school music lessons: 'Over the Seas to Skye', 'The Lincolnshire Poacher', 'Sweet Lass of Richmond Hill', 'Johnny's Gone Down to Hilo'. After the War with its 'Is your journey really necessary?' every and any trip in a car was a delight, a proof that the world was free again at last. Wasn't that reason good enough for singing? But my father quickly got impatient with me; 'Oh, for God's sake, Bruno, give us a break!' he'd say, 'it isn't even as if you ever sing in tune.' And I'd blush to myself on the back seat, though pride obliged me to sing on for a few bars before falling silent.

That car journey down to Dorset with Charles Compson at the wheel filled me with this kid's rapture I'd all but forgotten about. It was release, it was a new horizon, and several times – in the comparatively few pauses in our conversation – I caught myself singing aloud for joy just as I might have done years before. We passed woods crimson and gold with autumn and sunshine, and I had the sensation that Salisbury Plain was being unfurled and unfolded around and in front of us, as if someone were shaking a huge version of Joseph's many-coloured coat.

> 'Oh, wake her! Oh, shake her!' (I piped up)
> 'Oh, wake dat girl wid de blue dress on!
> For Johnny's gone down to Hilo,
> Poor old man!'

'You seem very happy, Bruno.'

'I am very happy!'

Though should I have been, I now ask myself, when I'd deceived Auntie Eileen about where I was going, and had surely hurt her with my so evident readiness to be off and away from Tanbury?

'Well, that's what I want more than anything, you should know that – for you to be happy,' came Charles Compson's reply. And swiftly, lightly he put a hand on my thigh. Here we go again, I tried not to think. For wasn't this whole expedition to Dorset a sort of compensation for that kind of interest in me? Not that I'd minded in the way he'd, almost instantaneously, surmised; I'd just, naively, been taken aback. Still it might not be at all a bad thing for me that Charles Compson felt I needed making up with. It gave me an advantage.

'Mr Compson –'

'*Charles* – I really must *insist*!' (And indeed he already had, and perhaps I'd only used the more formal address to have the pleasure of being told to do otherwise.)

'Charles – doesn't all this make you believe in Fate?'

'All what? That an old codger like me and a dashing young man like you strike up a friendship?'

I couldn't help myself. 'No, not that,' I said, 'no, I meant you being married to Verity Orchard – to *Verity Orchard*! And to think that the last time I saw you, I didn't know this!' (When we'd met last time, I had, of course, been at pains to suggest that my great interest was theatre design. How long ago that now seemed!) 'Honestly, I just can't see how it *isn't* Fate.'

'Well, I suppose at my advanced age I've got just a smidgen too used to a coincidence here and a coincidence there to go attributing everything to some Great Celestial Plan.'

I was hurting him, I knew it – and when he'd taken such pains over the organisation of this weekend! But I ignored his put-down, his stony glance, his pursing of the mouth, and rushed on: 'Are you really quite *sure*, Charles,' (there, I'd used his first name, and easily) 'that Miss Orchard didn't respond to my name when you told her who you were bringing down for the weekend?'

Charles spoke with cold languor: 'As I've explained already, Verity

28

gets too many letters from too many people to be able to remember –
just like that! – the name of any correspondent.'

'But she can't surely get many letters like mine. So long and
confiding. I went into such *personal* details…'

Charles' pooping of the horn was caused perhaps not only by a
careless young driver. 'So you've given me to understand!' he said.

'…and all the suggestions I made about how my experiences could
be used in *The Parkers*.' I was still hoping that suddenly his memory
would unblock and he'd recollect his wife saying: 'Ah, now I know
what I must do about Minty Macdonald! I've just had the most
fascinating letter from a younger listener, and he's made me see the
way I must go!'

'Doubtless she will have been very grateful to you,' said Charles
drily, 'but rather than try to anticipate her enthusiasm, shall we not let
ourselves enjoy this peculiarly beautiful part of England? It's only
necessary to be patient for an hour or so, after all, and then you will be
able to ply my wife with questions to your heart's content. I'm only an
old stage-hand and part-time junk-merchant, you understand, and
have, I fear, little to contribute on this subject.'

I was being rebuked; I ought to make amends. But no questions
about a past Shakespearean triumph of his occurred to me. Nor did I
feel inclined to make the effort to compose any.

I leaned back in my seat, half-closing my eyes against the afternoon
sun, and found myself saying in a voice dreamy but eager: 'Do you
know something, Charles? You and your wife will be the first famous
couple I've had the good fortune to meet. Funny! I'd have been very
shy at the prospect a while back, but now I've met you, I know that
famous people can be the friendliest of all.'

That did please him, I could tell, and soon he was telling me
anecdotes of places we passed most of which involved folk every bit as
famous as Charles and Verity (had I heard of them) and some even
more so.

Almost as soon as we'd seen the sign announcing Dorset, and had
begun on the descent towards Blandford Forum, Charles' tone altered,

and his anecdotes became less humorous, and more place-centred. He loved this country devotedly, that was very clear even to the youthful egotist who was his passenger. Ten years ago, he informed me, with *The Parkers* launched, and a successful theatre tour over, he and Verity had agreed the time had come for them to leave London – and where should they live but Dorset? As he drove us past the country-town Adam houses of Blandford, mellowed red-brick, shell-porched, solid and quiet, Charles told me:

'It's one thing to make a decision, quite another to find the right house. And then The Puzzle came up for sale. It was the answer to a prayer we'd never quite dared to ask.'

'The puzzle? How do you mean – puzzle?'

Charles Compson laughed. Already I liked him when he laughed. His thin, refined, tense face, so hawklike in eyes and nose, all at once became gentler, more expressive of a wistful ironic sense of humour, and it grew easy, even while confronting his old-fashioned aesthete's style of dressing, to imagine him young.

'Why do you laugh?'

'Because I realised that I'd quite forgotten to tell you the name of our house. And it's such a nice one! It's what first drew us to the place in fact. It's called The Puzzle.'

I tried this out aloud. 'The Puzzle. Yes, it's got a good ring to it,' I said, 'but why's it called something so peculiar?'

'Well, the local historians think Puzzle must be related to Puddle and Piddle, which are common enough Dorset place-names: Puddletown, Piddletrenthide etc., etc. I don't think either of those needs to be explained.' Another boyish laugh. 'But Puzzle's nicer than any of the others, more delicate, more intriguing. Though there's…' But he stopped himself here in mid-sentence, as if he'd thought the better of something. Had he been going to mention another, and perhaps even more indelicate, derivation?

No sooner had he said that word 'intriguing' than I myself felt a stab of excitement, the shock of which reached every part of my body. That was the moment when I knew that The Puzzle and its inhabitants were going to shape the years of my life. As we drove across a heathland only occasionally broken by clumps of pine, I pictured the unknown house as a physical expression of its name, as a maze under this late autumn day's cloudless sky, with myself following some thread through it, like that hero (Theseus?) in the Greek legend, until I reached its centre. And that centre would be where my ambitions, those secret creatures, could find the strength to take off – like a flock of birds leaving the ground to wing towards the sun. 'My cousin the writer,' Ian had said to me not so long ago, seeing me cover sheet after sheet of paper with proposals for *Parkers* incidents. Well, perhaps The Puzzle would turn that half-joking schoolboy's phrase into a statement of truth.

And suddenly it seemed strange that so short a time ago I had been so hurt by Nina Cardew that – go on, admit it! – I'd cried myself to sleep at the humiliation I'd received at her hands. Only a matter of days separated me now from Doctor Cardew's anger and my own father's sad disapproval. And yet already the girl's face had grown indistinct, as was the body I'd taken such rough unwanted hold of.

'I think, Bruno, you have a good deal to learn about women,' Daddy had said to me.

I'd blushed, and stared down at the carpet.

'In fact I think you have almost *everything* to learn about everything.'

Well, here I was, on the point of adding to my knowledge, yet I somehow didn't think my father would be very pleased with me, could he see me now. That, of course, only intensified my pleasure.

I wasn't prepared for the long bare green chalk wall of the Purbeck Hills which all but blocks the sea from heath and meadow, occasionally revealing it tantalisingly, in triangles of a blue deeper and intenser than the day's sky. Shining far beyond the greenness, it made me think of the few seaside holidays of my childhood, taken in Ramsgate, before my mother left us, those holidays which had begun with the car-rides during which I'd sung to the engine. Ramsgate – Victorian villas, all turrets and mock-ecclesiastical windows; steep sea-wall dividing harbour from esplanade and town; garish, jolly Funland, with winkle-sellers and jellied-eels stalls outside its gates; beach-huts and sands on which I tried to build castles; fishermen mending nets who, such a short time back, had taken out their small boats to bring home English boys (and the occasional dog acquired in France) from the disaster of Dunkirk. Sea, shore, and mother...

Many a day now I was completely unable to see my mother's face. She'd been pretty with hair red like my own. My father never voluntarily mentioned her name (Cynthia). She, for her part, had never shown anything but the scantest interest in me, even when informed about my tubercular patch and my being denied the chance to serve my country. Her life was over there in Florida and was closely connected with an organisation called *The Divine Pathway*.

It'd be wrong to dwell on the past, though, which was where my mother surely belonged. Only a few miles away, at the end of this very road indeed, The Puzzle and an interesting present and a brighter future were awaiting me.

And would, I'm often asking myself as I write this, I have turned out a better person if The Puzzle had remained a puzzle, a façade never gone behind? Would I have led a more admirable life if my knowledge of *The Parkers* had been confined to Auntie Eileen's radio at tea-time, and to *post mortems* with that kind, comfortable woman on her pea-green Maples' sofa: 'Do you think Miss Venables will...? Do you really believe Kevin O'Flynn has...?'

I'm tempted to answer: Yes!

It was twilight when I first saw The Puzzle. We'd driven through Senfrith, a compact, somewhat scruffy village of thatched cottages dominated by a tall-towered church (restored Norman) and a long pink-washed inn with a swinging sign in need of fresh paint: 'The Jolly Sailor': 'As a *Parkers* fan, you'll doubtless be interested to know that this church is also called St Luke's,' said Charles.

Imagination and reality were starting to converge. We crossed a little ford, the local name for which was a 'watersplash', and then took a narrow winding lane. This came to a stop by a farm, but before the dead end was reached, Charles had turned left, to make a way up a long and bumpy drive. Thick high brambly hedges grew on both sides, then the right hand one gave way to reveal a ragged-edged lawn, at the far end of which stood a small thatched stone summer-house. There was plenty of work for a Verges to do *here*, I couldn't but reflect. What was it he said so often to Elizabeth Parker?: 'The Good Lord just can't abide untidiness in a garden, that He can't. That were why He sent old Adam out of Eden-like. To teach folks how to keep their gardens proper. Because that Lord God, He don't like the old grass to grow too long!....'

'You should see all this in summer,' said Charles, 'May and June are best, with the world's tallest cow-parsley and great banks of hawthorn, and I don't need to tell you, I hope, that we never, but never, mow down daisies and buttercups. But it doesn't look so very dreadful now, does it?'

'Dreadful? It's beautiful!' I said, 'but –'

'But?' he repeated, as if offended, which was the last thing I wanted him to be.

'No "buts" really,' I speedily assured him, 'it really is amazingly beautiful, and so different from any place I've known. I was only thinking how it's not in the least like the *Parkers*' house and garden.'

Any more, I might have added, than Senfrith is like Greenfield End.

'Well, I wouldn't know about that, would I?' said Charles. I heard dogs barking. Festus and Mutt? 'Anyhow, we're about to be greeted.'

Charles had drawn the car up before the unlit porch (also thatched-roofed), and now I could discern emerging from its shadows a short woman well into middle age with straight brown hair worn long and loose like a much younger girl's. She was wearing a fisherman's shiny black waterproof over clothes of indeterminate colour and cut.

Charles and I stepped out of his Rover into the softness and stillness of deep-country early evening, a stillness which the dog-barks did nothing to mar. I felt the moist gentle air wrapping itself blanket-like round my whole tired travel-cramped body, and the multiple sounds of silence filling up my head as though it were a jug into which soothing ointment were being poured.

The silence was, if not exactly broken (it was too strong for that), then broken into. 'Late, Charles,' and the woman's voice was more of a bark than any sound coming from those distant dogs, 'late again. Cor blimey O'Reilly! I should have got used to it by now, but I flaming well

33

haven't! Because when I think what good time-keepers *goats* are…' She let the sentence trail away in something disturbingly like contempt.

'Unlike any goat I've known, I'm apt to encounter such things as traffic and dithery motorists – which perhaps makes arriving a mere twenty minutes later than the time I'd given a rather venial offence.' Charles, sighing, sounded a touch irritated.

So here before me stood the creator of now proverbial neighbourliness and warm family life. Her face was even more curious and unexpected than her voice, extravagantly blotchy and all wrenched to one side. She had a none-too-faint moustache and, on the right of her nose, a huge mole, of such a size it simply couldn't be ignored. Her tongue seemed to be positioned at the opposite end of her mouth to that which issued her gruff, cross words.

'Who on earth's *this*?' she said next, pointing at me with a long finger, the gesture of a pantomime witch.

'I've told you all about him. He's Bruno Armitage, a young friend of mine, our guest for the weekend.'

'Bruno? Funny! I didn't know they still gave that name to human beings. I was daft enough to bestow it on a goat once – did him no good at all, but then I'm not sure he was any good in the first place. I was never so relieved as when Caprice stables at last bought Bruno from me. "Bonny's your back!" I said.'

Hard to know how to reply to this. Most people tended to congratulate me on my rather unusual Christian name.

Charles reacted to this onslaught by looking weary, perhaps a bit bored, but not as embarrassed as I might have expected.

Crikey, what a disappointment it all was! And how unanticipated!

Nevertheless I was where millions of members of the great British public longed to be; therefore I must pull myself together and cast off my feelings of bewilderment and let-down. Also I surely owed Charles something. So I stepped forward, extended my hand, and said in my best public school voice: 'It's really a great, great pleasure meeting you after wanting to for so long, Miss Orchard.'

'Miss Orchard? Well, if that doesn't take the ruddy biscuit!' came the response.

Oh, lord! I should have said 'Mrs Compson', shouldn't I? I told myself. Socially I always so much wanted to do the right thing.

'This isn't Miss – Verity, my wife,' said Charles Compson, softly – I could tell that he was gulping back laughter, 'this is Nesta Coolidge who lives here with us.'

'And who works hard for her living, don't forget that part of the introduction,' Nesta said, 'it's no joy-ride here at The Puzzle, let me tell you! You should have seen the ridiculous mess Verity was making yesterday when in her wisdom she tried to repair that kitchen table herself. I laughed my blooming head off, I don't mind admitting. Glue all over the place; it's a wonder the silly woman wasn't stuck for ever and a day to the floor. A proper Charlie she looked; Fat Anna, the goat with me at the time, just couldn't get over the sight of her. But you couldn't expect *her* not to be amused, with her ruthlessly practical disposition.'

'I suppose not!' agreed Charles, giving me an unmistakable wink.

'Well, why are you both standing outside in all this damp November air,' said Nesta Coolidge, 'darned stupid, I call it, when the boy's had trouble with his lungs. We don't want him dying on us, and you had up in the courts, Charles, for criminal negligence.'

I was so surprised at this that I couldn't stop myself from saying: 'But I thought you didn't know who I was!'

'I didn't say that, did I?' Nesta Coolidge replied, 'you should develop your ears a bit, boy. I merely asked: "Who's this?"'

'"Who on *earth's* this?"' I corrected her.

Miss Coolidge thrust her face unnervingly forward and close to my own. 'When you know me better, dear Bruno,' she all but spat, 'you'll know that I often give people little tests. To get to know their worth. To sort out the sheep from the goats, as you might say.'

And she proceeded to laugh so loudly at her little joke I wondered whether her jaw might fall off. I appreciated even then (I think) that I had not come out of her 'little test' very well, though I couldn't see what I'd done wrong.

Charles opened the boot of the Rover and took out our two suitcases. 'We must do as Nesta says and move along inside!' he said, 'anyway, welcome to The Puzzle, my mis-named Bruno.'

A cupboard door opens to reveal a wooden staircase corkscrewing upwards – to the thatch itself, you suspect, but no! to encounter a door as near identical to the first as makes no matter. You lift up its latch, and find yourself in a small, white-walled room, a monk's cell snuggling beneath the roof. Latticed windows look out through thick walls on to a little copse beyond which bare Purbeck hillside rises. Through that copse a stream flows, so, when the windows are open, the sound of gently cascading water accompanies your every move.

The floorboards are bare; for furniture there is a bed, with a brass head and a feather mattress, a chest-of-drawers (scratched rosewood), two rush-bottomed chairs and a prie-dieu of varnished oak that Charles found in France. Those white-washed walls bulge in many a place, while through gaps in the plaster of the beamed ceiling you descry patches of roof-straw.

'I want you to describe your ideal bedroom,' said one therapist to me. And straightaway I was back in what I came to call 'my' bedroom at The Puzzle.

And yet the room brought me no happiness.

'You'll hear the gong going for supper. We'll be eating rather late tonight, I fear,' Charles Compson said to me, after telling me where I'd find the bathroom and lavatory. How stylish to have a gong; imagine one in Auntie Eileen's little house in Church Terrace! The Puzzle, in fact, wasn't at all a big house, but unfamiliar as it was, with its passageways and flights of steps and concealed back staircases, it gave off grandeur. It was certainly as different as could be from my Tanbury quarters, so unappealing to the imagination, so – well, *common*, in its furnishings (that three-piece-suite, that sideboard with the frosted glass front), its decoration (that dining-room wall-paper with its over-busy ivy-leaf pattern) and its dreary aspect (the fronts and backs of other houses in other Edwardian terraces).

I lay on the bed, excited but tired; I tired exasperatingly soon these months of deep-ray treatment, and how I despised myself for this! What would my life be like now, I wondered, if I had been medically fit and gone into the Navy. Sometimes, especially when lying under that great, powerful, relentless hospital lamp, I would imagine myself positioned above burning sea and under over-arching sky on some

Mediterranean destroyer or minelayer, handsomely at the ready, with a midshipman's badge on my cap, (plumes symmetrically supporting the royal crown). Anyway, if I'd been allowed to do my National Service, I wouldn't be here at The Puzzle. But – wasn't it entirely appropriate now, this household's latest guest, to see myself as some kind of sailor scanning new waters? I should banish all traces of the invalid from myself this evening: I had to be in top form, exuding youthful confidence, for my first meeting with Verity Orchard. A good job perhaps that she *hadn't* been there on the porch to see me stumble awkwardly out of Charles' car!

So presently I got ready for the evening. Doing so brought back all those lonely evenings of holidays in Swiss hotels with Daddy and his lady-friend of the moment, when, in the process of changing for dinner, I'd gaze down at my prick and wonder whether there was anyone in the hotel who could appreciate it, do justice to it, uncircumcised, eager, virile… I put on a cream poplin shirt with a horizontal-barred tie, a lovat sports jacket and fawn cavalry twills. I sprayed 'Eau de Portugal' on my hair.

But was the gong ever going to be struck? Again and again I looked at my watch. Had they forgotten perhaps what they'd said about letting me know when dinner was. Charles had said they would be eating late, but really… there was late and late.

I was just wondering how much longer I could contain my gnawing hunger when at last – boing! boing! in the hall below, the gong sounded. I veritably ran down that tortuous staircase and into the dining-room. This was a square room overlooking the front garden, in which – as the long brocade curtains had not been drawn – I could see dark forms of summerhouse and high hedges against the cloudless night sky. The room was lit by candles; they stood on the sideboard and on the dining-table, which was round, with, in its centre, a laden dumb-waiter and a jug of bronze chrysanthemums. In the fireplace logs were burning, and their leaping flames cast shadows on the wine-coloured walls. How undignifiedly aware I was of the fast beat of my pulse, of my breathlessness (probably occasioned less by the speed of my descent than by my excitement at imminent confrontation with a distinguished writer at her own board).

37

But in fact only Charles Compson and Nesta Coolidge were sitting there. 'Verity'll be a bit late,' Charles told me – he'd changed into a red velvet jacket worn with a deeper red shirt (almost the colour of the walls themselves) and a large floppy spotted bow-tie, 'she sent her apologies, and was most emphatic that we shouldn't wait for her. As a growing lad,' he smiled up at me, knowing surely that I'd stopped growing three years ago, 'you'll be in need of sustenance straightaway.'

'Parsnip soup's first course,' grunted Nesta, 'and if you don't like it, you know what you can do, don't you?'

I gave her a polite smile, sat down, and re-arranged my chair, so that I could stretch out my legs. My left encountered some warm, breathing lump, which, on contact, emitted a little grunt before shifting itself a few inches further underneath the table. Could this be Festus? Could this be Mutt? 'Oh, excuse me,' I said, apologising to myself as much as to Charles or Nesta, 'my foot brushed against your dog just then, and I've disturbed him.'

I found myself remembering how I'd longed, indeed begged for a dog as a boy, a Sealyham or West Highland White, and had not been allowed one – because I was away at boarding-school, and who would look after it?...

'*Dog?*' said Nesta, sounding, as she had at the porch, astonishingly like one herself, 'is the boy stupid or something? There's no dog in this dining-room. We wouldn't allow one of those creatures here, I can tell you. They're banished to the kitchen and the outhouses, and quite right too!'

'Well, I think one of them may have escaped,' I said, not wanting the poor animal to get into trouble, 'but leave him be; he's no inconvenience.' Just to make sure I'd not been mistaken, I extended my foot again, and yes, again it touched a heavily breathing body that surely could belong only to a dog.

'I'd better put you right. What you've found by your feet is one of Nesta's goats,' said Charles, ladling soup into my bowl for me, 'they have a sort of *droit de seigneur* here.'

I didn't know this expression. Nesta must have seen that I didn't, for, sticking out her misshapen head, she 'translated' for me: 'That means the right to go where they ruddy well want!' She gave here another dreadful little laugh, the jaw threatening anew to fall off her head. Then – 'Do you like having red hair, Bruno?' she asked.

A humorous approach was perhaps best. 'I've never been given any choice in the matter.'

While Nesta said something that I'm sure I heard correctly as: 'Looks darned awful in my view!' Charles was assuring me, 'It's something to be very proud of, Bruno; it gives you an enchantingly *quattrocento* look. Like someone in Botticelli.'

'I certainly wouldn't turn to that muck for my compliments,' said Nesta, wildly filling her bowl far too full of the admittedly delicious parsnip soup, 'I hope you dislike Italy as much as I do, Bruno.'

'My father once took me to the Lakes...' I began, always eager to show off the costly holidays I'd had. (And memories suggested themselves of a swimming-instructor in Stresa, and the mineral-collecting Milanese lawyer who'd spotted me on the hotel tennis courts and later took to watching me through binoculars.)

'The Italian Lakes ought to be drained,' said Nesta, 'though not before you've had a chance to drown a lot of Italians in 'em first. And I'll tell you for why.' She glared across the table at me. 'They eat *goats* in their country!! Charles here was daft enough – well, he's always daft, but on this occasion he was dafter than usual – to take me to Italy once, to Florence. Wanted to show me art treasures and all that sort of stuff. I was never more bored in all my life. Call that a picture, I'd say, I've seen better ones at Dorchester Women's Institute, and with ruddy sight better frames too. But that wasn't the worse of it. After a dreadful morning looking at Michelangelo's rubbish, Charles here says: "Lunch-time!" So in we go to one of their trattorias. Waiter recommends a dish. '*Capretto*', says the man, pointing to the menu with an idiotic grin on his face. Of course I had my suspicions right away; I'm not stupid, you know, just a bit mentally retarded.' I hardly dared meet her eyes at this point, but found myself blushing in something like agreement. 'And what's *capretto* when it's at home?' I ask. The fool waiter was very proud of his English. 'Goat, lady,' he says. 'Goat, is that right?' says I, and I'm proud to tell that I stood up then and there and socked him hard in the kisser.'

'She did too,' said Charles.

I felt wholly inadequate to this story, and now Nesta was looking at me with a grim intensity as though I were, in some way, in collusion with that Italian waiter. But the ensuing pause did not last long. For – and how this moment has stayed in my mind, to be brought forward from its stores times beyond counting – scarcely had Nesta pulled her aggressive head back from telling me her tale than the door opened. It took something like audacity to turn round, but turn round I did. And the woman who entered, softly, as if equipped with the padded paws of a doe, and wearing a plum-coloured housegown over a night-dress was, I thought, the most beautiful person I had ever set eyes on.

'What a *relief* that you've started without me,' she said in a gentle, low, rich voice that straightway brought cream and honey to my mind, 'I was afraid you'd been waiting for me, all pitifully hungry, and then your discomfort would have been *my* fault. I would have been so sorry! You do believe, all of you, that I would have been so sorry, don't you?' She smiled pleadingly about her. 'I want everybody in the world to be as contented as possible; it's as simple as that!' She glided up to the chair next to mine, and sat herself down with a light but noticeable attention to all the little movements that this process entails. I was just wondering whether she'd in fact taken in my presence, when she turned to me, and, another smile lighting up her pale face, with its grey eyes and almost Asiatic flat nose, said, and in a most musical manner, 'And you are our visitor. How nice you look! I hope you're going to be very, very happy with us this weekend.'

'I'm sure I am,' I said, my awe making me stammer, 'I've been looking forward to my visit here so much... I'm the Bruno Armitage who wrote to you, you know, your big fan who has so many ideas about the young people on *The Parkers*.'

Verity, continuing to look at me, her grey eyes seeming to grow larger by the second, put a finger to her mouth: 'Shh, shh! nothing professional, nothing Parkerish this evening, if you please. Tonight,' and she moved her glance away from me now, over the bronze chrysanthemums and towards the uncurtained glass of the windows, 'tonight one of my sadnesses has come upon me, and so I must have everything sweet and soft and soothing and subtle. Mustn't I, Charles?'

'That's how it would seem!' said Charles. He reached over the table for a bottle of red wine. 'Time perhaps to pour out some of this stuff! It must be pretty well *chambré* by now.'

I quickly worked out what this word meant, and vowed to use it myself at the next opportunity. Even Daddy, who thought himself something of a wine-connoisseur, had never to my knowledge employed it.

'It will be *good* to drink wine with food while the fire burns and the dark thickens outside,' Verity said, speaking as if she were reciting something from a foreign phrase-book, 'very, very *good*. And may I say again,' she turned back to me, 'how pleased we all are to have you here.'

'Pah!' said Nesta Coolidge, 'the boy doesn't know goat from dog.'

'Four people sitting round a table,' Verity Orchard went on, 'four *pleasant* people sitting round a *pleasant* table, eating, drinking, talking, laughing.' This last word struck me as less than accurate, and indeed it was hard to imagine anyone here doing so coarse a thing as laughing – unless, of course, you counted those strange barks of derision that Nesta was pleased to give out, 'such simple things, yet they are the very stuff of Heaven, aren't they?'

'One hopes!' said Charles, with something like a wink at me.

'Oh, but Charles, one *knows*! Aren't I a Vicar's daughter? Do I not write about a Vicar's family? I know that up there, in the Vast Beyond, there will be for eternity Chippendale chairs, and views of gardens, and round tables, and dumb-waiters, and log-fires, and damask curtains, and jugs of chrysanthemums, and....'

'No need, I think, for a complete inventory of the room,' said Charles.

'And red-headed young men with delicious cream poplin shirts,' finished Verity triumphantly, 'and with the most ravishing of smiles to match his dress.'

'Get a move on, can't you? and drink up your ruddy soup!' commanded Nesta Coolidge. 'My tummy's rumbling like an old lorry, and I don't want to wait for my grub much longer, thank you very much.'

'After supper,' Verity said, after doing as Nesta had bidden her, 'we will make music. We must! We shall! Tell me,' and once again her look at me was very full, 'are there any words in our whole wealthy and wonderful English language more profound than *If music be the food of love, play on!?'*

As my eyes met hers, so soft and grey, I could only agree.

In the sitting-room another fire was blazing, counteracting the damp night chill that had succeeded the fine November day. As guest, and one with a physical condition, I was given a deep and extremely comfortable armchair close to the hearth. Verity now stepped forward to the piano by the bay-window, and most eye-compellingly took her place at it. She settled herself down on the music-stool in a way that made me all but feel the curves of her buttocks beneath my carressing hands, and then lovingly stroked the ivory keys, as if they might, touched gently thus, yield music of their own accord. The lamp made her white-streaked fair hair shine gold. Somewhere out in the copse beyond the garden an owl hooted. I sank myself more deeply still in my chair, and congratulated myself on my distance from London and from North Oxfordshire alike. What were my Riverbury contemporaries doing now? Or those poor bastards I met at Tanbury Tech. battling with 'A' Level course-work? They wouldn't be anywhere like The Puzzle, I'd be bound. Bruno Armitage had arrived in a household of artists who lived the good life!

'What music do we think best for this late autumn night?' Verity Orchard asked. 'Is there any our guest – our so very welcome guest – would specially like?'

I was nervous about the limitations of my musical knowledge, having most of my life been decidedly bored by classical concerts. Wisely therefore 'Please play anything you want to, Miss Orchard,' I said, sycophantically, 'I'm sure I shall enjoy it!'

'Then I know what it has to be,' Verity said in a whisper that was almost amorous in its quiet certainty. And she stroked the keyboard again, but this time rippling chords of a lovely melancholy issued, to cast a spell over that quiet firelit room.

They were but a prelude, however, after which, to a captivating accompaniment, Verity – to my amazement – began to sing:

"Once a young maiden
Climbed an old man's knee.
Begged for a story,
'Do, Uncle, please!
Why are you single?
Why live alone?
Have you no babies,
Have you no home?' "

There was a pause here. Verity looked briefly away from the piano, almost pleadingly, I thought. And then from the depths of the armchair nearest to mine, a mellow baritone, Charles', took up her song;

" 'I had a sweetheart,
Years, years ago,
Where she is now, pet,
You soon will know.
List to my story,
I'll tell you all!
I believed her faithless,
After the ball!' "

A second's rest. Then Verity Orchard raised high her head, as though to the ceiling, to the stars, suspended her hands for a few instants above the keys, only to animate them further into a swirl of notes in waltz-time, the song's melodious chorus:

'Af—ter the ball was o—ver,
Af—ter the break of dawn,
Af—ter the danc—ers leav—ing,
Af—ter the stars were gone.....'

Charles and Verity herself and yes, even Nesta Coolidge, were all singing together now (pretty loudly too) and I felt at once strangely moved by this — tears actually pricking behind my eyes — and equally strangely uncomfortable as though I were attending some

initiates' ceremony I was not entitled to witness. Their voices swelled
to the chorus' finish:

'Many a hea–art is broken,
AF–TER THE BALL!'

'Oh,' said Verity with a sigh that sounded like some written-in coda
to the music, 'oh, the utter pathos! How can one bear it? That poor girl
with her beau thinking her unfaithful when she was only embracing
her beloved brother! That poor man tortured by jealousy into believing
himself not truly loved. But life's just too often like that, isn't it? The
wrong things happen! Yes, *the wrong things happen all the time*, and
we must never ever forget that!' She closed the piano lid as if in
conclusion of this judgement.

'*Sunt lacrimae rerum*,' said Charles Compson, lighting himself a
second cigar (he'd earlier offered me one, but I'd declined, because I
was afraid of what an ingenuous figure I might cut). 'Have you read
much Virgil, Bruno?'

I heard Nesta snort. 'Surely any fool,' she was pleased to observe,
'can see the boy's hardly read a book in his life.'

How could she have known! She was right, of course, damn her! I
felt reading was for people like my cousin, Ian Armitage, poring over
the *Oxford Junior Encyclopaedia*, *Pears' Encyclopaedia*, *The Observer's
Book of Trees*, *The Weather*, *Wild Animals*, *Architecture*, over volumes of
The King's England, dedicated to various counties of Britain, and – by
contrast, appealing to his fantasies – C.S. Lewis' Narnia stories and
The Borrowers by Mary Norton. Ian usually read with his tongue upon
his upper lip, and a finger in his tufty black hair. I hadn't been like
him four/five years ago. Even now, when I'd started reading a bit more,
inclinations to other activities (jerking off not excluded) usually
overcame me to such an extent I was unable to continue. I wanted to
be a writer, not a reader.

Verity moved closer to the fire, humming those wistful, philosophic
last lines of her ballad:

'Many a hea–art is broken, After the ball.'

She patted me on the head, 'I do so hope *your* heart won't be broken, young man. It would hurt mine so dreadfully if it ever were.'

It was then that I realised that she'd never yet called me by my Christian name for the very good reason that she didn't know it.

I was so tired I didn't undress completely, but lay on top of the bed. Up here it was even colder than downstairs, but, to warm the room, there was a little electric heater already switched-on which gave off a distinct scorching smell of damp. It was odd that I was here, was it not?

And suddenly it came to me – strongly, beyond refutation – the fact that my father, my Auntie Eileen, my cousin Ian would all dislike The Puzzle and its unusual (perhaps unique) atmosphere, dislike it very much. Well, *their* loss! I was different from my relations, a complex, open, and sexually needy individual who could inhabit many social domains and give something to them. All the same the realisation didn't make me feel either easy about myself or happy.

I heard through my self-questionings that cupboard-door below being opened, its latch rattling, and then footsteps, heavy and slow ones, making their way up the narrow twisted staircase; it was as when, watching a film, one sometimes catches, without taking them in fully, noises beyond in the cinema itself (and even in the street in which the cinema stands).

'Silly boy!' said Charles Compson, for of course it was he, 'you haven't even got into bed. I was hoping to find you all tucked up and ready for a good night's sleep.'

If that's what you were hoping, why come and disturb me? I felt like asking. But I knew, of course, that to someone enamoured the merest glimpse of the love-object asleep and ignorant of his presence will suffice... 'I felt too sleepy even to get undressed,' I replied, 'and I've had so many things to think about.'

A worried look came into Charles' eyes, as though he'd interpreted these 'many things' as both troubling and attributable to himself. 'I hope you're glad to be here, Bruno,' he said.

'Of course I am!' I replied, turning over on my side to face him, framed in the low doorway, the sincerity of my enthusiasm unmistakeable. 'I think The Puzzle is the most wonderful house I've

45

ever been in. I'm used to living in some style in Primrose Hill – not in *Tanbury*, of course, that's another matter altogether – but my home in London isn't *interesting* like this is.'

Charles moved towards the bed and me. 'You're saying exactly what I've been hoping you'd feel,' he said, 'thank you for those kind words, Bruno, thank you, dear boy!'

During my reveries on top of the bed I had been smelling Verity, the lily-of-the valley scent that encased her graceful body like an aura. It was dispelled now: the masculine odours of Charles Compson, ones I was far more used to, from house- and scout-masters, not to mention other older, conventional-faced, romantic-headed men I'd come across – odours of Old Spice, Havana, the accumulated cigarette smoke of years, and, not least, the adrenalin of erotic interest.

'My love for The Puzzle knows absolutely no bounds,' said Charles Compson, breathing too loudly and wheezily for his or my comfort, 'but, Bruno, let me tell you this, please – you, I think, will have little difficulty in understanding what I mean – I am not so very happy here.'

'Why not, when it's so beautiful?' I heard my own heart-thumps loud and arhythmic above the words I spoke.

'Can you not guess?' Charles sat himself down – very heavily, making the tightly wedged feathers under the covering of the mattress billow upwards like waves beneath a boat. 'Surely, you're shrewd and adult enough to guess, dear boy! I'm lonely here, lonely!'

Well, who could know more about loneliness than me? I was lonely even in dependable Auntie Eileen's house, just as I had been in Primrose Hill and at Riverbury. Wasn't that a reason for my love of *The Parkers*? Hadn't Elizabeth and Derek and Kevin O'Flynn and Tom Cavan relieved my solitude, filled a real and achingly felt vacuum?

Charles Compson was continuing: 'I thought that must have been apparent tonight, for all the act I – we – put on! I mean, doesn't it stand out a mile that I'm... I'm in need of a friend?'

Both our breathings were stertorously uneven now. They seemed to fill the whole little room, reminding me of the sea-sounds you hear in shells.

'Perhaps I might be so bold as to amend that remark: I'm in need of a *young* friend, even a *particular* young friend.'

I didn't reply, but such was my vanity then that I even had time, in the wheezy beseeching pause that followed, to imagine how I was looking, flat on my back on the bed, poplin shirt undone showing my navel, legs spread-eagled out so my crutch showed to advantage, one sock on and one sock off and the arches of my feet bare for a hand to be laid on one or other of them.

'I'm not speaking out of turn, am I?' Charles was saying now, bending closer and closer towards my head. 'We are friends, aren't we, Bruno? Good friends?'

'Yeah,' I said, 'of course, we are, Charles!' I was now aware that alcohol was another of the odours that emanated from him. We hadn't drunk so very much at dinner. (My father, in a hotel dining-room on holiday, could put far more away.) My own breath didn't smell of the stuff; I'd even tested it in cupped hands. So he must have had quite a drop more since I'd gone upstairs – of whisky rather than wine, surely.

What was going to happen next? Was anything?

'I could become so fond of you,' Charles told me in a treacly whisper, 'I repeat, I am happy you are here and are happy you're happy too! Thank you for coming down to lighten an old stage-designer's darkness.'

The 's's were far more slurred now than on entry to the room. 'I really am tired,' I said, adding – judging it best to capitalise on my condition, 'this damned T.B. thing gets me exhausted so easily.'

'Dear boy, I'm being thoughtless, no, selfish, as is my wont. I must not bother you any longer! Let me give you a good-night kiss – on the top of your Botticellian head, merely – and then I will take myself off!'

As perhaps might have been expected, Charles' bidding Good Night to me rather diminished if not my tiredness, then my sleepiness. I took off my clothes, folding them with the obsessive care that had long become automatic with me, vain youth that I was, put on pyjamas and climbed into bed, between sheets of a delectable roughness, cleanness, and lavender-fragrance. I was sexually aroused. Why? Because a man old enough to be my father (though in all other ways almost ludicrously unlike the man who actually was) had been all droolly over me? Surely not?

A book had been placed on the chair beside my bed. *A Year of*

Grace edited by Victor Gollancz. I picked it up (though as Nesta had so shrewdly divined I was not really much of a reader). 'Verity Orchard – her book!' was written inside in flamboyant purple ink, and underneath that in the same hand, but more shakily and in pencil, 'Her prop and her guide'. I flipped through it – it seemed to be an anthology, and of a sort of religious nature. The book opened more easily at some places than at others. The first of these showed me a longish poem with lines of oddly unequal length. Verity had written something in the margin. What? 'Wonderful! Derek P.'s favourite!'

Derek P.? Why, who else could that be but the Rev. Derek Parker of Greenfield End. So I began to read; the author of the poem was Thomas Traherne, and his spelling was as strange as his sense of line-length. He'd lived a long time ago, it seemed:

'New Burnisht Joys!
Which yellow Gold and Pearl excell!
Such Sacred Tresures are the Lims in Boys,
In which a Soul doth Dwell;
Their Organised Joynts, and Azure Veins
More Wealth include, than all the World contains.'

I still felt myself 'Boy' – even though I was also anxious to enter the vast, unmapped adult world. Now I ran my hands over my own limbs and 'organised joints', then, moved by something, I could not say what, continued:

'From Dust I rise,
And out of Nothing now awake,
These Brighter Regions which salute mine Eys,
A Gift from GOD I take.
The Earth, the Seas, the Light, the Day, the Skies,
The Sun and Stars are mine; if those I prize.

Long time before
I in my Mother's Womb was born,
A GOD preparing did this Glorious Store,

The World for me adorne.
Into this Eden so Divine and fair,
So Wide and Bright, I come his Son and Heir.

A Stranger here
Strange Things doth meet, Strange glories See;
Strange Treasures lodg'd in this fair World appear,
Strange all, and New to me.
But that they mine should be, who nothing was,
That Strangest is of all, yet brought to pass.'

I would never have read these lines, I imagine, if they hadn't been marked with Derek Parker's name, yet they have lingered in my mind, stirring me, and often touching me to the point of tears, for more than forty years, though I have no religion, no more than I had then. They've never altogether failed, I suppose, to bring back to me that first night I slept in The Puzzle – to awake to a day of being a presence in that quiet sea-fretted Purbeck valley, and in the life of the woman who had brought *The Parkers* into being.

But before I woke up to all that, I had a dream. The scent of the linen must in part have prompted it, for I found myself in a field of high and vividly blue lavender the flowers of which tickled my naked thighs and crutch. I was running – running very hard towards a stream I could see in the near distance, a margin for the field, burning silver in the sun. Was I being pursued, or was I trying to catch up with someone? Small butterflies, of a mottled brown that I later learned was peculiar to one Isle of Purbeck species (the Senfrith Skipper), flitted about, pointing the way, it seemed to that bright stream.

Piano music – and how odd to hear it *outside*! – made me suppose that when I'd got out of the field (had fought away the lavender) I would find Verity Orchard, playing with that sad beauty of touch I'd heard only hours before. With a special effort, and sending, with an impatient movement of my elbow, a great swarm of butterflies, scattered, to fly up high into the sky, I broke into a part of the meadow where the flowers grew less densely. The stream and its banks were clearer to me now; there was nobody about that I could see, however.

49

'I'm coming! It's only me, Bruno!' I called. The exertion of my cry must have carried me that last lap, for now I was standing on a mossy ledge gazing at sun-spangled waters. Then: 'I'm up here. Can't you see me?' said a voice, an intimately familiar one, but for the minute I didn't recognise it. I was gasping with breathlessness. It seemed to me that this dream (for by now I knew it to be one) had moved me on years, but maybe...yes, maybe, for all the optimism of the doctors, my lungs still weren't well, for here was I still panting and coughing hard after my run, and spots before my eyes were preventing my seeing my surroundings very precisely.

'Up *here*!'

I now lifted my head towards a willow-tree the branches of which dangled in the stream. A boy was sitting on the thickest point of one of these, and – it was my cousin, my cousin, Ian Armitage, and the tears were running down his red-cheeked, usually cheerful face.

'Bruno,' he said, 'you never should have gone away. You never should have fucking gone!'

And even in my surprise at seeing him, I wondered at his swearing, for I had never heard Ian use bad language, or say anything indeed that wasn't good-humoured and modest. At twelve he was how boys are supposed to be before the descent of puberty: at once robust and pure.

'What do you mean by that?' I asked. But if I had a reply I don't remember it. It died somewhere or other in the caverns of my mind, as I rolled over on that unbelievably soft feather-mattress.

Like so many young men of my age I found getting up irksome and difficult, and I finally left my bedroom at an hour I wouldn't have dared to back in London or at Auntie Eileen's. Something told me anyway that The Puzzle would not be unduly punctilious about hours. But when I arrived in the dining-room, I saw that the others had indeed breakfasted before me. There was a bowl and a plate and a cup and saucer set out for me, and on the dumb waiter a packet of cornflakes and a coffee-pot and a jug of cream. I helped myself to these, rather shyly, I have to admit, looking round all the time for someone to come in through the door. Whatever my health problem, I had a hearty appetite even in the mornings, and certainly one measly bowlful of cereal didn't satisfy it. However I couldn't find anything else. So I had a second and a third round of cornflakes until indeed I'd finished up all the cream.

The house was invasively still, stiller than any house I'd ever been in before, and the garden outside the windows no less so – there was almost no wind this morning; no birds were singing or rustling. My deliberate clattering of china and cutlery and my humming of good old 'Last Train to San Fernando' had aroused no-one's attention. Oh, well, it *was* five minutes to eleven.

I decided to go a walk by myself. Indeed what else was there for me to do?

The Puzzle, its garden and copse, lay below me now, and, further below still, the insignificant village of Senfrith, a huddle of thatched roofs out of which grey chimneys protruded like little pricked-up ears from a bunched-up group of rabbits. Beyond Senfrith the heathland over which Charles and I had driven the night before stretched towards undulations of rather more fertile and intensely farmed country. The brown of the heath was cut into by lines and scars of white chalk, the same substance as the cliffs were made of that I could see on the other side of the hill ahead; the sharp sheer falling away of the Purbecks into the Channel.

Inland, as your eyes travelled the heath, it was hazy, the haze seemingly delivered to the open country by fragmentary clumps of russet-coloured trees (for this countryside had few woods deservant of the name, far fewer even than the agricultural Midlands Plain of Riverbury and Tanbury). But, swinging your head round, you encountered haze elsewhere, first between hilltop and sea, and then, beyond water the blue of which was streaked with both turquoise and black, a vague, loose, torn shawl obfuscating any proper horizon. But over to the west I saw, defying these mists, a long, strong finger of land extending from a cliffless shore. Portland Bill! – I recognised it immediately from prep. school geography lessons with funny old Mr Midgley whom we'd teased so, and so pleased was I at my swift identification that I spoke its name aloud. 'Not Portland William,' I said, remembering The Midge's corny joke, 'but Portland *Bill*.'

'Right first time, how absolutely brilliant of you!' came a voice, 'I *am* impressed. I've witnessed many a confused body gazing out over there, to say: " Look at Land's End." But not you! No, not Bruno Armitage!'

Verity Orchard stood before me; she had come from a path that ran from the east along the ridge. She was wearing a blue windcheater and a blue linen skirt, and a mostly blue headscarf over hair that appeared more subtly and lucently yellow this morning even than last night.

Realising what idiotic words of mine she must have heard, I blushed. But I blushed also because, standing alone in front of me, she appeared so unlike the women I had been used to in my life: fierce school matrons; glum, grim housekeepers; Daddy's lady-friends with their business-women's lips and vaunted tastes for cocktails; homely Auntie Eileen. (To say nothing of my own mysterious, unsatisfactory mother.) How did one talk to such a female as this one smiling quizzically in front of me now, on this maritime hill-top, on which she'd arrived stealthily, seemingly out of nowhere?

'Miss Orchard, I'm so sorry I got up so late this morning. Country air, you know...'

Verity Orchard put a finger to her lips, as she had done last night when I mentioned *The Parkers*.

'I won't have apologies from guests,' she said, 'particularly such good-looking ones as you. It's me who ought to be apologising, for having been so unhostess-like as to leave you to your own devices. I do hope you slept well?'

'Oh, very –' I remembered erotic reactions of the night before, and blushed deeper still, 'very well indeed, thank you, Miss –'

'Thank you, *Verity*!' she corrected. 'Now can I tempt you to walk with me a little further or are you too tired? We are going to take great care of your health here, you know. But it's a gentle enough stroll, with no further climbing; all gradients are behind you. What I do most mornings, you see, is to go down into Senfrith, take the path just after the church, and then follow this track until...well, until I come somewhere I'd love to show you. I usually walk alone, not even a dog accompanies me. It's how I think over happenings in Greenfield End.'

What a thrill I experienced at hearing the so-familiar, so-loved name spoken by its inventor herself.

'But won't I be in the way?' I asked, or felt obliged to; for more than anything just now I wanted to be at her side and to be shown this object of her creative walks.

'Far from it!' she said, 'besides I've done my thinking for this morning. Bad news for Gillian Parker, I'm afraid – that Laurence of hers isn't anyway near as nice as he sounds. But good news for Kevin O'Flynn! He's got quite a literary triumph coming his way. And then there's poor good old Mrs Bobbington. It isn't only her corns that are going to plague her...'

Again a thrill passed the length of my spine. 'Mrs Bobbington!' I exclaimed, hardly believing I was where I was, 'Oh, Mrs Bobbington, I like her so much!'

'And so do I,' said Verity, 'but don't let's talk of her yet-a-while; my mind has been too much with her this morning already. I want it to travel elsewhere. To you, for example! That Nina – I shan't ever be able to forgive her for what she did to you.'

'Nina – ?'

'Nina *Cardew*. Why, oh why did she string you along as she did, hateful hussy, allowing you to take her out to hear The Strummers, and then insulting you – you, so obviously kind and sensitive, as well as quite *scrumptiously* handsome. I really feel like writing her a stinking letter, making my feelings about her conduct quite, quite clear.'

Naturally I didn't admit to Verity that Nina had already died in my mind and heart. She had dwindled into being merely the subject of my long first-ever letter to Verity which obviously had, for all my fears, made the intended impression on her. The script-writer and I began measuredly to walk along the ridge-path. Seagulls wheeled above us, the air tasted of salt as well as of that peppermint essence indistinguishable from the English autumn, sheep were cropping the turf, but for me it was as if everything animate and inanimate, to hand and in the distance, were infused by Verity's spirit. As for Verity herself, I was aware even then that – perhaps on account of her so often putting walks to meditative use – she noticed her surroundings far less than did her husband, Charles. They were backcloth for her preoccupations.

So I started, as best I could, living up to the idea of Bruno Armitage that my letter had (it would seem) given her. Not for nothing had I once entertained thoughts of being an actor! I made of my relationship to Nina a poignant thing, throwing in Parker parallels whenever they occurred to me, which was frequently. Indeed Verity was before long moved to say (just as I'd hoped): 'How well you know my Greenfield End! And how marvellous that your attitude to the people and places there is the same as mine.'

'What do you mean by that, Verity?' I dared to say.

Verity Orchard stopped in her tracks. We had reached that stage of the path where both sea and heathland temporarily recede and all we could see on either hand was rolling chalk-pocked greensward. Opening her eyes very wide so that her grey irises delicately shone, she said: 'That they EXIST! That if the moment were, in some mysterious way, propitious, and if we stood, let's say, on tiptoe, we might be able, quite literally, to peer into the leafy gardened streets of Greenfield End, and see our friends there for ourselves.' She was herself standing on *tiptoe* now. Though only sheep were in sight, it didn't seem ridiculous – quite the contrary – for her to say next: 'Why, I do believe the door of St Luke's Vicarage is opening. Who would you most like to come out, Bruno?'

'The Rev. Derek Parker.'

'The silly thing,' screwing up her eyes, 'he's forgotten his overcoat again, and you realise, don't you? that he'd put that important letter *in his overcoat pocket*? What *does* he think he's doing?'

'His mind's on higher things!'

'Of course, it is! He's thinking of a sermon about all those martyrs and saints of the Church who have believed in the souls of animals and tried to pray for them in the next world.'

'He preaches well?'

'Not altogether. Sometimes he's apt to go wandering off what his listeners have assumed was the point, on some course or other that takes his fancy. And of course his mind is almost over-stocked with information. He's very, very learned.'

'I think people of Greenfield End value him for his acts of kindness rather than for his sermons.'

The rays of Verity's grey eyes seemed to bore straight through me. 'How absolutely right!' she said, in a low, intense voice, 'how utterly true! .... And now I can see another figure coming along the road; he looks cheerful, and indeed he's whistling to himself.'

'Tom Cavan?'

'Tom, of course, who else? I do believe –' she wrinkled up her nose almost flirtatiously at me, 'that he's your favourite. You identify with Tom, and why not?'

'He's my age...' I said.

'And has your sweetness of manner. I have an idea – I must root among the old scripts – that we said that Tom was dark. But now that you have come into our lives, I want Tom to have red hair, red, curly hair, just the same as someone a few yards from me now. I can't think why I didn't see the colour of Tom's hair properly, some time ago.'

Flattered though I was by this, a horrid thought struck me: 'But there's a real Tom Cavan, isn't there? I mean, there's an actor who plays him, there's what's-his-name – Neil Micklewright.'

Verity's eyes seemed all at once to glaze over: 'Neil Micklewright,' she echoed wanly, 'such a *dull* fellow! Nothing like you at all.'

I should have been pleased to hear this, but I was too aware that somehow I'd said the wrong thing.

Verity now said; 'I think it's time we moved on, don't you? These sheep look as if they're a bit tired of our company.'

And so on we moved! Clearly there was going to be no further peeping on tiptoe to descry people at Greenfield End.

As the path descended, and both the sea on our left and the Dorset heathland on our right offered themselves to view again, Verity's good spirits returned to her, though, subtly but immovably, it seemed, the matter of her conversation had changed. Now she was talking about the cast of *The Parkers*, about the whole business of programme-making. Here was a subject which was now – indeed only these last two weeks – beginning to interest me. Previously I'd assumed, I think, that a programme came into being like some genie after the rubbing of Aladdin's lamp. But I mustn't betray my ignorance of its procedures, I must listen and learn. Verity gave me a good instance of her craft by speaking of Enid Berridge, who'd played the part of Elizabeth Parker from the very first. She'd had suddenly to undergo a minor operation recently, and this had necessitated ingenious stratagems by the script-writers for a convincing non-appearance of the programme's central character.

'You mean, that was the real reason for her having to go to Belgium, to see her aged Aunt Gertrude in Bruges who thought she was dying?'

'Exactly!'

'We were all so interested in what had made Aunt Edna summon her that we never really thought of Elizabeth being away from Greenfield End. And there were all the telephone calls she made to Derek, keeping him in touch with what she was doing over there.'

'Bang on again. But, think about it, Bruno, you never once heard her *speak* on the telephone.'

I thought how exciting it would be to meet such logistic challenges. I nearly said so then and there, but decided – surely wisely – not to declare myself so obviously and so soon. Rather I would make Verity appreciate just how lively and deep and how multi-faceted my concern with her programme was.

'Is Enid Berridge at all like Elizabeth Parker?' I asked.

Verity paused, as if uncertain how she wanted to answer this. (Clearly talking about the cast – in distinction to the characters they played – presented difficulties for her.) Then, wrinkling her nose up fetchingly again, she said, with something like a giggle, 'Well, she has a husband and a son and a daughter, and they all live in a large house, though it's not a vicarage.'

'And their names, I suppose, are Gillian and Davey?'

'I'm so sorry to have to disappoint you. They're called Adam and Cassandra – Cassie she's always known as.'

I do sincerely believe, so many years later, that, on hearing these names pronounced, I knew that missed heart-beat which is too often our reaction to the significant when – overtly or in disguise – it manifests itself to us. I am certain that I knew Cassie was to come into my life, and to be, not before so very long, the dearest person in it.

Perhaps the walk (when, for Christ's sake, would I be well again?)

had tired me more than I'd realised, for I felt ripples of giddiness speeding through me, forcing me to stop and steady myself. Verity showed concern. 'My fault, my wretched fault. Please forgive me! But we've more or less reached our destination; it's only yards away, and after that there's a gentle, totally downhill path all the way to the back garden of The Puzzle.'

A dell opened out below us, and – surprising the walker in that treeless land – in it six or seven yew-trees showed themselves, all with huge reddish boles that suggested the pressing together of several aged trunks. The yews were at most fifteen feet high, and their branches began at so low a point on them that the trees appeared shorter than their actual height, specimens of some metamorphosed dwarf race.

'No trees live longer than yews, and yews were here – in this country of ours – long, long before any of its tiresome invasions,' said Verity, with an unexpected wild little laugh. 'I feel at once old and young when I'm among them. I'm taken back over the centuries, on the one hand, and humbled by the trees' great age, on the other, into thinking of myself as little more than a slip of a girl – for all my wrinkles and crows'-feet.' Another laugh like the first. 'Come into the heart of this little grove, Bruno. You'll stand in the very spot where Verity Orchard's poor head has received what wisdom it has ever received.'

I think I was afraid to do what she asked of me. But while I could not do other than obey her (I owed it to myself as much as to her to be obedient), I trembled within at my own inexperience. I thought of Daddy in London and Auntie Eileen and Ian in Tanbury, just as I had last night, and now they seemed not merely distant but curiously insubstantial. Though the day had so little breeze and this dell was sheltered from such as was gently blowing, the trees, I could hear, were creaking, creaking, sighing and whining to themselves.

Verity Orchard threw back her head, and, with a theatrical gesture, undid her headscarf; 'I stand, the priestess!' she said, 'I thank you, my yew-trees, for my powers.'

Odd thoughts that I didn't want to have came into my head as I confronted her, my back against the widest bole of all: how Verity had not replied to my long, impassioned letter, how she hadn't been there to greet me, her only guest last night and had (in effect) kept three people waiting for their already very late dinner, how she hadn't seemed to know who I was, how self-indulgent had been her playing of 'After the Ball', how wasteful of feelings it surely was to sigh over the characters of that Victorian ballad's idiotic story when there could be so many other claims on them...She herself was leaning her graceful body against a bole now, and, speaking through branches of thin, leathery leaves, shiny and each shaped like a reaper's hook, she said to me: 'Tell me, Bruno – or shall I tell you? – what part you should play in my *Parkers*?'

2

I had lied to Auntie Eileen and Ian about where I had gone for the weekend. Why I did so I am not now altogether clear. Perhaps my aunt would have frowned on my going to stay with an older man whom I knew so slightly (little guessing that the side of his personality she might fear was one I was entirely aware of). I obviously couldn't have shown her Charles' letter, and how could I have expected to be believed if I'd said I was going to spend a weekend at the home of that nation-wide celebrity, Verity Orchard? But there was, of course, something else: I wanted to keep my entrée into *The Parkers* to myself, even though I had to acknowledge the fact that my aunt and cousin were wholly responsible for my interest in the programme.

I had told them that my godfather, Sir Leslie Ormroyd, had invited me to go 'motoring' (as he would undoubtedly have put it) with him for the weekend (thus making his telephone number an irrelevance). My father was away on a business trip to Hamburg, Cologne and Munich. Of course – I told myself as I sat in Charles' Rover, heading back for London – I have to accept the possibility that Daddy has returned earlier from West Germany than programmed. And perverse Fate might have made him get in touch straightway with first his old friend, Sir Leslie, and then with Auntie Eileen, mentioning the former to the latter. But... but it was jolly unlikely, wasn't it? The stuff of paranoia. Rather than think about such improbable things I should concentrate on what Charles, speaking against the busy working of windscreen wipers, was now saying. Rain had started to fall after Sunday lunch, and was coming down dense and fast, rendering the great sweeps of Salisbury Plain almost invisible, except for the roadway itself with cars emerging through the downpour to pass or pass by ours, headlights on, sea-lions with luminous eyes swimming at maximum speed through dark water. One could appreciate that the Friday of our coming down to Dorset was the last day of a season.

'Well,' said Charles Compson, 'you seem to have made a peculiarly favourable impression on my wife. I mean "peculiarly" in the sense of "particularly", of course. I don't think it's in the least peculiar for someone to find you quite compellingly pleasing and attractive. After all, I find you so myself!'

What had Verity said to him about me? What tributes, even fuller than those she'd paid me to my face, had Charles heard? –tributes to my powers of understanding, to my talents, to my remarkable fittedness to participate in *The Parkers*, to all she'd 'understood' about me in the yew-grove?

Aloud I said: 'I've never got on with any woman better; she knows things about me that I didn't know myself.' I had not thought this until that moment, but, the statement having occurred to me as a way of praising Verity's intimate and flattering manner, it at once seemed to me to be the truth.

Charles turned momentarily aside from peering into the rain: 'And you are sure these things are there to be known?' he asked. He didn't seem to expect a reply, and swung his head back to its forward-leaning position. 'Once upon a time – far back in the mists of the past – Verity convinced herself that she knew things about me that I myself hadn't quite grasped. But, now I look back on it all, I don't think she did. Not at all!'

I thought: I don't want to hear any more about this.

'The things I was thinking about had mostly to do with me in relation to *The Parkers*.'

Charles' thick, sensual lips curled in a by no means wholly agreeable smile. 'Ah, *The Parkers*!' he said, 'let us never forget *The Parkers*. We touched on that subject coming down here, if I remember a-right. Perhaps to speak of them again on the return journey might be a smidgin superfluous.' Watching him – he was a handsome man, as I was always to think, even when he was childishly put out or nursing injuries, even after so much had changed between us – I could see that he was wrestling with himself: should he or should he not say what he obviously wanted to?

He decided that, whether he should or not, he would.

'Verity has enthusiasms,' he said, 'just as she has –' he paused significantly, 'sadnesses.' His pronunciation of the word was not exactly sympathetic. 'Enthusiasms can pass – pass quite quickly – just as sadnesses can. Well, you had a good example of *that* this weekend.' And indeed I had found it hard to relate the Verity of that late entrance into the dining-room on Friday night with the talkative, teasing, trusting hostess of Saturday and Sunday. Showing me the animals in the stables and the adjoining field (an old donkey rescued from ill-treatment, a marmoset in a hutch, fantail pigeons), helping Nesta with her goats, exercising and feeding the dogs (yes, their names *were* Festus and Mutt), making a Salad Niçoise, guiding me round her *Parkers* office, she'd struck me as not only imaginative but capable, resourceful, practical.

'So, in my humble view, if you want to persevere with all this *Parkers* stuff, then you – or should I say 'we'? – must keep her to the mark. You don't want Verity flitting off and away from you in some different direction, do you?' And I saw, uncomfortably sharply, another young man penning her a long, confiding letter and another young man coming down to The Puzzle for the weekend, and entering the unexpected dell full of yew-trees.

'No!' I said, emphatically, 'no, I don't!'

'Well, the person who usually guides her along the straight-and-narrow, to coin a phrase, is none other than Yours Truly, your chauffeur of the afternoon.'

I saw how this could be true, and made a resolution on the spot to be considerate and yes, respectful in all my dealings with him, and, even, to please him as best I could.

'Idiot!' said Charles, as an E-Type speeding through the swirling rain all but brushed our car, 'scum!'

He himself was a careful (rather than a cautious) driver, who relished all subtle nuances of control over a car. He had strong, gentle, creative hands, darkly hairy on the backs.

'What project are you working on at the moment, Charles?' I decided to ask, 'I've felt shy of asking you until this minute.' (Liar!) 'I'm sure you're working on some stage-set right now that's going to take London theatre-audiences by storm.'

I'd hardly got things right – Charles Compson was helping a friend out with décor for a revival of a Maeterlinck play in a small private members' theatre in Bolton. But he was pleased by what I'd asked and by how I'd asked it, and pleased too by the work he was doing.

So he talked – "Maeterlinck is so undervalued these days, it's positively tragic. You, I think, would respond to him very differently from all the other young insensitives of today. You, I think, would see the point of *The Death of Tintagiles* at once.' While he went on – and on – I asked myself what at The Puzzle I'd really like best. In my head I heard the old donkey bray again, and the tumbling pigeons musically coo. Whatever my faults and empty pretensions my heart has always gone out to the creature-world. Ask my wife, who always tells the truth!

Across the chasm of years, but through that day's downpour, objects in the dimly lit shop – P. Dickinson, Antiques (it was not called 'Treasure Trove' until later) – stare at me as though with animals' eyes: a grandfather clock, its face painted with a country scene, a wooden wine-cooler, a Georgian chest-of-drawers, glass decanters winking with what wan light fell on them, floral china pieces, jugs, tea-pots, plates, with their patterns of neat rosebuds and leaves on creamy-white. 'You'll know us all better,' they seem to proclaim, 'one day! And to think how little notice you took of us on our first meeting!' (And think, too, what *objets trouvés* they all had to vie with when P. Dickinson became 'Treasure Trove'.)

Not true, your rebukes! I want to counter. For I can see now the Fulham Road that early evening, swept by rain as by an energetic broom, and, inside the shop, that fine grandfather clock (made in Edinburgh, date 1858) pointing with elaborately wrought hands, positioned over stylised trees and crofts and burn, to one of those hours which are dividers of your life. If I felt nervous, while Charles fussed about the damp little back-kitchen making us tea, this was by no means an unpleasant sensation. It was the necessary apprehension of any artist or craftsman about to have his talents put to the test.

The flat above the antique shop was extremely small; Charles had been right to disparage it in his first letter to me. We approached the bed in silence – however had they got a double one up that staircase and into so tiny a room? they'd certainly never get it out again! – carrying out, as if acting rehearsed parts, the rite we had both known (from the beginning) was to be ours.

Rain roared as it fell off the inadequate guttering.

'You realise, I suppose,' said Charles, 'the gravity of all this?' (But he was already naked.) 'Two law-breakers, that's what we both are. With me by far the more serious offender!'

'I wasn't born yesterday,' I said.

'I'd almost convinced myself you were, dear boy! Why did you rebuff me that first day we met!'

I smelled that taxi's leather-pungent interior all over again.

'Didn't know you well enough!'

'That was all it was?' (spoken a little anxiously).

'Yeah, I think so!'

And to create the necessary respect and desire for myself, I could truthfully have added.

Charles stretched himself out on his bed; his large cock was rising slowly. 'Good!' he said, 'that's very good!'

He was comforting, as well as arousing, in his size and years as he lay underneath me, awaiting my attentions. I knew what I wanted to do, what I would be good at doing; self-admiration swept tinglingly through me. Stripped of clothes, he looked so much younger than I'd hitherto seen him, and yet his eyes, as they shone upwards to admire the whole of me, from face to stirring loins, had the appreciative light of the seasoned older man. I was being compared, judged and found meritorious. Did I really think then (as it seems to me now that I did) of my mother, her of the *Divine Pathway* (which she'd obviously preferred to her only son) or of my cold, ever-judging, ever-disappointed father, or that snobbish doctor's daughter (Nina Cardew) who'd set her sights on quite different young men from one who lived in Eileen Armitage's house? No, perhaps I didn't, perhaps I only thought of the figure I was cutting in Charles' admiring, excited eyes... I would do both of us proud. And I can honestly say that I did.

As I spoke of Wiltshire, Hampshire and Dorset, to my aunt and cousin, it occurred to me that I didn't (wouldn't) deserve the term 'liar'. After all, most of the places I was describing in such detail I had, in truth, been to that weekend. 'Did you see Shaftesbury, Bruno?' Ian asked, his dark eyes bright with memories of the *King's England*, 'it has one famous old street by the name of Gold Hill. It stands at an altitude of 900 feet.'

'No, we didn't go to Shaftesbury, I'm afraid,' I said, hoping this was consistent with what I'd already related of my travels.

'Blandford, then?'

Here I could rely on memory.

'There are *two* Blandfords,' Ian informed me, 'Blandford Forum and Blandford St Mary. Blandford Forum is the one we usually mean when we talk about Blandford. Perhaps you'd like to know how it got its unusual name?...'

I thought it well to hear him out, while preparing sentences to describe the Georgian houses I'd seen there.

'You really do bring places to life, Bruno,' Auntie Eileen said, 'I hope one day lots of people apart from ourselves will have the benefit of your talent!'

'*My cousin the writer!*' said Ian, as he had before, 'that's what I shall be able to say, isn't it?'

My cousin the writer! How the phrase has come back to haunt me!

How dreadfully difficult it was to sit through *The Parkers* that next week, having met its author and having been let into secrets about imminent developments. Auntie Eileen wondered if Laurence Tomlinson's new partner was entirely straight; I knew that he was not. She hoped that Davey Parker's sudden trouble with his eyes would not prove serious (couldn't it have the gravest consequences for his veterinary work?); I had the knowledge with which to reassure her. And guilt, of an intensity that I hadn't ever quite known before, but was to know many times again, broke over me.

Three items came for me in the post during the week following my visit to The Puzzle, the provenance, indeed, of the first and second of these.

Dear Bruno,

I did NOT enjoy your visit to The Puzzle. Fat Anna didn't either, and Lord Kitchener and the Air Commodore were distinctly hostile. I hope you don't come again. It isn't in my power to veto guests, otherwise I would veto you, believe you me!

Don't get me wrong, and think that I am objecting to you only because of your inability to tell a goat from a dog when it brushes against your foot. That is truly a sign of great inadequacy but I would be prepared to pass it over. Other things, however, I am not.

You think yourself irresistible, and that anyone who doesn't find you so isn't worth bothering about. On the other hand you are quite capable of picking and choosing where those who have gone all silly about you are concerned. If they're useful to you, you'll bother; if they aren't, well, you won't. Just now poor old Bruno Armitage is in a terrible fix. He doesn't know which should concern him more, gooey-eyed Charles or equally gooey-eyed Verity. And he's not such a simpleton as to be unaware they're in some sort of competition for him, the silly fools!

Well, I hope this letter will have the effect of making you not want to come near The Puzzle again (though I don't suppose it will). You spell trouble as far as Senfrith is concerned, and we've already had enough of that, thank you very much!

I'd like Lord Kitchener to butt you in the bottom (butt you in the butt, as our American cousins might say). That's the sort of treatment you deserve (and which you've got coming to you, you mark my words).

So stay away from Dorset, and take your red curly-mop to another county, if you please.

Yours faithfully,
Nesta Coolidge.

The second (accompanying a parcel which I had to collect from Tanbury Post Office):

My dear Bruno,

I've amused myself these last two days by unearthing some old scripts for you. They can show you – not least by the alterations etc scribbled in the margins – how we go about things with The Parkers.

One of these you yourself commented on during your wonderful, wonderful weekend with us: the episode in which Tom Cavan tells Elizabeth Parker of his feelings for Minty. (And how wretched I still feel about its consequences for you. It's just as well that I don't know that deplorable Nina Cardew's address, otherwise, now I've at last met you, that poison-pen letter I wanted to write her would be trebly poisonous.)

I feel so proud and honoured and grateful at the feeling you have for my programme. Get in touch with me soon, please, to let me know your responses to these scripts (which obviously are yours to keep).

Best love,
Verity

And the third?:

Dear Bruno,

Another 'away' assignment – this time thorny problems with a major British chemical company in St Helen's.

The letter I had from the consultant at Tanbury Royal is remarkably assuring. We shall have beaten your problem in a few months, he reckons, and he also thinks you could – and should – have a break from the treatment at Christmas.

I trust you are still getting on with your course work. Mixed reports from the Metropolitan College of St Alban's, I'm afraid, though better than ones you collected at Riverbury, and I hope to have a lengthy meeting with the staff tutors at the Tech. before the end of term.

Now for some very sad news. Your 'Uncle' Leslie died last week. He'd gone into the Hampstead Royal Free for an operation –you're old enough to know what it was, a prostate, which can be a simple op. but always, for some reason, carries a mortality risk. Well, poor Leslie died. He was my oldest friend from London University, so I can't help feeling sad. The funeral is being delayed until next Wednesday (27). I'd like you to be there, and enclose a card, with time and place of ceremony.

Good wishes,
Daddy

My reaction to the first of these letters surprises me the most now – on account of its tepidity. Surely Nesta's disapproval and dislike must have preyed on me, must have caused me to think about myself and the dishonesties of the relationships I was embarking on with both Verity and Charles? And surely I read in the letter disagreeable signs for the future?

I am today far from certain. I would answer the first question by countering that I was no stranger to being disliked. From my first day at kindergarten – when I complained about how hungry I was and expressed my anxiety that other children were being given helpings of food bigger than my own – many a teacher and many a fellow-pupil had regarded me unfavourably. Nor had my times at summer-camps and winter-sports courses been free of difficulties with others. Nesta appeared merely as the last and most tedious of too long a line. Of late, though, my fortunes had changed (deservedly, I thought) for both Auntie Eileen and Ian, the two principal nurses at the Hospital clinic (one female, one male), and now both Verity and Charles themselves all plainly admired me – in fact I could say surely that they were *besotted* by me. Why then bother about the opinions of a cracked old gentlewoman who sounded like a dog but looked like one of her goats?

That she *was* cracked seemed to me beyond disputing. One particular little incident came back to me:

I'd been crossing the backyard of The Puzzle, after a solitary walk, to keep my 4 o'clock appointment with Verity, who was to show me some analyses of listeners' comments. Suddenly I heard Nesta bark out from one of her stables: 'Bruno, if you wanted, you could give me some advice?'

'Yes, Miss Coolidge?'

'Come a little closer. You're not someone who goes all silly when things get stinky, I hope?'

'Not at all.'

'Stinkiness is part and parcel of life's richness, Bruno.'

'Of course it is, Miss Coolidge.'

'You see, I'm preparing a little musical for our Christmas show here in the village. No prizes for guessing what my theme will be.'

'I suppose......'

'Its title is a most amusing one –' she gave a coy chuckle here which I found distinctly irritating considering her gruff rudeness to me earlier on, '*Oklagoata*, a Rodgers, Hammerstein and Coolidge production.'

The very successful film of this very successful stage musical had recently been released, and we were all familiar with it – with its checked-shirted or bonneted folk singing out their sentimental optimistic numbers.

'I'm afraid I can't stop now, Miss Coolidge,' I apologised, 'I promised to be in Verity's study at four o'clock sharp.'

'But I'm in such need of a young man's comments on my lyrics.'

And she began on:

'Oh, what a beautiful udder!

Oh, what a beautiful teat!

Cow's milk's contemptible rubbish,

Goat's milk's a permanent treat!......'

'Must press on, Miss Coolidge!'

I was already regretting this impatience!

I now tore Nesta's letter up, angry at a contemptuous view of me that sought to impose itself on my appetising present and future. Rip –rip–rip– into the waste-paper-basket with it!

That night, however, I had a dream. I was standing on a lawn at some garden party or other (not Buckingham Palace, though this possibility occurred to me) dressed in a linen suit, and holding a megaphone. An announcement was expected from me; many people from the huge crowd had turned to me smilingly, clearly looking forward to whatever I was going to say. I was aware in the distance, however, of Nesta Coolidge, most strangely attired. For, far from wearing the shabby, eccentric clothes I'd seen her in, she was dressed in a gorgeous robe that shone as if diamonds and rubies had been sewn upon it, while on her head was something remarkably like a crown or coronet.

'Speech! speech!' came several voices.

Wanting to oblige everybody, I smiled in my most winning way and then raised the megaphone to my lips. I knew what words I should say. But the moment I opened my lips, I heard the the obscene crackle of peculiarly loud farts.

Some people in the crowd giggled nervously, but most looked shocked, disgusted. I blushed and tried again. Worse still, this time. The noises were those of someone with a serious bowel upset, and, to my consternation, I could now see shit flying from the mouth of the megaphone's horn, in all directions, spattering the smart garden party attenders.

One voice now raised itself above all others. 'Well, if that doesn't sum up Mr Bruno Armitage to a T.' It was Nesta Coolidge, stepping out from the horde and holding her crown high above her head. 'What a revolting exhibition! Can't I ask –' and she lifted her sparkling crown higher still, 'ask a kind someone to help me hang him. I'd so like to see him strung up as he deserves.'

I woke fearful, with people (it seemed) rushing at me to do me harm. Had I been a young child, I would have fancied I'd fouled the bed. But I hadn't done so; my body, as usual, was clean and dry. Well, I told myself relieved, if that isn't further proof that Nesta Coolidge is a dotty and unpleasant piece of work! Don't let me bother myself about her another minute.

In retrospect it seems to me that truly I did not.

That letter from Verity, accompanying the parcel of scripts, had me replying by return of post – in tones even more effusive, were that possible, than those in which I'd thanked her for my weekend at The Puzzle. As for the scripts themselves I studied them with an assiduity which I'd never given to anything before.

I had been so lazy, so lacking in interest all my schooldays. My shortcomings had not gone exactly unremarked; even to this day I can quote numerous condemnations of me by my mentors. But it is my deep conviction that both laziness and uninterestedness are unnatural vices; the natural virtue with which they contrast is the delight in particular matters that makes an individual, so grateful for their existence, feel that nothing is too much trouble that furthers knowledge of, and involvement with them. Rather the trouble itself becomes both agreeable, necessary and life-enhancing, helping to define you and your days, to give them their individual and unique colours.

That's what I thought as I began my scrutiny of *The Parkers* scripts. Bruno Armitage was becoming more Bruno Armitage – and less an attempt at him made by others – as he saw how a radio script was brought about, how one episode of a serial related in a hundred complex, subtle and hidden ways to previous ones, how each had its own rhythm, its pauses, its fade-outs, its climaxes, its movement towards cliff-hanging end.

What had been a predisposition to fall in love now became love itself. Ian had called me his 'cousin, the writer'. Well, so it was, so it should be.

I come to my reception of the third letter, from my father. Almost before I reached its appalling last paragraph, I was seized by hysterical panic. Yes, here was Fate dogging me, persecuting me yet again just as it had done so many times before – for example, during those exams when so many boys had cheated and only B.L. Armitage had been ignominiously found out.

How to prevent the conversation between my father and my aunt which would give away my deceitful behaviour and might even undo the most important friendships of my life? Rats seemed to gnaw at me within even as I articulated the question to myself, and bats to flap and fly about in dark mental caverns.

Panic begets ingenious solutions to distorted problems. That which it made me arrive at now changed my life no less than the weekend at The Puzzle had done, or my subsequent immersion in Verity's scripts.

I decided to confide in my cousin, Ian.

3

The episode of *The Parkers* for Thursday, November 21 was as good as its most enthusiastic listeners could have hoped. Mrs Bobbington tried a quack remedy for her corns, but it made her feet swell up, obliging her to clean The Vicarage ('from top to bottom as per usual') in a pair of floppy carpet-slippers; Elizabeth Parker, understandably though uncharacteristically, lost patience with Irish writer, Kevin O'Flynn ('I'm very sorry that it's melancholy you are about your childhood in Limerick, Kevin, but just now some of us are busy working – and it wouldn't be a bad thing if you were working as well!'). And then, who was this curious man who turned up at the private hotel, The Elms, announcing he'd known officious church-worker Miss Venables 'in circumstances it might be – shall we say, *prudent* – not to relate'? (Even I, who'd had a glimpse into the *Parkers* future, knew nothing about this little mystery.) As I listened, I found myself gratefully parodying *Round and About Our Vicarage*: 'It's ever so cosy at tea-time in Eileen Armitage's little Tanbury house. The rain is pattering away at the bay-window, but the sound of it only emphasizes how snug and safe we all are here in the sitting-room, and besides, Eileen's row of potted cyclamens on the windowsill look so cheerfully sturdy that you know bad weather is powerless to do anybody or anything any harm. We're beautifully warm inside because, as always, Eileen has turned the gas-fire on very high. Behind the sofa stands the trolley with its tea-tray and welcome plates of toasted scones and jam-filled sponge-cake. From the Bakelite radiogram come the strains of "Sellinger's Round" which means, sadly, that our favourite programme, *The Parkers* is coming to an end.'

But as usual the signature tune hadn't quite played itself through before Auntie Eileen and Ian came out with their comments: 'Well, I must say Kevin O'Flynn had it coming to him. For Elizabeth of all people to say that to him... perhaps it'll do him some good!' 'Do you remember, Mum, we've already had a hint that there might be something odd in Miss Venables' past? About a week ago. She was talking to Derek and Elizabeth, and she said she'd never been to Bristol in her life, and then that bloke who's Dr Macdonald's locum popped round, and she forgot herself and made it clear that she knew Bristol pretty well.' Auntie Eileen said ruminatively, as she turned the radiogram off: 'Why, yes, Ian, how clever of you, I do recall something of the sort. Bruno, have another slice of the sponge, won't you, dear? – it's never so light and feathery again as it is the afternoon it's made... And talking of Dr Macdonald, are we to take it that Minty's set her sights on this young man she met at the dance and so won't have time for poor Tom? If he ever plucks up the courage to tell her how serious he really is!'

Ian looked across the hearth at me, his cousin who might well be expected to know about dealing with girls. There was a quizzical brightness in his dark brown eyes as he said (for my benefit, I couldn't help thinking): 'Oh, I'm sure Tom Cavan can look after himself okay, Mum, even though he is a bit shy. If Minty Macdonald isn't interested in him, he'll find someone who is easily enough.'

Was I blushing? After all Tom Cavan and I were as good as the same person. Hadn't his creator said as much? But there was a real Tom, of course, Neil Micklewright. A dull sort of person apparently. But had Verity just been calling him that to put me off a scent? Suppose he meant as much to her as I did, or more? Or to Charles. For I wasn't at all sure that Verity was unaware of her husband's tastes, and he must have had opportunities to get to know the various *Parkers* young men...... Oh, wasn't this the beginnings of paranoia? I was in difficulty enough without adding further complications to my life.

I smiled back at my young cousin (what a child he seemed, inhabiting a different universe from that of Verity Orchard, Charles Compson and Nesta Coolidge!). 'You could well be right there,' I said, 'anyway, I must be getting back to my old labours, mustn't I, Auntie Eileen? whatever the situation in Greenfield End... But if you'd like to look in on me, Ian, in, say, about an hour's time, when I'll have got through what I'm doing now, I daresay I'll be glad of a few minutes' distraction.'

Pleasure and gratitude instantly suffused Ian's round, red-cheeked, cherubic face, as always after I'd condescended to admit him to my room, or shown him that his company wouldn't be altogether objectionable to me. What a heel I was, what a jerk! I'd had so many opportunities of making him happy this autumn, and yet had chosen to be, for the most part, aloof, I who knew only too well what a lonely boyhood was like, with no-one around to chat away to or simply muck about with.

In truth, for all the concentration I was to give my French texts, Ian could have come up to my room then and there. (Could anything be less interesting than Racine's *Andromaque* anyway?) But Ian had his own prep. to do, which he usually got on with in the warmth of the kitchen, his tongue sticking out as he pegged away. I must, I told myself, bear in mind that he's just a kid, knowing nothing of Life (into which I felt the weekend at The Puzzle and its aftermath had truly initiated me). He'd need to be flattered, and – after he'd agreed to support me in the story I would tell – to be coached and rehearsed. The tiniest gaffe on his part, and I'd be for it, the victim not just of reproaches and accusations from father and aunt (though these would be painful enough) but of questions it'd be death to my very freedom to answer.

Did I have any moral misgivings about what I was going to persuade Ian to do for me? No, because I thought making him a confidant would bring him such joy, and afterwards I would be as sportingly nice to him as – well, as the nicest big brother (or cousin) in those adventure stories we read at prep. school (Malcolm Savile, Arthur Ransome, Enid Blyton).

The conversation that hadn't as yet taken place replayed itself over and over in my head, with many variations, while the pages of Racine grew blurry to my eyes, and the little radio I'd placed on my desk vibrated with the pop songs of the day. In a way, I thought, listening to these was like following the characters in *The Parkers*: you knew exactly what was coming next, and the knowledge only intensified your delight. But then (I thought) sooner or later – sometimes quite abruptly, but mostly by a gradual but unspoken consensus – these seeming indispensables were heard no more, entered some limbo of silence and forgottenness, and no-one spared them a thought. Right now I knew every bar of 'Diana' (Paul Anka), 'That'll Be the Day' (The Crickets), 'Whole Lotta Shakin' Goin' On' (Jerry Lee Lewis) and felt as if I would never stop hearing them. How could you tire of something so vital, so sure of itself? But already I was detecting that that favourite of mine for singing or whistling in the bathroom, 'Last Train to San Fernando' was receding; soon the radio would relay its strains no more. Something else would have taken its place, and we'd all be wondering why we'd bothered about the earlier number the way we had.

Could the same fate be Tom Cavan's, Kevin O'Flynn's, even the Rev. Derek Parker's? It seemed implausible; *The Parkers* was such a fixture in our lives.

But so had Johnny Duncan's 'Last Train to San Fernando' seemed – inseparable from the period of my move from Primrose Hill to Tanbury. But – admit it now! – what was it compared with this pounding item from that rubber-limbed black giant called Little Richard, appropriately enough playing just as Ian gave his none-too-soon well-bred little knock on my door: 'Keep a-knockin', but you can't come in'?

Ian, on the contrary, was most welcome in (though my temples were throbbing, and there was a tightness in my guts). 'It's great this one, don't you think, Bruno?' he asked, indicating the radio with the gesture of an embryonic rock'n'roller.

'Mm!' To sound too enthusiastic would be to put myself on Ian's age-level; it was very important in the handling of this whole situation to appear not just cool but sophisticated (even dauntingly so). 'Mm,' I re-affirmed, 'it's *okay*.' It was advisable to keep the rock'n'roll programme on, I thought, less danger of Auntie Eileen's overhearing us.

Ian was looking up at me with soft brown dog's eyes. Did he *love* me, then? No sooner had I asked myself this than it occurred to me – as if I'd seen the words suddenly on a screen on the wall: 'I don't know any more about Ian than he does about me. I've no idea what he's like in school, how he talks when he's among his pals. Not always as the cherubic mother's helper surely?' What sort of Ian Armitage did Tanbury Grammar School's 3A see and hear?...

'Good you could come up here for a chat,' I said, with a touch of drama in my husky whisper that'd have done credit to the boards of the Riverbury stage, 'I'm in need of some help right now – help and advice – and where better could I get them from than my cousin, Ian Armitage?'

Ian looked more astonished than overcome by joy. 'Help? advice?' he repeated, 'why, whatever's wrong, Bruno?'

'Wrong!' I shrugged the word off as unsuitable for one of my years and experience, 'I don't know about *wrong*! Anyway, I'd better begin at the beginning, hadn't I? Take a pew, Ian.' He obviously didn't know this expression, so I had to say: 'I mean, sit *down*. On the bed, that's right...'

Suddenly I didn't want to go on with this talk. Perverse of me. It still wasn't too late to abandon its intended subject. I could surely improvise something else for which I needed assistance.

But on the other hand how otherwise to get out of the mess – the very considerable and ugly mess – that I was in, except via Ian? So I forced myself on.

'Last weekend,' I got out, 'last weekend I bet you don't where I was.'

'Where you were. Of *course* I know, Bruno – you were with your godfather, what's his name, your Uncle Leslie, touring Dorset.'

I tried not to see that man's face first contorted in agony and fear, then drained of life, empty eyes of a cold corpse on a mortuary slab, but I did so nonetheless. 'Well, that's where you're wrong, Ian. I was somewhere different, somewhere very important – particularly to all of us in this household. Can't you guess?'

'How the heck can I guess a thing like that?' Ian's eyes had brightened with interest (and suspicion?), and he was leaning forward with his head held up as if to ray their beams right into me.

'Have a try!'

Ian gave a schoolboy's pert laugh: 'New York?'

'No, you're not even "warm".' Pointless, I saw, to continue the guessing game. 'I was with *The Parkers*.'

'*The Parkers*? How *could* you be with *them*, Bruno? I mean, they're not real.'

This remark sounded all but blasphemous. *The Parkers* not real? What an idea!

'Well, I don't of course mean it *literally*,' I said, realising that my opening ploy hadn't been as judicious as I'd imagined it would be, and extricating myself from it quickly by means of a condescending smile.

Ian, cupping his cherubic head in his hands, and swivelling it to scrutinise me, said, softly, but in a voice, for all his Murillo-like appearance, by no means without menace:

'In what way *did* you mean it then, Bruno? You're obviously not telling me you went to Greenfield End?' The look on his face did not suggest (as in my anticipations) that for a minute he thought his admired older cousin had gone off his head. No, he clearly sensed straightaway that there was something fishy in what I was about to confide, in perhaps the whole situation of this summons to my room. He was going to be as careful and canny as he could in his reception of anything I said.

'I'm hardly likely to tell you *that*, am I?' I gave a brief derisive laugh, 'because there's no such place as far as I know.' Though hadn't there seemed to be, on Sunday, on the other side of the cliff-path? 'No, what I'm trying to say – and maybe, Ian, you haven't shown much patience so far; I'm sure your teachers at school would advise you to listen for a bit longer before you rush in with comments – what I'm trying to say is that I spent the weekend,' and even in the midst of all my difficulties I couldn't keep a certain satisfaction and, worse, pride, out of my voice, 'with the *creator* of *The Parkers*. So in a manner of speaking you could say I spent it with *The Parkers* themselves.'

Ian's voice was now no more than a whisper, hard to hear above the continuing rattle and twang of the pop. record programme, 'You mean Verity Orchard? You spent from Friday to Sunday with *Verity Orchard*? But you don't know her!'

'I most certainly do,' I said grandly, 'I'd hardly have invited you up to my room to give you a pack of lies, would I?'

Ian considered this. 'How come if you knew her, you've never said anything about it before?'

This was where I'd thought striking a note of young-man's mystery would be most appropriate. 'Gosh, there are lots of things about me you don't know, Ian. Lots about any bloke my age, I'd reckon. I've been around, you know.' And I couldn't but see myself now, vigorous and resourceful, with Charles in the little room above P. Dickinson, Antiques, 'I must keep some things secret – you do see that, Ian, don't you? – otherwise I simply wouldn't have a life to call my own. It's called freedom,' I finished pompously.

'So how long have you known Verity Orchard?'

This was a hard one.

'Not so very long really.'

Ian's voice had risen now – though from the radio Elvis' 'Teddy Bear' was vibrant and strong enough to win against his words: 'Do you mean to say that while we've been sitting there, Mum and you and me, listening to *The Parkers*, wondering what's going to happen, you've actually been *friends* with the lady who writes the scripts...'

'Well, I haven't exactly been *friends* with her all that time,' I said, thinking – too late – that perhaps an edited, differently slanted story (with gaps, of course) in which Charles Compson played the central role would have been a happier idea, easier to carry out. I'd thought a fabrication – based on my undeniable love of the programme – would prove a better stratagem than the ramified and question-provoking truth.

'*How* long, Bruno? *How* long have you known Miss Orchard, and kept it from Mum and me?'

Today I am convinced that I still at this point had the chance to save myself: if I'd answered truthfully, that I hadn't met her until the Friday of last week, Ian would in some way (after a real effort on my part, doubtless) have been appeased. But how could I make this fact credible without giving away more of the story of my friendship with Charles than I wished to be known? 'It's so hard to measure time,' I said, ' I mean I haven't known her as long as I've been living here in Tanbury obviously – well, you remember what a *Parkers* ignoramus I was when I first came to live with you. But I've written her and all, and she's appreciated the various ideas I've sent her, enough anyway to.....,' and I gave a modest cough of a laugh here, 'invite me down to her house in Dorset to talk them over. (I really *was* in Dorset, you see!) She's going to base forthcoming scripts on things I said to her.'

I hadn't delivered this at all well; my words were neither well-chosen nor well-spoken. I was aware of a very different expression in

Ian's dark eyes from the moist devotion he'd displayed on entering my room. Once again I thought how limited my knowledge of him was.

For a moment I thought he wasn't going to say anything further, would simply sit there staring at me stonily but interrogatively for a bit longer, and then get up and leave the bedroom. Then into the room flooded that pop. favourite of which no-one so far seemed to have tired, that number which more than any other turned thoughts to sex and fun and liberty (but not, I'm afraid, to a flat above an antique-shop in the Fulham Road) 'A Whole Lotta Shakin' Goin' On.' Guitars twanged, Jerry Lee Lewis' pumping piano sounded away, and his words were oily, insistent, seductive while I contended with my cousin's now released invective. Positively impassioned he was, the silly bastard, choking over some words while spitting out others, and now and again repeating himself to make time for other and stronger phrases. I would never have believed my kid-cousin to be capable of such prolix indignation or to be bold and articulate enough to express it so forcibly. My loins jellified with (merited) guilt.

'You weren't just a *Parkers ignoramus*, Bruno, you'd never even heard of *The Parkers* before you came to live with us in Tanbury, you didn't even know what time of day it came on the radio. No, you didn't know a *thing* about the characters and had to ask lots and lots of questions about them, some of them pretty stupid I thought at the time, though I was too polite, and sorry for you also (with your illness and all), to say so. And in the beginning you were even a bit snooty about the programme – I could tell that, even if Mum's too nice not to of noticed – yes, you thought Mum and me a bit dim, a bit common, way beneath you and your Riverbury friends, 'cos we followed the programme so regularly. You only listened because you thought, well, what else is there for me to do in a dump like Tanbury when I come from the highest class, used to smart London ways. Though I admit you got fond of the people in the programme quickly enough, and picked up on their situations… And so now you're an *expert* on them, huh? a real expert with important ideas that people take notice of, and you write away to Miss Orchard without ever telling us, and you get replies and you still don't tell us – don't tell Mum and me who introduced you to the programme, and don't have all that much excitement in our lives, and would have given such a lot to have heard all *The Parkers* news you've gone and got. But no, you don't mention a *thing* about it, do you, Bruno? not a thing. And then you're given invitations to visit Dorset to discuss *Parkers* ideas with the Maker of the Programme Herself. And still you don't say a word, but just let Mum and me think that what you're doing at the weekend is touring round with some silly old gaffer who's your godfather. But all the time you're being consulted about England's most important programme, but you don't let on until a week later and then in a hole-in-the-corner sort of fashion.'

He was red in the face and out of breath, but, though he spoke as with a lump in his throat, he wasn't actually crying – though I feared that any moment he might do so. Auntie Eileen was either watching the news or very busy in the kitchen; surely she was likely to catch the strains of this outburst and think something very peculiar indeed was happening up in her nephew's room.

'Steady on!' I said, when he enabled me to, 'hold your horses! You keep on saying I've never told you a thing. True, *up to this evening* – when I *have*. Can't you understand that I was going to tell you all along and that I was merely *waiting for the best time to do so*. They're very temperamental people, these creative BBC types, you know.' That, as far as Verity Orchard was concerned, was certainly very true. 'And do you seriously believe,' I attempted righteous indignation now, 'that I haven't told Miss Orchard how I came to be a *Parkers* fan, and how I have this unusually intelligent younger cousin, Ian, who's extremely keen on the programme and can give you more accurate information about it than even a member of the BBC staff. "You've simply got to meet Ian," I said to Verity. Can't you believe me? Otherwise why would I have asked you to come to talk to me in this room?'

I have, as I've already confessed, told many, many lies in my life, in fact I sometimes wonder if I've ever gone a day without telling them. But I don't think I've ever felt worse than I did when I told this one. Ian – whom anger and hurt had abruptly made appear older – now looked a child again, eager for any consolation.

Nevertheless: 'But *Mum*,' he said throatily, 'have you told Verity Orchard about *her*? She's even more devoted to *The Parkers* than I am, even if,' a touch of a boy's conceit here, 'even though her memory isn't

79

as good as mine. She'll want to know about your new friendship and your plans for the programme, and she'll want to meet Verity Orchard also.'

Really it had all worked out just about as badly as I could have feared. And I still hadn't come to the worst part, the actual reason for admitting to the lie, the trouble (and humiliation) that would come to me if (when) it was found out.

'I'd love Auntie Eileen to meet Verity,' I said, almost laughing at the picture of my comfy, unsophisticated, dowdy aunt at The Puzzle – listening to Verity's theatrical effusions, sipping port and exchanging remarks about Virgil with Charles, entering into the spirit of Nesta's *Oklagoata...* 'but the time isn't right yet, though I'm working on it. Verity isn't like any other woman I've met, you know. She is an extraordinary person, and...' The return of that stony expression to Ian's eyes alarmed me. Whatever else he was, my cousin clearly wasn't a fool, nor a complete child either; he knew that in my hesitations lay a certain social embarrassment at his mother, that I thought her somewhat non-U (that dreadful word of the times) and therefore unfitting to be introduced to Britain's leading scriptwriter. I must get now to the point, I told myself – to the main reason for confiding in Ian.

'The thing is,' I began, 'when I decided – under pressure from Verity, you know; don't let's forget she's one of the most famous people in the country; all those interviews and articles on her in *Radio Times* and *Everywoman* and *The Sunday Express* and *Country Life* – when I decided *(for her sake)* that I should keep it secret that I was going to Dorset, I told a stupid lie, I'm afraid... I don't like lies, and of course never tell them as a rule. But there *are* times...' When it's best to tell a lie, I was going to say, but Ian's glare was so fierce I faltered, and then changed course to: 'when you go against your better judgement and lie nonetheless. So, as you know, I said I was with my godfather, Sir Leslie. But the dreadful truth of the matter, which I couldn't have foreseen, is...'

Laurie London's skiffle number 'He's Got the Whole Wide World In His Hands' (which I didn't care for at the time and have never liked since) and the engulfing external and internal emotionalism of our conversation had quite prevented the pair of us hearing the telephone downstairs. Now came a knock on my bedroom door – Auntie Eileen's, who else's? – far less diffident than her son's (but then it was *her* house) – and with a perturbed perplexed expression on her face she entered the room. 'Bruno, it's Raymond – your father on the phone. He's ringing from St Helen's, so you'd best be nippy going downstairs to answer him. He wants –'

I knew it all now before she finished her sentence, knew it from her not being able to look me in the face as she spoke.

'He wants to have a word with you. About your godfather's funeral on Wednesday.'

Ian looked up at me from his seat on the bed, with, on his Murillo face, something not far from moral horror.

Most decidedly Bruno Armitage didn't have the Whole Wide World in His Hands.

Supper was shepherd's pie, a dish which Auntie Eileen could do really well, all brown and furrowed on top, with the mince juicy and well-seasoned underneath; it had already come to be known in the household as 'Bruno pie'. This evening, awaiting us, in its earthenware dish and decorated with little sprigs of parsley, it provided as vivid a rebuke to me as I could not have hoped for. ('And yet,' began an inner voice, one I soon came to fear and detest above the others, 'what have you done that's so very dreadful? Leaving aside the question of sex with an older man – maybe, in a fairer, more sensible world, *not* leaving that aside – isn't all this fuss a pretty ridiculous storm in a tea-cup? Why, it wouldn't even be reckoned strong enough for an episode of *The Parkers*.')

Daddy, muffled by the distance between Oxfordshire and South Lancashire, had merely said in that cold bemused but basically indifferent voice that, my whole life long, he'd employed with me: 'Eileen says you spent last weekend touring with Leslie, but knowing what I know, and what you yourself know now, that obviously wasn't the case. I suggest you get the mix-up about your doings and whereabouts sorted out pronto. And I'll be expecting you to do a bit of further touring with Leslie, so to speak,' the bitter humour was so obviously mirthless it struck at me far more violently than any proper reprimand could have done, 'I want you here by ten thirty on Wednesday, which gives us good time to get to the cremation service at midday. And there'll be "baked meats" afterwards, which there is no question of you not attending.'

The phone call over, silence prevailed for an appalling length of time, though measured by the watch it probably didn't last more than a couple of minutes. As I helped myself to the pie, Ian watched me with a strange intentness that made my hand tremble as it operated ladle and fork. It was almost as if the scales had literally fallen from his eyes. Another watcher was my late uncle whose framed photo stood in place of honour on top of Auntie Eileen's hideous cheap-reproduction sideboard. I had memories of this man, blurred and non-consecutive ones admittedly, because when my mother and I had been sent out of London during the bombing to a Suffolk village, he had visited us, being stationed not so far away. I'd thought him silly, I now recalled, full of compliments that he obviously thought would make me like him. But I hadn't. Now he seemed to be saying: 'Well, you haven't fared any better than I did, Bruno. Tell a silly lie, and it's sure to trip you up sooner or later.'

Now why did I fancy that *that* was what his round freckled face was saying?

Meanwhile his widow, Auntie Eileen slowly poured water for us all, a quite tragical expression on her face. It was all I could do not to hum my bathroom stand-by 'Last Train to San Fernando' in the teeth of all this disapproval. But my loins for the second time that evening had gone like jelly again. Finally Auntie Eileen said, with a lightness of touch I wouldn't have credited her with: 'You gave us such a lively account of touring Wessex with Sir Leslie, Bruno. As I remarked at the time, Ian and I felt we'd been there ourselves. All those bare chalk hills and thatched cottages – very different from a private room in a London hospital I'd say.'

Blushing so deeply it hurt, I said: 'But I didn't go to any hospital.'

Auntie Eileen said: 'Why doesn't that surprise me, Bruno?'

'But I *did* go to Wessex. To Dorset anyway.'

'You tell Mum who you stayed with there,' said Ian.

Auntie Eileen turned to her son: 'You know then, do you, Ian?'

'Bruno told me just before you came into his room,' said Ian, his gaze still on my burning face.

I gulped water.

'So who did you stay with? I'd be most interested to find out. Better late than never! Now we know you weren't having a long vigil with the dying man who's left you money....'

I gulped more water. 'Left me money!' I echoed, and the words came out oddly (as well they might).

Auntie Eileen clapped a hand over her mouth, just as the schoolgirl she'd been would have done. 'Shouldn't have said that!' she apologised, 'you're not meant to know. Sorry I spoke.' It was she who was blushing now, and our eyes, each imploring the other to be merciful, met. 'But having gone as far as I have, I'll break my promise to your father (naughty of me, I know) and tell you – in exchange for information about your weekend, of course.'

This morally dubious proposal seemed fair enough to me. Anyway what other course of action had I? I gave my aunt more or less the same story as I had Ian who never stopped studying my face, as if he could detect in it inconsistencies, discrepancies, the tentative beginnings of a lie proper. In fact my account was short of the truth only in its (admittedly very considerable) omissions. After all (and that most dangerous of voices congratulated me for these self-reassurances) I had written to Verity Orchard with proposals for *Parkers* episodes, she had been interested in my ideas about Tom Cavan's relationship to Minty Macdonald, she had sent me scripts (I could get them down from upstairs by way of proof) and already I'd found them outstandingly interesting – in a life which had contained so few things that interested me.

Had I then been of a more philosophical cast of mind, I could have been given much to think about that evening concerning truth and our relationship to it. How by carefully steering my story I avoided any falsehood, and yet, leaving Charles Compson out as I did, produced a tale that bore slender relation to reality even where Verity Orchard herself was concerned. One further thing – I came closer to the facts of the case this second confession than I had the first. Without giving precise dates I contracted the time of getting to know Verity Orchard so that an impartial listener might have arrived at something not so unlike how it had been in life.

Auntie Eileen wasn't – or didn't let herself appear – as jealous of *The Parkers* as her son, nor did she impute (even by implication) any feeling of social superiority to me, as if I considered herself and Ian unworthy of meeting the Queen of Radio Drama. She herself – as could have been expected – used the words that best described her manner: 'I'm speaking, Bruno, more in sorrow than in anger.' *Sorrow*, I suggested silently, by raising my eyebrows, what for?

'For feeling that you couldn't trust us. Oh, I admit, I've insisted you're regular in your treatment at the hospital, and I've insisted you get on with your "A" Level work – partly because I promised Raymond that I would, and partly because I feel sure these are the best courses for you. But surely you can *hardly* say I otherwise play the part of the heavy aunt, and, believe you me, I often turn a blind eye or a deaf ear, when I know you're paying more attention to the radio than to your books... So why the evasions, Bruno, why the failure to tell me the truth?'

My loins felt so softened up now, mightn't they be in danger of melting away? 'I was going to tell you,' I mumbled, and once again, if I'd been content to leave well alone, all might have been redeemed, 'I was going to tell you *everything*.'

Use of that last word must count as one of the greatest mistakes of my life. But I was weary, was longing to be free of this supper-table and this situation (though I continued to tuck into a shepherd's pie excellent even by Auntie Eileen's high standards), and I wasn't as mindful of the implications of what I was saying as I should have been.

Ian's voice was starting to break, but right now it rang out with the bell-like clarity of a child's: 'Everything?' he sang back at me, '*everything*, Bruno? You were not! I *know* you weren't! You invited me up to your room to help you concoct –' he seemed horribly pleased with his (not inapt) choice of word, for he repeated it, 'yes, to *concoct* a story for Mum's benefit about where you'd been at the weekend. You'd *just* got to the point when you were going to confess to me that your Uncle Leslie was, without you knowing it, very ill and had since died, when Mum came in after speaking to Uncle Raymond. But it's all very clear to me: you were going to try and get me on your side so that together we could concoct,' that word again! 'something that would satisfy Mum about what you'd be doing and that I could back up... Right, aren't I?'

I felt myself change from someone hot and scarlet with blushing to someone blanching, from whom the blood was draining away. Auntie Eileen, who normally would have rushed to solicitude at seeing me unwell, put down her knife and fork, and said in the chilliest voice I'd ever heard her use:

'Is this true, Bruno? Assuming you know the meaning of that little word?'

I was beaten. 'I suppose so!' I said.

'Suppose so? What does that mean? I asked you, is what Ian said true?'

Beaten, beyond any fight-back. 'Yes!' I replied.

'I'm quite a broad-minded person,' said Auntie Eileen with a hurt, insulted look that has remained with me, that gets imposed on her face of a few years later, exhausted and yellow with the cancer that was killing her, 'and if a young man of nineteen wants to go off to have some fun – whether with Verity Orchard or some girl from the streets – I'm not going to poke and pry. I know what the male of the species can be like, particularly if he fancies himself; I was married to one, my dear Bruno, to Raymond's brother, and a right fool he was! But one thing I won't countenance is deceit. And another is the attempt to make other people – particularly impressionable young boys like Ian here – parties to that deceit.'

'Now if you'd kindly leave the table so that I can regain my temper and finish my meal in some sort of peace, I'd be grateful. The two of us may talk further later on tonight. On the other hand I might decide to leave things till the morning. Either way you can take it from me you've well and truly blotted your copy-book, my lad.'

I looked back across the room to the sideboard photo of Ian's father, Uncle Brian, and saw now a decided smirk on that 'right fool's' foolish face.

That evening I chucked my copy of *Andromaque* into the waste-paper-basket. What was all this to-do about 'A' Levels and qualifications anyway? I didn't need them. I was going to have a different future from any my father and aunt envisaged: I was going to write radio serials; I was going to be Ian's 'cousin the writer'.

Carefully I took out one of the *Parkers* scripts that Verity had sent me. As if actually in a studio I saw the characters moving about, speaking to each other, lovingly, angrily, informatively, evasively – and beyond them I saw the houses and gardens and church spire of comfortable, comforting, busy yet ultimately tranquil Greenfield End.

And – perhaps an indication that I was, after all, a genuine script-writer – a bold idea came to me. Why shouldn't I turn my present horrible plight into a *Parkers* story? Why shouldn't Tom Cavan experience something like what I was going through now?

I picked up a biro and began to jot down some sentences.

I am not lying when I say that it wasn't until an hour or so later that I remembered what Auntie Eileen had said about Uncle Leslie having left me some money. Perhaps, in addition to being a valued member of the BBC staff, a cherished colleague of the esteemed Verity Orchard herself, I was shortly to become a rich man. That too would show them.

4

If I haven't said much so far about Sir Leslie Ormroyd (knighted for his services to British commerce and industrial relations two years before his death in his mid-fifties), it's because I have so very little to say. He bored me – just as I, and indeed any young person, male or female, patently bored him. He was a tall, gaunt man with thick grey-streaked black hair that sprang back from his scalp, highlighting his high intellectual forehead; his hands were a conspicuous feature, with long sensitive strong-seeming fingers, and Daddy had often remarked on what a fine pianist he'd been when younger. And indeed insofar as he ever permitted himself pleasures, attending concerts, nearly always alone, of up-and-coming instrumentalists was one of them.

Nothing seemed to satisfy Uncle Leslie but work in its various but demanding forms: the long-drawn-out work of committees and conferences (and just how many he'd sat on, participated in and chaired I was to hear at interminable length at his funeral); the grinding work of computing figures both precise and conjectural; the exhausting and essentially combative work of persuading others of the merits of your proposals and of defeating those short-sighted and ill-informed enough to oppose them. Even an apparent social situation – a drinks party, a rendez-vous at one of his clubs, the Reform, the Travellers', or lunch at Claridge's or the Savoy – invariably turned out to be work in disguise, a meeting with an important West German, a discussion with an opinion-maker on the *Financial Times*. He and my father – as far as I could gather – talked work together, as they must have done when serious and ambitious students at London University, about the Common Market's Inner Six and Britain's failure to wake up to the opportunities the set-up offered, about our national reluctance to accept modern methods in management. Both men were enthusiastic champions of obligatory Union representation at any company's Board Meetings, then widely considered a suspiciously leftist and unBritish notion. But I can't rid myself of the idea that Uncle Leslie believed in this cerebrally – as doctors today will go through the motions of saying they accept the merits of holistic treatment. I doubt he had any real interest whatever in what he would have called 'the British working-man', let alone in the 'working-woman'.

Outside his convoluted complex of committee- and conference-rooms and his chambers high above a Mayfair square, he could only be at ease choosing items on a menu for a guest in a highly mannered, slow-moving and curiously furry voice. I know, because every holiday he invited me to a meal (in club or smart restaurant or hotel) and I would try (from my early adolescence onwards) to relieve my boredom by wondering if he'd ever been tempted to have a purely personal, let alone a sexual relationship with anyone – and how, if he had been, he'd dealt with the temptation.

And now the man was dead. Had he known he was dying? Had he been frightened? regretful? resigned? Did he imagine the life beyond the grave (well, beyond the urn of ashes; in his will he'd been adamant about cremation) as a vast, indeed endless system of committees on which he could be of literally cosmic use? Or did he realise, as he prepared to sail off into the measureless amorphousness of death that in no way could he be as useful and revered and important as he had been on earth, that he would find it – to a greater degree than most of us – a serious and solemn diminution of himself?

And yet this man – who must have judged me culpably frivolous ('without a brain in his head, poor chap,' I could imagine him saying), whom he must have dreaded having to entertain but always dutifully did, holiday in, holiday out, asking questions answers to which interested him not at all – had thought enough of me to remember me in his will.

Even at the time I realised that his doing this was a tribute to my father, to the Raymond Armitage who'd given him the only companionship he'd ever enjoyed.

I'd come already to the portals of death, it seemed to me, when I reached the flight of steps leading up to the door of the house I'd for so strangely long called 'home': tall, with a white-painted façade, and situated in a quiet cul-de-sac off the Regent's Park Road that spoke unequivocally of good salaries and good bank balances – and not perhaps of all that much else. And my feeling was reinforced when I actually stepped inside my father's inappropriately large ground-floor flat. It was only my second visit back here since I'd gone to live in Tanbury, and, on this damp, lightless November day, the apartment struck me as itself a form of tomb – or, to pursue the literal fate of Uncle Leslie's body – of urn: clasically proportioned, hushed, quite devoid of life. How much better was the sometimes fuggy but always snug sitting-room of Auntie Eileen's terrace-house: the cyclamens in the window, the Bakelite radiogram and Ferguson television set, the large standard lamp with its tasselled shade of appalling custard-yellow, the pea-green three-piece suite and the fitted carpet the busy patterns of which clashed with just about everything else, the trolley laden with tea-tray and plates of goodies – all that I'd catalogued in my pastiche of *Round and About Our Vicarage* – Christ, what wouldn't I give to be back there just now, and on our old good terms?

Well, maybe, to be strictly honest, there were things I *wouldn't* give. Things to do with freedom – freedom of thought, life-style, activity, movement. Of sex.

The sitting-room seemed so large, so still, so dreadfully flawless in its blend of soft colours and its immaculate arrangement of furniture. What, in all the past years, I wondered, had I ever done here? What (an even graver question) had I ever *felt* here? Unease took hold of me, as much at the thought of the life behind me as at the ordeal now ahead (which was essentially a social ordeal, not an emotional one; I was honest enough to concede that.)

Gabriella, the plump middle-aged Italian woman who was the new housekeeper here (no housekeeper lasted very long), had informed my father I'd arrived. Wouldn't most fathers have called out: 'Won't be a minute, son!' or 'Just make yourself comfortable, boy, and I'll be out in a jiffy!'? Not mine – though I was forgetting, of course, that not only was he in mourning but I, his only son, was in deep disgrace. In a double sense I was – suddenly I became aware of the sickly scent of great waxy creamy-yellow lilies – in a house of death.

Death? Had it ever come into *The Parkers*? I couldn't remember its ever having done so, and it would have somehow cheered me up if I'd been able to. Yet who saw more of death than a Vicar? When he wasn't posting his gloves instead of a letter, or listening to the garrulous officiousness of Miss Venables, the Rev. Derek was, as likely as not, ministering to a death-bed or pronouncing words over the lowering of a coffin.....

'Ah, there you are!' My father's severe, smart, formal appearance had the disconcerting effect of making him look younger, so I was aware of him as he walked across the room to shake me by the hand of all the strength and energy he was able to bring to the opposition between us, 'you don't look too much like a dandy in disguise, I suppose.'

I was wearing my best – dark blue – suit, and a black tie (bought at Tanbury's best tailor's only the day before) but with one of my cream poplin shirts and smart pointed Italian shoes. It could easily be said that I looked what I was, a reluctant mourner.

There followed a long, by no means unprecedented silence. Then Gabriella came in to offer us coffee before we set out (she hadn't thought to offer *me* any while I waited there for Daddy). My father – talking to her as if she were some new cabinet-filer for his office – said, yes, thank you, we had just about got time for some. Gabriella left the room, it filled up again with silence. Finally I said: 'I'm sorry.'

My father turned his head away from me, and, with a surely self-conscious gesture, straightened some magazines (*The Economist, Scientific American, Investors' Chronicle*) for the crookedness of which I had not been responsible. And as I looked at him, I was reminded – to my consternation – of my cousin, Ian. Something in his profile. Had my father's appearance been a Murillo-boy's when younger? Odd to think so. And if he looked like Ian, did I resemble his younger brother, my dead Uncle Brian at all, whose hair indeed had been reddish (though not my own 'carrot-top'). 'Well,' my father was saying, 'death's something we have to accept, the only trouble being we never know when we're going to be asked to do so.'

The tension of the situation – physical as well as emotional – made my next words come out all wrong: 'I wasn't meaning about Uncle Leslie, Daddy, I was meaning about what's happened with me at Auntie Eileen's.'

90

Daddy slowly swung his head round to look at me more directly, and, as he did so, he resembled Ian even more closely, I thought: Ian sitting on the bed and receiving my confession of deception, Ian hostile, trouble-making and admonitory at the supper-table... 'Is it possible, I wonder,' he said in perhaps the coldest voice he had yet used to me in a lifetime full of his cold voices, 'is it possible to find a bigger egotist than you are?'

His tone suggested that there were some people too morally inconsiderable to be worth much expenditure of time and trouble, and that I was conspicuously of their number.

Nevertheless, after Gabriella had come in with two strong black coffees served in elegant thin bone-china cups, he was pleased to remark: 'I'd prefer to leave the whole sorry business of *you*, and the mess that *you*, not for the first time in your life, have caused, until a decent interval after the important event of Leslie's funeral.'

I longed to ask, like a wayward child determined to behave badly: 'Decent interval? What does that mean? Hours, days, months? Whatever I've done, don't I have any rights? any say in things? I've been left money, it appears. I'd like to know about it; in fact I think I *should* know about it.'

But, of course, I didn't say anything of the sort. In fact I didn't attempt to break the prevailing silence, but in my head played the tune 'Sellinger's Round' over and again. It was almost as if I could at will step into an episode of *The Parkers*.

Mist penetrated even North London's upland and outer regions, robbing all its streets, all its gardens, all its eruptions of heath and parkland, of colour. Even a tree still rudimentarily leaved in faded orange-yellow or a bank of cotoneaster full of red berries did nothing to relieve the pervasive damp dullness. Isn't this how it all *should* be for a funeral? I said to myself, but even so I wished the weather were different. And when, after what seemed like many featureless miles we arrived at the crematorium – my residence in Tanbury had altered my sense of the scale of London; how truly vast 'my' city was! – I found myself resentful of place and atmosphere. A young man like myself

91

should be somewhere pleasant and interesting, not in a dripping garden for the dead beneath a heavy grey sky, one of a large but ill-assorted group of 'special' mourners, trooping eventually – after shiveringly standing about in the drizzle – into a chapel more like a public lavatory than a building for solemn religious rites.

Special funeral services for agnostics were not as common then as they have become since. Uncle Leslie's was an unconvincing listless amalgam of the conventional Church of England affair and the secular send-off he doubtless would really have preferred. Not so unfitting, I couldn't help thinking, perhaps his entire life has been a similar compromise, the right, the intelligent thing carried out, with neither convention flouted nor tradition blindly upheld – but how lacking in any kind of intensity, personality or sense of community it was, undenominational hymns, the singing of 'To Be a Pilgrim', the clichéd praise of him – 'a man who never spared himself, who never ceased unstintingly to draw from the resources of his superb mind' – by someone who had never known him. Give me St Luke's, Greenfield End, any time, I thought: and the Reverend Derek's sonorous voice reciting that beautiful poem by Traherne that I'd found by my bedside at The Puzzle, assuring us – and the dead man – of eternal joy, and fulsome hymns and prayers of a congregation made up of people who knew each other well. Daddy, beside me, and yet aloof from me too, had a remote, tight-lipped expression on his face; it was as if he had just won a war against all personal emotions, including fondness for Leslie Ormroyd and sadness at his passing, and as if these feelings, like devils in the Bible stories, had departed from his bodily form, leaving him drained, gloomy but prim.

Though I could and did play 'Sellinger's Round' internally during the service, its efficacy was limited. Dull, pompous words and bars of doleful, conventional hymns obtruded. And then came the ghastly gliding forward of the coffin to pass between curtains en route for the incinerator. My imagination had never dwelled on this event that was, in truth, not an event.... A lump of sick panic worked itself into my stomach, and only after some moments was I able to get the better of it. A terrible notion had come into my head: just as after the *Parkers'* closing signature tune the radio was switched off, so too now had been the knob of Leslie Armitage's life. Never to come on again – the wireless was defunct. He who had made vows on my behalf, and had with dismal gallantry entertained me all those years, he who had been so kind as to leave me money had become in seconds a handful of ashes. A wind could blow them all away and it would be as if he'd never existed.

The gathering afterwards, at a big house lost down foggy rich residential roads was awkward, being formal yet without helpful structure, and wholly cheerless: no noisy children, no embarrassing relations, no clamorously grieving lover. Daddy was plainly as eager to leave as I was – he was not a man with much small-talk or general charm, even though, well-dressed and courteous, he had a certain social presence – yet he took long enough to decide it was time to go. I for my part was by this time actively hungry but nobody else seemed to be, so I was shy about helping myself as amply as I would have liked to the chicken fricassée and potato salad provided by a catering firm. A well-known judge whom I'd met before but had totally forgotten talked to me about Riverbury under the impression I was still there. I hadn't the heart to tell him I wasn't. A large woman in an ocelot furcoat she never took off trapped me in a corner to tell me that she'd had a premonition of Leslie's death, having dreamed one week beforehand that he was floating down the Thames in a coffin. I was something very like pleased when at last my father came to me and said: 'Time to be leaving now, Bruno, I'm afraid! The mini-cab will be here any minute.'

I was surprised as we made out way to the front gate and the waiting car to find that the dark had not yet descended. No streetlamps were on, though the headlights of many cars were, on account of the fog; it was barely the middle of the afternoon. Service and 'baked meats' had seemed to last so long, and the battle against depression and hysteric revulsion had been so protracted that I could have sworn it was already advanced evening. There had been an understanding that I would stay this night at home in London, yet, as I sat there beside the stern, laconic man I so incongruously called Daddy, I could see no reason why I should do this: it was hard to believe I was wanted, let alone needed. And yet to return to Tanbury, Auntie Eileen and Ian.... that, with its prospect of spoken and unspoken reproaches, didn't appeal either. I needed a friend to go to!

I knew from the palpable increase in physical tension in my father the nearer we got to Primrose Hill that he had composed in his head the talk he was to have with me, and had determined to have it just as soon as he could.

Understandable, unavoidable, and probably agreed on with, and pledged with Auntie Eileen. But I would get in my word first.

Gabriella brought tea to us in the drawing-room. The mist, in our neighbourhood so close to Regent's Canal, was denser than it had been elsewhere; the Italian woman drew the green velvet curtains against it. When she'd left us, Daddy helped himself to a brandy; he didn't offer me one, a symbolic gesture (I supposed) to emphasize my child's status in relation to himself.

'Well, Bruno,' he said, after slowly, so slowly, swirling the gold-brown drink round in his glass, 'well...'

'I'm glad we can talk about things at last,' I said, quickly, and probably more nervously than I appreciated, 'so how much has he left me, then?'

'I'm afraid I'm not with you.' Spoken more into the brandy-glass than to me.

'Uncle Leslie. He's left me money, I understand. I can't help being interested in how much. And when I'm to have it.'

My father said: 'I asked Eileen not to tell you.'

'Well, she did,' I said quietly, 'and I must say, I can't see *why* she shouldn't. I mean, either Uncle Leslie did leave me something, or he didn't. And if he did – which is presumably the case – I've a right to the details.'

To my credit I delivered these remarks in a manner suited to their surely indisputable logic. Perhaps (I like to think) I, for once, looked and sounded more young man than youth, or, else, pained by the whole matter though he was, Daddy decided to get the matter over and done with; anyway he gave me my answer:

'£3,500.'

I had to stifle antic expressions of incredulous joy. I had not imagined so large an amount, a nice sum indeed at that time, especially for someone kept on a less-than-generous allowance all his life. '£3,500!' I repeated, 'that really is – *was* – amazingly kind of Uncle Leslie.'

'Amazingly indeed! Thank goodness he never knew how you told lies about being with him in order to – in order to do what exactly, Bruno?'

I took no notice of this (apart from blushing). 'When am I to receive my legacy?' I persisted.

'Legacy!' Daddy repeated to himself with distaste, 'when probate etc's been attended to, I imagine. I've no idea how long that will be. And anyway – there are strings.'

I might have known it, I said to myself, I might have known.

'Strings?'

'Until you're twenty-one, you have to have *my* approval for how you use the money.'

'So it isn't mine?'

'Yes, it's yours, but I have to administer it.'

Well, fuck that, I said angrily to myself, why can't something go Bruno Armitage's way for once in his wretched life. But aloud, I said: 'Oh, well, I expect we can reach agreements about the matter. I can't see that stipulation being much of a problem.'

'I'm so glad you can't,' said Daddy, once again more to the gold-brown Cognac than to me, 'because *I* can see many a one all too clearly hovering on the horizon. You haven't shown yourself exactly dependable or prudent of late, have you? You've thoroughly upset your aunt and cousin and betrayed their confidence in you, you've got yourself into a sordid tangle with childish and gratuitous lies (at which, I may add, you're no novice) with none of us knowing what, and what not, to believe, and – I still don't know where the hell you were on that lost weekend.'

'But I've *told* Auntie Eileen, I've told her all, and I can't believe she hasn't passed on the good news to you by now.' And I'm not a fucking child, I longed to add. But didn't, of course.

'Please don't be impertinent, Bruno. It doesn't become you, it doesn't become anybody.'

Tiredness broke over me like a wave over a bather; perhaps, what with the tubercular patch and the sun-ray treatment, I got exhausted more quickly than most young men my age. I certainly didn't feel like a row, not even a mild one, on the other hand I had points to establish. Their establishment concerned nothing less than the course of my life ahead.

'I went at the weekend to see the script-writer of *The Parkers*.'

Daddy batted his eyelids in boredom, a habit of his, and an unsympathetic and offputting one too.

'Oh, yes, Eileen did tell me something about a radio serial, but I thought that was just a blind you were giving her.'

'Why should you think that? *The Parkers* happens to be very important to me.'

It was as if I'd never spoken.

Daddy put his brandy-glass down on the carpet, beside his armchair, took a deep breath almost as if he were doing some hatha yoga exercise, and then said: 'Tell me the truth – for once, please, Bruno. Are you a virgin?'

How to answer this and be truthful? For I could reply 'Yes' and I could reply 'No!', and in neither case would be telling the truth. Nevertheless, interpreting the question as: 'Have you so far abstained from fucking?' I said: 'Sorry but no!'

A deep sigh. (Rich, I thought, from someone who'd taken his son on holidays with several different women, all, undoubtedly, short-term mistresses.) 'Well,' my father said, 'if you'd gone into the Navy as you hoped, you'd have lost your virginity a lot sooner, I suppose. Not that, if you're someone like my brother Brian, you necessarily have to wait until you're in the armed forces...'

Later I was to think it somewhat comic that my father had assumed (correctly, as it happened) that my sexual initation had occurred only *after* I'd stopped being a public-schoolboy, and that for parallels for a young male's antics he went to his younger brother, Ian's father, rather than to (his admittedly rather austere) own self.

'I do hope you're being careful, Bruno,' my father said, 'I haven't been – I mean, I've never said much...'

Only in retrospect – after months? years? – did I appreciate that my father was here putting himself on trial for his bringing-up of me, for the whole haziness of definition in our entire relationship. Fleetingly my mind moved back to my mother, and what she had felt – or not felt – about the man questioning me now. I saw her on that war-time Suffolk farm standing in its walled garden while Uncle Brian took a snap of her, cornfields and oak-woods at her back, I saw her, bored by husband and son on those brief, heavy, joyless 'family' holidays of ours, I saw her (later) pouring out gins-and-french for her new American 'friend', Uncle Edward (no blood-uncle he) – and realised that most certainly it had been a case of not feeling rather than feeling.

'I can take care of myself in that respect,' I said – and I suppose that here, for once, I wasn't making a false claim, 'Daddy, when I said I'd been to Dorset with *The Parkers* script-writer I was telling the truth. For a change. I'm sorry for having pulled the wool over Auntie Eileen's eyes, but –' I came near to saying; 'It had nothing to do with sex!', as in a sense it hadn't, but luckily – for whatever angelic record or general karma we make for ourselves – I stopped myself short here. 'I have to talk to you about *The Parkers*. I must.'

'Oh, must you?' Spoken as if the scene had gone on quite long enough already.

'Yes, really! You see, it's what I want to do more than anything else, to think up and write scripts for that programme. It's what I've always wanted to do.'

Daddy gave me a sad wry smile, and looked down again into his glass clearly wishing there were more brandy left in it, but reluctant to pour himself out any more. 'Such nonsense, Bruno!' he said, 'how could you always have wanted to do *Parkers* scripts? I should think you'd only just about heard of the programme when you went to live in Tanbury; I'd be amazed if you'd ever listened to a single episode all the way through.'

Undeniably true. 'Well, I've now become so interested it feels like always,' I answered, feeling small again as a result of the dry disdain of my father's argument.

'Why on earth?'

And I couldn't answer. Later I thought I might have indicated with a sweep of the hand the tasteful barren loveless room in which I was sitting (and the rest of the flat beyond it), and said something along the lines of: 'Because it stands for a way of life where people interact, and where they like (and even love) one another.' But all I could manage, after a pause that only confirmed my father in his view of my interest's built-in evanescence: 'Because it's part of the life of this country.' Having delivered myself of the statement, it didn't seem to me unimpressive – and any journalist and cultural commentator would surely have agreed with me. Think of *Radio Times* and its circulation, think of *Everywoman* and *The Daily Mail* which only last week had featured a photograph of Enid Berridge, 'the universally loved Elizabeth Parker', prompting me to thoughts, yet again, of what her daughter Cassie might look like! If these organs didn't amount to 'the life of this country', what did?

'Her Majesty's Prisons, Tottenham Hotspurs, Littlewood's Football Pools, the British Museum, the National Trust,' said my father, that disconcerting prim smile of his returning, 'they're all beyond doubt part of the life of this country, to use your rather vague phrase, but as yet I haven't detected any eagerness on your part to attach yourself to them.'

No satisfactory dialogue was going to take place between us; that I could now see. Better therefore simply to stick to my own wishes for myself. 'Well, a bloke can be attached to only one of these at any given time,' I said (rationally enough, surely), 'and the BBC's most popular programme is the one I've chosen. There's nothing I want to do more than write for it. I'm re-sitting my 'A' Levels next month (not that I'm going to do much better this time round than last) and hospital treatment will be finished in mid-December too. So though I don't *want* to, not after all this stupid fuss about the weekend, I'll return to Tanbury, but after that I want to devote myself to scripts.'

'Perhaps,' my father was swirling round once more the small amount of brandy in his glass, an obvious nervous irritability now fighting with the manner he'd decided to assume wherever possible, but most of all in his dealings with me, one of knowing detachment, of well-informed boredom, 'perhaps when the exams have been taken – and passed to satisfactory standard –and when we have the official all-clear from the doctors, then we can discuss this whole matter. Until that time it strikes me as somewhat premature. And you never know,' there was an oddly bright malice in the look he gave me now, 'you never know, you might even have tired, just a little, of *The Parkers* by then.'

This contemptuous superiority was too much for me to bear. 'I don't agree with you, Daddy,' I said, 'what's the point of working hard for examinations and putting myself through all the discomfort of hospital treatment if I don't have a plan of the future in my head. You've said in the past that I don't seem to have any sense of urgency about time ahead.' This was a verbatim quote. 'Well, now I have. More than just a sense, I've an actual blueprint. And you refuse to discuss it.' As no interruption came at this point (the last remark was surely a throwing down of the gauntlet to him), I hurtled on: 'I want, when it's legally possible, to have the money I've been left by Uncle Leslie, and to use part of it – only part of it, mind – to support myself while I get a few scripts together. But these scripts will eventually be paid for, because they'll be done under the supervision of Verity Orchard, who has already implied that she would like me to be a member of *The Parkers* team. And Verity,' I couldn't resist calling her by her first name *tout court*, 'is the lady who actually invented *The Parkers* and for some time wrote it single-handedly –'

'I'm perfectly aware who Verity Orchard is,' Daddy replied coldly; I'd forgotten how copious his general knowledge was, 'I read the papers after all, but I'm afraid I can't wax enthusiastic about this scheme. And as you have to await my consent for use of your money, I would advise you,' now he did get up and make for the bottle of Cognac, having overcome any inner doubts as to whether he should indulge himself in this way, 'to curb this enthusiasm. Until,' once more the smile, 'January, when things may look very different.'

I got up too. I'd half a mind to help *myself* to the brandy (and, to give him his due, my father wouldn't have objected) but the urge to ask a question arrested my movements: 'What is it that you want me to do?' I asked. 'We're always talking about what I haven't done and what I can't do and what I shouldn't do and what I mustn't do, and what I, almost certainly, *won't* do. But never about what I could do, or might very well do.'

This burst of rhetoric had an adverse effect rather than otherwise. My father shut one eye and stared with the open one into his new measure of rich liquid. 'You've only yourself to blame,' he said, 'you've defined yourself so continuously in negatives, it's become almost impossible to think of you in positive terms...'

That did it. No wonder my mother (and what had she *really* been like?) had left him. 'No wonder Cynthia, your wife, left you!' I said, though I still refrained from shouting, 'you haven't got a heart, you really haven't. It must be made of *glass*, like the brandy-bottle.' So distant had Daddy consistently been that my boyhood had contained none of the usual 'scenes'; he'd never let me get close enough to him to permit rudeness, the normal insolence of a youth to an older man. There was about this present confrontation the excitement of novelty. I stepped nearer to him, aglow all of a sudden, with urgency. He stepped back – without, I think, appreciating that this is what he'd done.

'I'll do what I said, what we've agreed on: go back to Tanbury, take the bloody exams,' if he minded my swearing (mild, but strong enough in this particular situation for those times), he chose not to show it, 'and finish with the hospital. And then – without your assistance, without the damned money – I'll get myself onto *The Parkers* team, with Verity's help. And don't worry, I'm not even going to stay around to add to your miseries this evening. I don't know why we even contemplated the idea of me doing this, since neither of us likes the other's company. I'll be going to a friend's – I *have* friends in London – and I'll stay there overnight, and tomorrow Auntie Eileen can ring you and assure you I'm still alive, and then you can forget all about me until January and examination-results, which are, of course, so much more important than a guy's happiness and his own hopes for his future.'

I think my father was too knocked back by my outburst to do anything but acquiesce in my leaving the flat, the white-fronted villa, the quiet cul-de-sac, for a different roof over my head from his, for the rest of this misty November night. Wednesday, November 27th, 1957, the date of change.

When I saw the bus rounding the bend, lit up against early evening's grey wetness, I silently saluted it: deliverance. It'd bear me decisively away from a home where I was not wanted, where I was

100

made to feel unworthy – of just about anything. I climbed to the upper deck, to join the smokers and dog-owners, categories of humanity I felt more at ease with than the hard-hearted respectable. The interior of the bus smelt of rain-spattered hair and rain-spattered coats – far from displeasingly – and I found a seat next to a duffle-coated, bearded student absorbed in Bernard Shaw's *Major Barbara*. Borne along in that crowded smoke-filled space, down long darkening tree-lined avenues, lights of houses and of cars criss-crossing as they pierced the increasing drizzle, I felt I were on some ferry-boat, one of many craft making the slow two-way crossing from one end of the capital to another, indifferent to the weather, indifferent to the jolts and slowing-downs it had to endure, and taking me over to some port more cheerful, more appreciative of me, more enjoyable (hardly difficult!) than the one I'd just quit.

And that port was called......?

Did I really not know?

On, on the bus took me, now into a West End far fuller than in any mental picture I kept of it of bumper-to-bumper traffic, full too of scurrying identityless unknowable pedestrians, and awnings that dripped, and shop-window after shop-window down which raindrops sped. No wonder people preferred the Greenfield Ends of this world; I could even imagine pining for Tanbury's Horse Fair with its grass verges and chestnut trees and golden-stone old houses. Was I really a Londoner? Wasn't I rather a general passenger through places and times, one unsure of where it was he was heading? Well, take a grip of yourself, man. Make a choice about where to go next.

But maybe I'd never intended to go anywhere else.

Oxford Street asserted itself, then the great curve of Regent Street, the lights proclaiming shops with associations for me, Liberty's (where my mother had bought things for herself, never minding the bored small boy exasperatingly at her side); Hamley's, where the few toys that had been given me had been purchased, all of them expensive, none of them played with for long – I quickly tired of pursuits; Austin Reed's where regularly my father, who had an account there, 'kitted' me up. 'So you're outwardly passable at any rate.' What a life mine had been, so dull, so very dull – and already it appeared long to me.

I'd have preferred one closer to the vulgar neon blaze of Piccadilly, which presented itself next. Piccadilly, and the pleasures and dangers of 'town'... Oh, yes, now I *knew* where I was heading for. And a change of bus was required.

The Fulham Road, once St Stephen's Hospital had been passed, was longer, far drabber, and far more monotonous than I'd remembered. Every so often I thought we'd reached the terrace of late Victorian houses in which P. Dickinson, Antiques stood, having forgotten quite how many similar (not to say identical) terraces of late Victorian houses were strung out all the road's length.

Indeed the bus had overshot the stop I was seeking by the time I recognised the little shop. I hurried down the stairs to the lower deck like a madman, and jumped off the bus onto the slippery-wet pavement, as if I had an appointment of vital importance ahead of me, to miss which would mean missing the chance of a lifetime.

Well, sometimes in retrospect this is how it has seemed.

I ran like an anxious small boy down the street to where the antique-shop was waiting for me, the light in its front dimly shining through the murk. I ran as though, if I didn't make the front door in two minutes or so, the building would become, at a stroke, deserted. The Fulham Road (remember how long ago all this is!) had a far more forlorn aspect than any part of London with which I was familiar, and I wouldn't have wanted to find myself abandoned and shelterless in it. Luck had clearly smiled on me with Charles Compson so plainly in; I knew how he spent only a limited portion of his time in London, so he might only too easily not have been at home.

I rang the bell and hammered on the door with the dolphin-shaped knocker in a near-frantic manner that would have alarmed any even moderately nervous person inside. For the feeling persisted that – as a result of my abrupt departure from my father – I was now carrying out some magic rite, and that this magic could very easily fade.

Through the window I recognised the grandfather clock with the country-scene painted on its face, and the wooden wine-cooler, and I felt the better for doing so.

And then – the relief of it! – here was Charles – a version of himself rather than the man I was expecting to see – flushed, breathless and apprehensive-looking, braced for an encounter at the door with some aggressive 'ted', but dreading it.

He said nothing for a whole charged, chilly, trickling minute. Then: 'My *quattrocento* angel,' he said, 'whatever's responsible for your glorious, unexpected visitation?'

We had sex – or made love, as we'd have said in the Fifties – many times that night, he and I; I hadn't known how quickly an appetite renews itself, or mutates, after gratification. How beautiful to feel so appreciated, to have him lying there wanting from me whatever (anything) I chose to give him – in the mouth, in the groin, in the arse, all territories proffered so gladly, so eagerly that, as night slowly wound itself on, I surrendered to him my own domains, not compromising myself (as up to now I'd have feared) but completing what I'd begun. P. Dickinson, Antiques was all wrapped in fog off the Thames, and the guttering never stopped dripping so that it sounded even through those shallow dreams that came and went more briefly and less consumingly than orgasms. Dreams in which I saw the coffin slide between the curtains at the far end of that dismal building-block chapel towards the flames, and somehow I knew its occupant was my cousin, Ian; in which I saw the officiating clergyman dipping his hand into Uncle Leslie's urn to find – what else but bank-notes, £3,500s worth. I dreamed that I returned back to Primrose Hill, opened the door of Daddy's flat and found – not fat, morose Gabriella, but one of Nesta's billygoats who charged at me with horns big and sharp enough to kill.

'You funny boy!' Charles said to me, as I fought my way out of this last nightmare, 'you funny boy, and you sweet one, too.'

But now I edged myself away from him, so that I could sleep unhampered by another's touch. I needed stillness, bodily calm if I was to have any rest. Drip-drip-drip went the drainpipes outside; probably everything at P. Dickinson's, from the antiques for sale outwards, needed repair. Awareness of Charles's proximity, and the strangeness of this kept me uncomfortably tense and alert for some time. Nevertheless I finally did fall into proper sleep, and when I surfaced from it, morning was breaking over the brown-grey brick walls and interlocking yards of Fulham, and Charles was standing over me, a mug of tea (brewed specially for me) in his hand.

And when I'd drunk it, feeling delivered of all the apprehension and trouble of the past few days, well – how could we not have sex yet another time?

'You like *doing* all this, *carissimo*, don't you?'

'Doesn't it seem as if I do?'

Charles altered his sitting position on the bed so that I was obliged to alter my kneeling one at its foot, and look up at him. I saw in his jowly, pouchy but still unarguably handsome face, with its copious morning stubble, a convergence of widely differing emotions: simple pleasure, grateful tenderness, unrepentant lust, and just-about-repentant greed, together with confusion, doubt, and even a measure of anxiety.

'Oh, yes, it all seems all right. It's just that I wonder – well, how real it all is.' Later I was frequently to take this question out of the files of my memory, first to resent it, then to applaud it for its dark wisdom. For, of course, the whole situation – my being here in these cramped, damp, dusty quarters above the antique-shop, my paying these attentions to an older man I didn't know well, even my 'comings' with what seemed heroic frequency – was *not* altogether real to me. I was not merely detached from Charles, whose deepest feelings and thoughts I could scarcely guess at and wasn't really interested in, I was detached from myself.

'To think,' said Charles, 'that all the good things we've just been doing to each other are forbidden by those who govern us. But do you know who we do have on our side, even though it doesn't, by and large, altogether approve?'

'No!' To tell the truth I wasn't much concerned; I've never been able to get political, even on the simplest level, about matters of personal behaviour.

'The Church of England. The good old C of E, and may it prevail!'

'How d'you mean?'

Charles explained that in September (on the 4th, to be precise) a report had been published, known, after the chairman of the committee, as the Wolfenden Report, which recommended that homosexual acts between consenting adults shouldn't be criminalised. Voluntary sexual behaviour, this document said, was 'not the law's business'. There'd been a tremendous amount of brouhaha as a result, all of which I, who read the papers so seldom, had missed; a great many punitive and acrimonious things had been said 'about those who like our way of loving' (said Charles). But then – on the 14th of this very month, November – into the debate had come the Church of England, backing the report's recommendations.

'So,' said Charles, 'so the Reverend Derek Parker, no less, would be on our side.'

The Reverend Derek Parker! He and his family had been the cause of my walking out on Primrose Hill. To serve him and the public which so cherished him was my ambition, was to be (for the foreseeable future anyway) my life's work. He was, in truth, why I was here in this bleak stretch of the Fulham Road in an unlawful bed with a comparative stranger, and the guttering drip-dropping remorselessly! And I hadn't thought, let alone (and more importantly) spoken of *The Parkers* once since I'd turned up on the doorstep of P. Dickinson, Antiques yesterday evening.

'The Reverend Derek,' I said, 'there's such a lot I've been thinking about him and the doings at Greenfield End. Such a lot I've been wanting to discuss with Verity.'

'Oh, *The Parkers*,' said Charles, precisely as he'd done on our rain-swept journey back to London from Dorset and The Puzzle. 'By no means let us ever forget *The Parkers*. Our life's blood, or perhaps better, our bread and butter.'

I judged it better to continue with a bit more dalliance – and probably to get dressed – before pursuing any further this all-important subject. But for the first time, since Charles and I had had sex, twinges of guilt and shame beset me: not indeed at what we were actually engaged in doing, but at the thought of Verity. Verity who had been helpful and encouraging to me (and whom I wanted, in fact required, to be more helpful and more encouraging still!) Verity who was, after all, Charles' wife! (And what did that make me?) I saw her walking on the cliff-top path, with Portland Bill like a cautionary finger extending from land to the reaches of the sea, I saw her enter that yew-grove and embrace the wide matted boles of those most mysterious of trees.

Did she know about Charles? And if she knew, what did she think?

Her lovely face in my mind wore a coldly Olympian expression, fitting for one who exercised life-and-death powers over a whole oh-so-real community. No, I decided, after briefly arguing with that face, she didn't know about Charles's predilections, she was too lofty.

Charles went out, to a nearby general shop, to get us provisions for breakfast. He returned to make – small and greasily untidy though the little kitchen was – a delightful repast: Grape-Nuts with milk and double cream, fried eggs, fried bread, fried tomatoes, and toasted wholegrain bread with salty butter and Cooper's Oxford marmalade. 'Dear boy,' said Charles, 'prepare the table properly so that we can eat *à deux* in style. And talk business.'

'Talk business?'

'Business, yes. I have a proposition to make.'

This proposition did not come as the surprise I feigned. Hadn't I been angling for it? Hadn't its possibility been present in my mind, if not precisely articulated, throughout my long wet bus journey down from Regent's Park last evening?

After I had finished my exams and hospital treatment in Tanbury I should move to the Fulham Road, where I could live over P. Dickinson's free. In return for:

(a) A certain number of hours a week serving in the antique shop, and coping with business matters arising out of it. (I could telephone The Puzzle any time if I had a problem; I didn't need to feel frightened of responsibilities.) For any hours over this agreed number I would be paid, (far more, Charles added, than the previous assistant, now dismissed, thank God!); this included obviously paper- as well as shop-work.

(b) Being Charles' lover when he came up to London. 'What you do when I'm not there, well, that, *carissimo*, I wouldn't dream of poking my nose into. Let alone other parts of my anatomy. But already I feel so

106

– *fond* of you, so *close* to you. If you didn't want to love me on my appearances in London – which I only make *de temps en temps* – then I would be too hurt for my little plan to work. And I can't bear being hurt, Bruno. I've been hurt so many, many times in my life. By – oh, well, we won't go into all that just now. Let's just say, I don't want any more of it.'

Lest being his lover might not appeal to me enough, (might even – dreaded thought – have the reverse effect to the hoped-for one) a further inducement was added: Charles would intercede on my behalf with Verity (with whom, he understood, I was already in communication), and impress on her that a reason for my living and looking after an establishment belonging to them was – so to speak – its proximity to *The Parkers*; I would be there on hand to suggest, receive, develop and generally work on ideas for the programme.

Only afterwards – after the inevitable sorry débacle which cost us so much suffering – was I able to review the terms offered me, and amid so much blaming of myself, appreciate: 'Charles knew everything about me, at least everything necessary to make me submit.' And righteous anger would comfortingly surge over me.

'Does the scheme find favour in your eyes, Bruno?'

'Find favour? I'll say it does.'

The train-journey from Marylebone Station to Tanbury I passed in a kind of trance; I was inhabiting the future, not the present – and the night just past, over which some might have lingered in their thoughts, occupied me hardly at all. It was the implications, the beneficial consequences of all that sexual activity with Charles that engaged my mind, not that activity itself.

As the train made its way through light rain and late autumnal countryside, I heard, all but literally – the audial equivalent of those drizzle-piercing head-lights in yesterday's Grove End Road – *Parkers* voices intersecting over my head, above the carriage roof, even making waves in the air beyond the windows. The Reverend Derek, Elizabeth, Gillian, Glyn Pritchard, Kevin O'Flynn, Tom Cavan.

From here it was no step to imagine myself officially welcomed onto the team of Parkers script-writers. I'd probably break a record for youth. I rehearsed a scene – was it a Christmas dinner, or a tenth-anniversary celebration in The Savoy? – when Verity Orchard graciously, fetchingly confessed to a host of media personalities that her 'loved child' of a programme had damn' nearly foundered, but for the luck of meeting – 'well, I've no need to name names, have I? because he's seated right beside me: Mr Bruno Armitage.' I even – we were just leaving the narrow wooded valley in which High Wycombe sprawls – went on to envisage the Director-General of the BBC himself (whatever *was* his name now?) grand, grey-haired, but smiling on a young man with that sweetness he reserved for those of undeniable promise. He'd summon me to his office, and say:

'Well, Bruno,' for we'd be on those terms by then, 'you've done a great job on *The Parkers*, saved the programme and increased the number of listeners threefold. So what have you next for us? I'm all ears.'...

Into the prison of my self-centred daydreams the farmland of North Buckinghamshire/Oxfordshire – the countryside in which I'd gone to school and was now, however briefly, resident – broke, commanding some attention. Perhaps there was a part of me – little as I would ever have imagined it – that felt more at home here than in London, where my weakness of identity had always been emphasized, where I'd been made to feel unwanted, unnecessary, expendable.

Well, all that would change soon enough. In London I would taste success. Nevertheless when I'd 'made it' as a radio scriptwriter, I might very well choose to live in the country. For a start Verity might want me to live near her in Senfrith, but assuming she didn't – well, how about that silver-grey stone farmhouse over there? Or that row of dormer-windowed cottages at the end of the lane leading out of that wood? The walls between them could be knocked down, and the three could charmingly be made one.

As an extra home for Charles and myself? As a supplement to The Puzzle and P. Dickinson, Antiques, Fulham Road?

Not fucking likely!

The train would be pulling up at Bicester in a minute. Tanbury next station. Everything had a rained-on look: the tiles on the roofs, iridescent in the weak sunshine, the platforms ahead, the raindrop-laden banks of the railway line, and, beyond, plashy arable fields and cattle-pastures. I saw a thin, sinuous, sleek black cat running through the wet grass, in pursuit of some creature or other. Such a pity that movement so graceful, so perfect, was inextricably connected to a death so cruel!

At Bicester a fair number of people got on – into my compartment stepped a fat woman with a basket bulging with vegetables, a boy with a spotty face and a transistor radio, and a girl in a blue mackintosh whose light-brown rain-sprinkled hair was tied in a pony-tail at the back.

She was very pretty. I liked pretty girls – and, to give myself my due, girls didn't have to be pretty for me to like them. I'd liked Nina Cardew (who indeed had been pretty) but then *she* hadn't much liked *me*. When she'd brought this home to me, I'd nevertheless pulled her roughly over towards me and kissed her as I, and emphatically, not she wanted. What did that tell you about me?

The train took us all northwestwards, deep into the damp, featureless, fertile Midlands countryside.

Much to the irritation of the others the acne-troubled boy turned on his radio. The Everly Brothers. What a year for them it had been! Their two voices wove harmonisingly round each other while their guitars twanged, in 'Wake up Little Susie!'

This song had inspirited all young America and Britain with the most delectable erotic thoughts. You'd have to have no sex in you to resist its lyrics (as well as its tune). To be caught by the world in the enchanted small hours of the morning (four o'clock the song specified) with a girl asleep beside you (and maybe Little Susie looked like the one opposite me now, from whom I must avert my eyes: she might well get embarrassed) – what could be more romantic? what could make you feel more of a man?

Well, yesterday – no, today! – the world would have caught me at four o'clock *actually making love*. Shouldn't then I be pleased with myself? My partner had been pleased enough.

But Charles Compson wasn't Little Susie. That was the sad truth of the matter.

In Tanbury Auntie Eileen said: 'Bruno, I might as well be honest with you and tell you that Raymond – your father – had to work hard to persuade me to have you back. You're here on sufferance, and perhaps it's as well that you know it.'

I said: 'That's the story of my life.'

PART THREE

(More) Documents

Dear Bruno,

I want to tell you how sorry I am that you're not here any longer. That may surprise you considering how I was those last weeks of your time in Tanbury. I suppose I was still angry that you hadn't taken me properly into your confidence. I'd have liked to have been your friend not just a kid relative. But I didn't go the right way about becoming one, did I?

Tea-time doesn't seem the same now you aren't here to make your amusing comments on *The Parkers* and your clever guesses about what's going to happen next. Mind you, I don't think the programme's what it was. Perhaps *I* don't feel quite the same way about it either. I mean, do you honestly believe there's anywhere under the sun where you could meet such "awfully nice" people who never get into a "hairy" about anything, and would you like them if you did? A new mate of mine, Robin Maclaine, whose mum is also a *Parkers* fan, said to me the other day: "If I came across the Rev. Derek in Tanbury Horse Fair, I'd give him a sharp kick in the bollocks!" I can see what he means. Can't you? (And don't kid me!)

This term I've been greatly enjoying cross-country running. It's an activity that gives you a chance to get away from a lot that gets on your wick, and if you've got a mate with you, you can cheat and pause for a bit in a field or wood and light up a fag. But seriously, one of the senior prefects here told me he thinks I've got what it takes to be a quite good cross-country runner – and his opinion of me is clearly high enough for him to look the other way when Rob and I have a smoke – I actually saw him do this. It was exceedingly cold that afternoon, with the ground all hard frozen and patched in still bluish frost, and we could see all the way to those hills which are said to be the beginnings of the Cotswolds, and our breaths (Robin's and mine) and the fag-smoke itself made marvellous silver patterns in the still air, and we both felt GREAT.

Now I'm reading *Out of the Silent Planet* by C.S. Lewis, and it makes me feel how I'd like myself to go on some great quest like his hero does, though it needn't be as far away as Mars!! There's plenty of places left on this planet of ours after all. Perhaps Tom Cavan should leave that boring old arsewipe Kevin O'Flynn and go on some exciting expedition of his own. To Spitzbergen or Lapland. There's a bright idea for a *Parkers* script, don't you think?

So I'm sorry about the past, Bruno, and hope that everything's going as well for you as you want it to. And that you go on having 100% good health and are feeling happier now you have no examinations hanging over you.

With best regards from

Your cousin the writer (*this* time round)

Ian

[LETTER NOT REPLIED TO]

(ii)
Tanbury School, Friday, February 14, 1958

Dear Mrs Armitage,

Half-term is upon us once again, and though I don't normally at this stage write to parents of boys in my form, I have, after much thought, decided to do so in your case. Don't be unduly alarmed by this, and please believe that I am concerned with nothing but your son's progress and happiness.

The fact of the matter is my colleagues and I have all seen a big change in Ian this term. Now, before I go any further, let me assure you that I'm very mindful (as how could I not be after so many years of teaching?) of the fact that Ian, in common with every one of his contemporaries, has reached a proverbially difficult time of life, which tends to take us all by surprise. The most unlikely boys suddenly become alternately wayward and dozy (and even both at the same time!). Small wonder so many teachers like to have as little to do with the 3rd and 4th years as they can. I sometimes, on my darker days, wonder why Muggins Here ever opted to be particularly responsible for them. The answer is – the responsibility has its own rewards. So it is in a spirit of experience and of a certain anxiety shaped by that experience, that I say to you that I am worried about Ian and his general comportment in almost all domains of school life.

He set himself high standards to be judged by, I know. I have taught him English from IA upwards, and he struck me from the very first as a most responsive, likeable and intelligent boy – always maintaining a good level, and at times doing excellent work. Last term in my own subject he consistently turned in satisfactory stuff (and not infrequently stuff a good deal more than just satisfactory). Maths and the Sciences were always weaker subjects with him, but neither Mr Terry nor Mr Felsham (his respective teachers here) had anything but good words to say about him, and saw no reason why in due course he shouldn't pass his "O" Levels perfectly respectably.

But this term – what a difference, what a sad difference! Ian has handed in constantly shoddy work, yes, even in English, and is almost more inattentive than attentive. Mr Terry has complained of persistent sullenness and even of rudeness on several occasions. Last week Ian swore quite badly at him, under his breath but so the whole class could hear. And I should tell you that Trevor Terry is someone averse to making fusses. Indeed if I had to answer the question: 'Do you know a member of staff who takes everything in his stride?' then Trevor Terry would be the man I'd name.

Some of all this seems due to a determination on Ian's part to change his image. To speak quite honestly I was conscious even at the start of his career here in Tanbury School that Ian is one of those boys (more often than not, only children, or at any rate only sons) who very much need the approbation of others, of those 'sets' they consider important or power-broking. Now I'm not going to name names; it'd be highly unethical. But whereas the Ian Armitage we knew in 1A and 2A and for most of last term aspired to join the ranks of certain serious and able boys (with, beyond doubt, some future Oxbridge scholars among them), he has now gone all out to be found acceptable by a very different group (one or two of whom will be lucky to stay the course here, or go through without serious trouble). Apparently Ian has already had to be told off for foul language and for physical coarseness of gesture and, even, conduct.

It's all a question of degree and perspective, isn't it? In another boy some of what Ian has done and some of what he has most regrettably not done would be a matter for, at the most, a few raised eyebrows. Again I shan't name names. But, given his past record, and the overall picture we have built up of him, I feel we have at the moment grounds for real concern. I know you to be a conscientious parent who enjoys a good relationship with your son, and I am sure Ian can be steered 'back on course' (otherwise I wouldn't be taking the trouble of writing to you).

I also think this letter would fail to be as complete as it is trying to be if I didn't mention that in *my* opinion – and others, when asked, have endorsed it – the boy seems far from happy, by no means the cheerful bright-eyed member of the community to whom we had grown accustomed.

If you wish to discuss this further, I would be most willing to do so. But my advice would be to digest what I've tried to say here and then exercise your own powers of observation and judgement. By Easter this letter may, let us hope, have become quite redundant.

Yours sincerely,
William Daley M.A., B.Ed.(Oxon)

(iii)
For February 14

A Valentine greeting to my favourite young man. He won't have got my *other* Valentine greeting to him, but I'm going to spill the beans and tell him that this afternoon as ever is he will hear (to be continued in later episodes) his 'own' story of Tom Cavan trying, with sad lack of

114

success, to disguise where he's been for a weekend. Of course the plot-line had special conviction – as well, as for me, special interest – because (or so you say) it was founded on your own personal experience. My poor Bruno! I wonder where you went, and who you lied to, you who seem the very soul of candour and truth! I can't bear to think of a whole network of insensitive people trying to put curbs on your freedom. Young men (young women too, for I am an upholder of the rights of my sex) should be free as birds, to fly, even to fly away, but above all to SOAR!! How fortunate – once again! – that I'm down in Dorset and not able to deal with these tiresome people (from whom you've now clearly broken away), otherwise I would be shaking a fist in their faces, and generally making my standpoint all too clear.

Now, I'd like you to do me a favour – I was going to say 'in return', but then it's me who has to be grateful to you for the wonderful Tom Cavan episode, isn't it? But could you, do you think, go from strength to strength, and as quickly as you can? (I feel sure you'll be able to, so this request is made in a spirit of the greatest confidence.) What I'd like you to do is to scribble down for me three ideas for *Parkers* stories, all of them emphasizing the pleasure and privilege the characters feel *to be living at Greenfield End*. I know I'm preaching to the converted here, but this is an extremely important point, and I can't stress it enough. Each story should reveal the rich satisfactions that come to the Parker family and their circle just through daily living round and about St Luke's.

Life goes on very quietly but busily here at The Puzzle, though the weather's been bad, with dramatically turbulent seas. Charles really enjoys digging himself in by the fireside on the worst days. (Never tell him I said so, but he is rather a stick-in-the-mud, an old stay-at-home. Now, be honest, Bruno, don't you think so too?) I, on the contrary, simply adore striding in the face of fierce wind along that cliff-top path – the same on which, that never-to-be-forgotten day, the two of us coincided –and watching the furious play of the waves, steel-grey with hissing white crests, ending always with great crashes against the rocks and cliff-walls. And as I watch, my heart goes out to all my 'friends and family' in Greenfield End, and I think what an honour it is to present them all to the great-hearted British public.

Don't get too lonely in the big city, Bruno! But, with charm like yours, how could you ever be this? I expect there's a Minty Macdonald (a nice receptive one) in every Fulham street by now, and probably as far as the World's End (I speak of Chelsea, not of the cosmos, but it might even be true of the latter as well). There, I've probably turned your head, so I'll sign off by saying – THREE GREENFIELD END IDEAS, ALL SINGING G.E.'S PRAISES, AS SOON AS POSS.

Don't break too many hearts this Valentine's Day,
Love, Verity

(iv)
February 14, *Valentine's Day*

For xxxxxxxx, my only true lover, infinitely precious, infinitely good, good in body and good in spirit. Whose company I can never have enough of, sadly rationed though my enjoyment of it is (perforce). Whom I *cherish* awake and asleep – and, most especially, in that precious interval *between* waking and sleeping, when desire rears its head and reigns o'er us without let or hindrance.

Your most constant (and besotted) admirer,
C C

P.S. I hope to be able to break out of 'prison' here next Wednesday DV. Though no doubt the two ladies here will be as ingenious as always in thinking of a reason why I shouldn't/oughtn't/mustn't/can't.

I'm pleased you have a buyer for that wooden wine-cooler, one of my favourite objects, but think the figure offered a bit on the low side. Could you up it by about £20?

You seem to be getting the feel of the antiques world (or rather our end of it) pretty well, in between your bouts of *Parkers* work, of course, which must be positively Herculean. In reply to your queries the first of the addresses enclosed with this Valentine should be good for *fenders* (I agree, there does seem to be something of a vogue for them right now), the second is *the* place to look out for High Wycombe balloon-backed dining-chairs, which I relish very nearly – only *nearly*, I said – as much as I do certain individuals of *quattrocento* appearance. (We could

116

talk on Wednesday, if I come, about the price ceiling here – for the chairs, of course, not for you whose worth is beyond computation, so infinitely more than that of jewels or minerals.)

(v)
February 14, 1958

Dear Miss Orchard,

Here are some thoughts about *The Parkers* which may be of use to you.

How many nights a week does Derek Parker shag Elizabeth? Or is he a bit past it? Can't he get it up?

Has Davey Parker got a big cock? Why doesn't he yank it out so everyone can see how big it is? He's always dating girls and never going steady with them. Perhaps the reason is simply that the girls don't think his cock's a good enough size.

Glyn Pritchard, with all his cats and his private hotel, is pretty wet, a silly old queen. Does he have *wet* dreams? Does he wear women's undies?

Did Gillian like it when her young husband first shoved it up her? She's sounded a bit miserable since she got married so my guess is she didn't. Frigid, is she? She ought to have used a banana or a cucumber earlier on by way of practice! Isn't it your duty on the programme to give girls advice?

Dr Hector Macdonald is the kind of boring old man who farts a lot. It'd make the programme quite a bit more interesting and realistic if we could actually hear him doing this. The BBC shouldn't find the 'sound effects' too difficult.

I may write to you again with some more ideas, but I think I've given you enough to be getting on with for the time being. I like your programme and have been listening to it for years, as you can perhaps tell from my knowledge of the characters.

Yours faithfully,
Ian A.
(and a few of his buddies down in Oxfordshire)

117

February 14

My dear son, Bruno,

It was quite some surprise to receive your letter just before Christmas, which I never celebrate because *every* day is Christmas, isn't it? Mother tried hard in the past to keep up with her little boy, you know, but then he turned out a *bad* little boy who only did what his hard-hearted father wanted him to and never (or almost never) wrote back. So his poor mother sighed deep and said to herself: "I know when I'm not wanted. What a blessing I'm already set on *The Divine Pathway* – beneath the good Florida sun which warms the recesses of the SOUL as well as of the body."

Darling, you will never know what a trauma it was for your mother to be cast out by Raymond Armitage. He never did believe that a loving woman – and I am a loving woman, Bruno – should occasionally lend her body and the *good* things it harbours to another than him, but behaved instead as if he had exclusive rights over it, and him not always so very loving, I'm sorry to have to tell you, often so very far from loving. Eventually she left her home on account of his coldness and pride, feeling such despair and such heaviness of spirit that if she hadn't met up with Dr Jack Weinberger, I *shudder* to think what she might not have done. But Dr Jack lifted her up and redeemed her, he told her that what oppressed her were in truth but dark SHADOWS, and that what she needed instead was to be in the LIGHT, where the SUN is shining and making the good into the real. You, darling son though you are, are for me part of those dark shadows, together with your father and his dreadful, dreadful lawyers, and London (and even England itself). But now, you see, Bruno, I have my own life, and dear wonderful friends, Eric and Frank, and Gene and Clayton – and Antonella too, for every woman needs a SISTER. All of us are securely set on *The Divine Pathway*, the BEST place to be, as I hope, my darling, you can discover for yourself one day.

So you really mustn't try to disturb me and shatter that peace which passeth all understanding by your talk of examinations and hospitals and quarrels with Raymond and wrangles over money. (What *is* money, after all? Just paper and metal!) None of these things are REAL, you see, they're all dark SHADOWS. Bring yourself, Bruno, just a little bit further into the light and you will see all this for yourself. I want my boy to be as happy as his mother, and I am convinced that one day he will be. I was talking with Eric and Frank about this, and they said such wonderful words: "Wouldn't it be the strangest thing if a woman already firmly advanced on *The Divine Pathway* didn't have a son capable of placing at least his toes on it?!" You see what wise friends I have.

You know so little about my life here I don't think I have any news that could interest you. And besides you might tell Raymond and spoil things for me. Through the kind recommendations of Gene and Clayton I have gone into property a little and have just acquired the most darling little summer home by a lake about a hundred miles from Orlando. When I'm there I can truly feel the Pathway shining in both directions, very bright and assuring. I'm wondering if you've ever read *Lighting Up and Lighting In* by Suzanne K. Hutchings? It's a most profound book and may be of help to you in your present troubles. I imagine its publishers have UK distributors. So take heart, Bruno,

Your loving
Mom

(vii)
Monday, February 17

Dear Mr Daley,

I am very grateful to you for writing to me as you did. I have to say the letter did not come altogether as a surprise, though I had been hoping that the changes in Ian which you describe with such accuracy and understanding were more apparent at home than at school.

A mother bringing up a son by herself has obvious problems, and these, I suppose, must inevitably increase with the onset of adolescence. Up to now Ian has been a gentle, amiable sort of boy (well, of course, he still is these things – we mustn't exaggerate how much he's altered), and I've perhaps deluded myself that the rest of his growing-up would be as pleasant and as problem-free. I was always afraid of providing too feminine an atmosphere at home (which I probably did nonetheless), and so I was very pleased, as Ian himself was, when his cousin (my brother-in-law's boy, also, by coincidence, an only son living in a single parent household) came to live with us. As is the nature of boys of Ian's age (particularly if they have no siblings), Ian looked up to him greatly, thinking him the very model of how a young man should be – which, I have to say, he wasn't. (I believe he handed in to you last term an essay on the subject of Bruno, which you awarded high marks.) Well, without going into too many details Bruno let Ian down – or, perhaps it would be fairer and more honest to say, Ian *feels* Bruno let him down. Bruno was all set to go into the Navy and couldn't; he got interested in a girl who wasn't in the least bit interested in him – pretty usual stuff, and obviously way over Ian's head. But Bruno blew hot and cold with his cousin to a degree positively painful to witness. Ian never knew whether he was in favour, and would be welcome in Bruno's room for a chat, for listening to pop records together or having a quick game of cards. Or whether he'd be greeted with obvious boredom and be sent packing within a few seconds. Inconsistency is almost the worst failing in dealing with the young, as I'm sure you'll agree. And so Ian got his feelings badly hurt.

It all ended with a falling-out beteen the two of them because Bruno told Ian a pack of lies, the intention behind which was clearly to keep him out of the way, and then tried to get him (if you please!) to help him cover up these untruths. It's a long story, and I won't trouble you with it. I nearly sent Bruno packing, but didn't. Nevertheless the last weeks of his stay here were very fraught, and the two boys just glowered at one another when they met, and otherwise kept to their own rooms. Certainly something seemed – sadly – to have come to an end.

Bruno doesn't live with us any longer and so Ian is cooped up, once again, with only a woman for company. And the outcome is – Ian has a broken heart.

Broken hearts aren't things young males are supposed to have – and they'd be the first to agree with that statement. (Ian, who, as you say, is trying to show himself a bit of a tough at the moment, would most definitely dismiss the idea out of hand.) But I believe it to be true, and I hope what I've said here will help you and your colleagues in your handling of Ian in his present crisis. Funnily enough, there was rather a good treatment of the young male's reluctance to acknowledge his emotions in, of all places, *The Parkers* (which I don't expect you ever listen to, though your wife might) only the other week. Tom Cavan, usually so cheery, was persistently awkward and moody, and the reason – a broken heart.

Obviously I'll do what I can to see that Ian hands in work worthy of himself, and even give him some (I hope) subtle hints on how to behave himself. I suppose the bright-faced boy has gone for ever now, but I have confidence enough in him – and in Tanbury School – to believe that he'll turn out well enough in the end.

We can have a talk at the end of term about all this, when Ian's had time to recover more fully, and any stratagems we've evolved have been given a chance to work.

Yours faithfully,
Eileen Armitage

(viii)
Excerpt from *The Parkers* (Tuesday, February 18, 1958)

ELIZABETH PARKER: February's a treacherous month, I know, but it can give you days when you feel that spring is truly to hand, and you can even sense the promise of summer itself – it's like that now in Greenfield End. The snowdrops are particularly lovely this year – especially that patch of them in the south corner of the churchyard, but already I'm noting, as I always do at this time of year, the shy but unstoppable flowering of old favourites: the Grey Poplars at the bottom of the Vicarage garden, the Wych Elm by the lychgate and the Hazel, and down near our little stream the cluster of Winter Aconites which is the most brilliant yellow, and I have to remind myself – and others –that this pretty plant is poisonous. Yes, the year is rolling round again, and as so often at this point in it, when the sun is shining and the sky a fresh blue with fleecy white clouds sailing across it, I have a feeling I've come to welcome: that everything in life will go on for ever, bringing, yes, anxieties, and even downright sorrows – but also a deep contentment, an inner security. But it would be a mistake to think that changes may not take place, and the most surprising people can – well, surprise you. Who would have thought that my gentle dependable Derek would be the harbinger of disruption to the gentle satisfying rhythm of Greenfield End?

(Sound of footsteps – a man's brogues on a flagged floor – getting louder and nearer, and then an inner door opening)

ELIZABETH: There you are at last, dear. I was beginning to think I ought to be sending the bellman after you. I know that the trains from London can be subject to delay – but *(laughing affectionately)* I also know that a certain clergyman's not always as good at finding his way around as he might be, and might even forget which station he's got to get out at.

DEREK *(with an equally affectionate chuckle)*: Now, I wonder, Elizabeth dear, who you could be talking about? Let me assure you I got to my West End destination and back without any hitches whatever. I don't deserve the reputation I've got. *(A slightly nervous pause)* No, it was the Bishop who took his time over things.

ELIZABETH *(taken aback – but beware of theatricality!)*: I'm sorry, Derek, but I didn't quite catch that. Did I hear you say – the BISHOP!! You couldn't mean *our* Bishop, Harry Hertford himself?

DEREK: I do, dear. I just couldn't bring myself to tell you yesterday (which was when he rang up) that he wanted me to meet him in town. And even today, I'm sorry to confess, I invented a reason for having to go up to London. The way I argued with myself was: 'I can't be sure exactly what Harry wants to talk to me about, though I have a pretty good idea.' And I was right too. We met, him and me, in a little hotel he knows near the British Museum, and he – well, he had a very important proposition to make me... *(Another pause. Derek Parker clearly isn't at all sure how his wife will take this news.)* Shouldn't we have a pot of tea, dear? It's not like you to miss an opportunity for making us one.

ELIZABETH: There are times when tea just has to wait, Derek, and this sounds to me like one of them. Whatever could it be, this proposition of Harry's?

DEREK: Simply that he'd like to recommend me to the living at Newstead. St Jude's, Newstead.

ELIZABETH: Newstead! But I hardly know where Newstead is.

DEREK: It's in the same county and diocese as Greenfield End.

ELIZABETH (*for her, quite sarcastic*): Is it really? How most interesting, I must make a note of the fact. And what is so special about Newstead, may I ask, that you should be summoned up to London to discuss an appointment there?

DEREK: Newstead, Harry says, truly deserves its name; it stands for a new kind of living. Oh, he told me such a lot about it, he made it seem really appealing...

ELIZABETH: In what way?

DEREK: It originated as what's known as an overspill for London: there was actually a small old village on the site already – but everybody there's determined for it to be a community in its own right. It's been most imaginatively planned, with gardens and woods coming right into the centre, and there are many facilities completely lacking in older-style towns.

ELIZABETH (*her curiosity roused, despite herself*): And what would they be, Derek?

DEREK (*with a genuine enthusiasm*): Places for all those children too young to know what they want to do with themselves, where they can play in the way that suits them best; places for their tired young mums. Places for the old whom we tend to forget so easily, even in Greenfield End; places for the less able-bodied amongst us. (Who knows, dear, whether *we* shan't join their ranks some time in the future? It's quite on the cards.) Places, in fact, for just about everybody. And a church that caters for everybody too.

ELIZABETH (*impressed, for all her reservations*): You make it sound very attractive, dear. Of course I have heard a great deal these last years about New Towns and what they've got to offer people – people of every kind and need, which of course is supremely important – but... I've never thought of living in one, I'm afraid.

DEREK (*laughing*): Well, no more have I.

ELIZABETH: But now you *are* thinking of it?

DEREK: Dearest, *I'm* not thinking of it unless *you* are. I really mean that. And anyway Harry, bless him, was absolutely adamant on the point; you've got to arrive in a New Town such as Newstead eagerly or not at all, was how he put it. Elizabeth and you, he said, stand as models of happiness for so many of us, and the Vicarage is the very pattern of a contented and giving home. If there were resentment at the move on either of your parts, he said, I should have deprived Greenfield End of something absolutely invaluable, and Newstead wouldn't be the gainer either. No, this is something to think over and talk over carefully, sensibly, not losing sight of either our duties to each other or my duties as a clergyman.

ELIZABETH: Oh, but Derek, Greenfield End!... I don't think I could bear to leave the place. This Vicarage and its lovely garden, just beginning once again to put forth flowers and shoots; Verges, always so painstaking; Mrs Bobbington – whoever would listen to all her stories about her corns if I wasn't around? And then to be near Davey and Gillian, that's such a constant source of pleasure, and Davey's veterinary practice is only just taking off, and I'd so like to be around to see it become a proper success.

DEREK *(lovingly, but with a hint of good-natured mockery)*: You're speaking as if we were asked to go to the South Seas or the Arctic rather than to somewhere barely twenty miles away. Besides who knows... Newstead is full, truly full, of opportunities for old and middle-aged and young. We might be setting an example.

(The knocker on the front door is heard, first gently, then rather more loudly and excitedly, and TOM CAVAN's merry voice calls out: 'Hullo, people, anybody at home?')

ELIZABETH *(a touch sadly)*: There, you see what I mean, Derek? Whatever will we do without Tom bursting in on us to tell us of the latest mix-up he's somehow found himself in (with the best will in the world, of course)?

Dear Verity,

You didn't know your Bruno (or perhaps you did!) I'm always ready to rise to a challenge. Your request was my command (and after today's episode I obviously appreciate the reason behind it). These three ideas just came to me as if some power (the great Scriptwriter in the Sky perhaps) had, in response to my prayers, just turned on a switch in my brain. I'm pretty sure they'll be exactly what you're looking for. GREENFIELD END FOR EVER could be their motto, or GREENFIELD END IS BETTER THAN ANYWHERE ELSE:

(1) A jumble sale in aid of the church. Everyone eager to give good sellable things to it. Tom Cavan, who probably isn't much of a reader anyway, decides to present two books, both of which get him into difficult situations. First, he gives away one inside which is a copy of a love-letter/love-poem he'd written to Minty Macdonald when he was first keen on her. It's she of course who buys the book at the sale, and obviously she finds the letter/poem and is, in spite of everything, moved. So.... The second book is a copy of one of Kevin O'Flynn's own novels, perhaps his latest title, the one that's brought him such success, inscribed to Tom by his 'affectionate uncle, the author'. Obviously this is a complete mistake on Tom Cavan's part, he mistook the book for another, but it is Kevin – surprise, surprise! – who comes across the book at the stall. He's deeply offended, and there's a prolonged misunderstanding (following a blazing row), though all will come well in the end. It's *The Parkers* themselves, Derek and Elizabeth, who bring about the reconciliations, and everyone says it takes living in a place like Greenfield End to have mistakes between people righted, cleared up as though they'd never been.

(2) Easter-time is approaching, and people's thoughts turn to religion, and who better to talk to than their kindly Vicar? There could be a scene when someone has doubts about the meaning of life, and in a place like Greenfield End isn't shy to contact his Vicar for guidance.

Derek recites to him or her some beautiful spiritual poem that makes him or her feel a great deal better. The sort of poem I have in mind would be like the following: (I wonder if you know it; it's by Thomas Traherne.)

'A Stranger here
Strange Things doth meet, Strange glories see;
Strange Treasures lodg'd in this fair World appear,
Strange all, and New to me.
But that they mine should be, who nothing was,
That Strangest is of all, yet brought to pass.'

The episode mustn't get *too* solemn, of course, and perhaps should end on the familiar humorous note of Derek Parker's absent-mindedness – giving the person he's just inspired a mug of tea into which he's put salt instead of sugar in it, something like that.

(3) Miss Venables goes to a shop where she isn't known (perhaps not in Greenfield End itself, maybe somewhere in London proper) and is accused of shop-lifting, the assistant (or store-detective) having got it into his head that middle-aged ladies are apt to commit this crime. The accusation is, needless to say, completely false. Miss Venables has the shop ring up the Parker household, and of course they come out in full force. Maybe it might be better if it was Elizabeth and her son Davey who defend her rather than the Vicar himself. As a result of this horrible business everyone likes and appreciates Miss Venables better (for a while, anyway), and we all have the feeling that Greenfield End is a place where people really know and care about each other, even if they don't always like each other, because there's a sense of harmony in the community – brought about most of all by Derek and Elizabeth and their church, St Luke's.

Of course I've been enjoying *my* little dramas – lived again by Tom Cavan – enjoying them immensely. Certainly it was the best Valentine greeting I've ever had. (Where are all the glamorous women who are going to send me the other ones?) But if anything I think the subsequent episodes are even better. You are a great writer, Verity, do you know that? Thank you very much – though can't I thank myself a little too? Talking of which I do feel that I'm entitled now to attend a real genuine *Parkers* rehearsal in Broadcasting House. Could you arrange this for me in the very near future?

(x)

So, Bruno, you think I'm not worth bothering to write to!!! Well, *fuck* you! Next time you go down to Verity Orchard's, or whatever swank household is on your list, I hope there's someone there to ram a red-hot poker up your arse. Or when you next try sex with a girl, I hope her cunt has sharp teeth which bite you hard as you go in.

No, I don't really mean all that. But I'm not crossing it all out because I want you to know how I'm feeling. Why can't you be a bit more forgiving, Bruno? *I've* said I'm sorry. (That wasn't easy, because I still think I had right on my side.) So can't you at least do the same?

I'm not enjoying school at the moment, and Robin Maclaine says T.G.S. is a first-rate dump, and we should be somewhere far more enterprising. I came first on Lower School cross-country last week, but don't expect that will interest you very much. Now I've finished *Out of the Silent Planet* I'm in the middle of *Voyage to Venus*. Terrific! Instead of dithering about whether to go to Newstead, why don't the Parkers get hold of a space-ship and head for somewhere in the remoter regions of the Solar System? One of the moons of Neptune (which might actually be quite nice) or there's always Pluto. Who knows what strange creatures might crawl from underneath the dense surface ice to listen to the Rev. Derek's sermons?

You may (sort of) be able to tell that I feel myself moving in a new direction. (And I don't mean the outer planets!) I'm not the same kid you knew back in the autumn. Others are saying the same about me.

Your cousin the writer (again)

Ian

P.S. Do you like 'Whole Lotta Woman' (Marvin Rainwater)? And 'At The Hop?' (The Danny and the Juniors version, of course!) 'Great

127

Balls of Fire' is still my very favourite though; I don't want it ever to leave the charts. But I don't like 'Kisses Sweeter than Wine' one bit (F. Vaughan) – it's nothing but slush.

[LETTER NOT REPLIED TO]

(xi)
[UNSENT LETTER]
Monday, February 24

Dear Auntie Eileen and Ian,

I ought to have written to both of you light-years ago but you know me, full of good intentions etc. (Don't complete the proverb, please!) I hope you don't mind me writing to the two of you in one and the same letter – killing two birds with one stone, etc (and that's the *last* popular saying I'll use in this epistle) – but it does save a bit of time and trouble (and there – I nearly put another proverb in!) especially when I think you will both be interested in the news I have to tell you. *Parkers* news, of course, and Bruno Lawrence Armitage's part in that estimable programme. Cometh the hour cometh the man, you might say (how can I stop this rash of proverbs? it's worse than measles, what's wrong with me?)...... Ian, I know you're not as great a fan of the serial as you used to be, but you *do* still listen to it, I note, and, I expect, support it against all its new enemies. For me it provides opportunities for showing what I can do scriptwise, and I will surely be able to use my present connection with the show as a stepping-stone for other and bigger things in the not too distant future.

Well, Friday morning last, your loving nephew/cousin presented himself at no lesser place than Broadcasting House itself, and I must say I was pretty impressed by the way the guys at the desk had my name all registered in advance. And it was "Yes, Mr Armitage! We're expecting you, Mr Armitage, Miss Orchard has phoned us our instructions: she's arranged with Miss Betty Reed that the two of you meet in this foyer." (Yes, THE Betty Reed, Arch-Producer of *The Parkers*). "I'll just give her a ring, Mr Armitage, and tell her you're here!"

He did, and with amazing quickness Betty (as I call her) had appeared to guide me through the fantastically complex labyrinth of Broadcasting House to the studio where the *Parkers* rehearsal was to take place. I don't quite know what to make of Betty; she speaks in a funny little-girl voice but she's obviously quite neurotically sharp, never missing a trick and often quite brusque with the actors, ticking them off like any old schoolteacher. She doesn't have much dress-sense, I have to say; she was wearing a very bright and very tight emerald-green "costume" which was a mistake with a bum as big as hers, and, on top, a small round yellow-plumed hat, also emerald-green, which for some reason she never removed, exactly as if the recording studio were Church (which, I suppose, it sort of is as far as she's concerned). She doesn't have anything of the charm and poise and brilliance of Verity herself, or of Elizabeth Parker (I mean, Enid Berridge, or Enid rather, for she, too, insists on first names terms). Betty gets pretty fussed (her job, I suppose) about timing and cues, and where everybody is standing in the studio, and once or twice she clapped her hands and said to the cast (with variations): "Boys and girls, let's get through this thing a bit more nippily than we're doing!" This *thing* – I ask you! I don't think Verity would care for that way of talking, and of course if I have go to more rehearsals, I shall, if I need to, tell her all about it.

But to give her her due, Betty said to the actors: "This is Bruno Armitage, a good friend of Verity and Charles'. Make him welcome! He's someone Verity trusts a lot for his views on *The Parkers*."

Of course I could have let certain cats out of certain bags here, but I restrained myself, though in the break, in the canteen, over the most delicious yeasty doughnuts I've ever eaten, I couldn't resist dropping a hint or two. "You may never see Newstead!" I said to Derek Parker, and, to Dan Whittaker (Davey Parker) and Neil Micklewright (Tom Cavan) "I'd say the veterinary practice has two pretty permanent recruits in you two." You should have seen the grins of satisfaction on their faces.

Hard to explain the ins-and-outs of a rehearsal, it's so *subtle* a business – a matter of knowing when to pause, in fact when to be silent, as much as when to speak or make a noise. For radio you've

129

obviously got to convey a sense of movement or atmosphere because listeners only – er, listen; they simply *can't* see. I certainly learned a lot about such matters during the course of the morning, and Betty and the whole cast were good teachers. The episode I witnessed being rehearsed for recording concerned Miss Venables and her past, and her shyness in telling the Parkers about it – a good script, and all the actors – with the exception in my opinion of Nigel Coombes (Kevin O'Flynn) who is far too pleased with himself by half – pulled their weight really well. It was, of course, a pleasure to hear (and watch) the queen of the programme – and I may say of the rehearsal room too – Enid Berridge herself. If she wasn't so spontaneous and warm, you might say that her behaviour was almost too much like that of a queen. She has her own corner of the studio, with her own chair, table and carafe-on-a-tray, and woe betide those who don't respect all this. Even the sound-effects people have to organise themselves round Where Enid Likes To Sit, but then why shouldn't this be the case, when she's the lynch-pin of the programme and, the real Queen HM apart, the most famous woman's voice in the country? She was most gracious and friendly to Yours Truly. At the start of the rehearsal she said with a girlish giggle: "I'm going to do my all-out best today, because I can see such a nice red-headed young man in the room. Better even than sunshine on a winter's day. Introduce me, please!" And when she had to speak the lines: "I'm sure I shall miss the little children of St Edmund's School here at Greenfield End quite horribly if and when we go to Newstead!" she unmistakably winked at me – me and no-one else.

Don't think, Auntie Eileen and Ian, that I don't realise that my ever-expanding experience in the world of script-writing is really due to you. Of course I still have a long way to go. However fast my progress, I realise that much....

[And on that note of irrefutable truth and (I fear) false modesty this never-sent letter ends.]

One of the (many) things I didn't know when I wrote the above was the effect on me, and on my life, of one of the *Parkers* cast in particular, of Neil Micklewright who played Tom Cavan. We eyed one another for at least half the rehearsal just like dogs when their owners meet. Would we get on? Should we demonstrate our respective sharpnesses of teeth and depths of growls? Were we more suited to being antagonists? or were we essentially the same breed?

Neil Micklewright as he was then! His hair was smarmed back with brillcreem, with his 'cowlick' in front combed and greased to stand up like a wave. He had a bony triangular face and narrow brilliant light blue eyes, which became perfectly slit-like when his face creased with amusement (sarcastic amusement as a rule). A little less tall than me, he walked with a rolling gait he'd obviously assiduously cultivated, deliberately transferring weight from one foot to another. As Tom Cavan his voice was ringing, with a male's ingenuousness and a youthful loudness; as himself it was soft (if well-articulated), perfectly fitted for asides or outrageous remarks which he intended only one person to catch.

At the canteen, over those delectable doughnuts I've mentioned, he relaxed his watchfulness. At one point he said: 'I'm quite the big new guy of this outfit now, you know, these last two weeks or so.' I said: 'Of *course* I know, Neil, I don't advise Verity Orchard for nothing.' That went home, I could tell at once. Neil started to try to impress me – yes me, the newcomer to the studios. He told me he'd done radio work even as a schoolboy; his father has an administrative job with the Beeb, and so has contacts. We could have said a lot more to each other but along came ghastly Nigel Coombes, who so plainly considered himself several cuts above all other cast members, and broke in on our talk. But when the whole session came to an end – when, in other words, the episode had been actually recorded – Neil Micklewright edged right up to me, and in a low, ticklish, sexy voice delivered right into my left ear, said: "How about having a swift half with me, Bruno? I know quite a few good little pubs round here."

"Good idea!" I said.

It took us longer than I'd anticipated to arrive at the particular pub Neil had in mind, small, snug, dark and already pretty packed. Getting served at the bar was a slow process. But eventually we had frothing glasses before us, and then it was that Neil asked me, voice very low, eyes very bright: "So what's it like then, being old Charles Compson's new cat?"

131

"Cat?"

Neil laughed – or chuckled rather. His eyes had gone extra-ordinarily narrow, they appeared like a wildcat's in fact. "Catamite, you thicky! His bum-boy!"

These words changed the way I looked at just about everything.

To Julian Cornish, Head of Entertainment Drama, BBC Home Service
Monday, February 24, 1958

Dear Julian,

I enclose three story-line proposals from the young man I have already mentioned to you. I've jigged them up a bit, but they are virtually as he submitted them. He is, I would say, highly representative of his generation, not at all clever, not in the least talented, merely – for our purposes – *interestingly* average. I think you'll agree that what comes over above everything is his *passion*, nothing less, for Greenfield End itself, as a moral, tradition-minded, somewhat easy-going and (yes, why not have the courage to say it?) *middle-class* community. This is precisely the world in which millions (literally) of my listeners live. The very people who deluge dear 'Auntie Beeb' with letters about *The Parkers* and send flowers and get-well cards to the actors come from it. It may not be radical and kitchen-sink-y to recognise this basic social truth, but – if only for reasons of commercial prudence – recognise it you should. And another thing – you know me, Julian, I am a democrat to my very finger-tips, who's supported Labour for I dread-to-think-how-long – we mustn't ever throw away the baby with the bath-water. There IS something precious to people – and to England herself – about *The Parkers'* Greenfield End life, and as I (and many others) have remarked before, it relates back to what we all knew (and fought for) in our darkest wartime hours. So heed the clamour that demands the keeping of the whole shebang where it has so happily been for a decade.

You may think I'm employing an argument against myself, but I received a most horrible and disquieting letter the other day, not exactly anonymous, just signed 'Ian A (and a few of his buddies down in Oxfordshire)', a string of really repulsive obscenities which it took me quite some while to forget. Now *there*, Julian, is your anti-Greenfield End, anti-middle-class standpoint, which wants everything sordid and disgusting and reduced to the messiest sort of sexual impulse. The Royal Court may be pleased to take up this way of looking at life, and no doubt Mr Kenneth Tynan would not only admire Ian A. and his Oxfordshire buddies but make them all script-writers-in-chief for *The Parkers* itself. But you and I have a different philosophy of life, Julian, we have standards by which we have stood for twenty working years. Let me prophesy: in another twenty the kitchen-sink will have collapsed utterly, but *The Parkers'* Vicarage will be go on being a place of strength and refreshment.

I was a good girl and have duly introduced Newstead and the possibility of a 'living' there for Derek, as my masters bade me, but in such a way that *quite honourably and logically, with no loss of face on anyone's side, or any ideological let-down*, the Parkers could remain in Greenfield End if it were so decided. (You listened to the Feb 18 episode, I trust!) I most certainly hope, however, that the whole matter can be laid to rest ere long, and that the enclosed three pages will tell you that a whole generation of sometimes Confused but very far from Angry Young Men need *The Parkers*, 'our' *Parkers* more than ever. Incidentally the un-A.Y.M. in question felt involved enough to ask to attend a rehearsal of the programme which I duly arranged with Betty Reed herself. He also is wildly keen on the Tom Cavan story-line, about which next week's *Radio Times* will feature a short piece. Think on *all this*, if you will.

As always,
Verity

(xiii)
Feb 24, 1958

Dear Director,

I have seen with the greatest interest several ads for your interesting Outward Bound Academy up in Sutherland. I would be most pleased if you could supply me with further particulars of the courses you run. You say you develop self-reliance and survival techniques within a peaceful environment. Suits me. I'm not interested in my school's CCF, I am not of a military turn of mind, but tough activities like cross-country running, orienteering, canoeing, mountain-walking, climbing appeal to me a lot. I'm also keen to observe animals and birds in a serious way. Living as I do in the Midlands, in a fair-sized town (20,000 people) in flattish country, I don't have the opportunities for these pursuits that I would like.

I am at Tanbury Grammar School (Form 3A) and I have to say that I don't think it offers all that much scope for the kind of person I am. It says it believes in both the Classics and the Sciences, but I personally don't believe in either. I don't know Scotland at all, but I have read many a book by John Buchan with pleasure, and often, when I read C.S.Lewis and J.R.R.Tolkien, I place the northern wilds in which both writers delight up in your part of the world. Living and working in such places as you do must avoid the disappointments towns and schools and families inevitably give you. For example, you have a cousin you trust and he prefers to cultivate some important snobby person to being with yourself; you listen to a radio programme that you think will go on for ever in the same likeable place, and you find out it's under threat.

I've looked on the map and seen that Scourie is where moutains and sea meet – islands to boat out to, peaks (further inland) to climb up. I long to see it all for myself. I have pleasure in enclosing a stamped addressed envelope. I had better add that I am not at all well-off. My mother is a widow who works mornings as a dentist's receptionist. I hope you will bear this in mind when giving me details of fees and so on. Can one get help from the County?

Yours faithfully,
Ian Armitage

From Julian Cornish, Head of Entertainment Drama, BBC Home Service
Feb 25

My dear Verity,

Thank you for that characteristically impassioned screed, and for the three enclosed plot-suggestions. I have to say that, although doubtless very gratifying and pleasurable to receive, these last didn't strike me as so very remarkable. Obviously it was their provenance – from a *young man* and not some *middle-aged lady* – that impressed you, and was intended to impress me. Is this the same young man whom you drew on before for the Tom Cavan lie story? I remember you admitted to me over a few gin-and-cins 'across the road' that you'd had to do so much surgery on what he submitted to make it work that you wondered if sticking to your own inventions as usual wouldn't have been better.

You know as well as I do that we can all find members of the public to back up our hobby-horses; people who think the world is flat; people who believe fairies exist and can be photographed; people who are sure the United States and the Soviet Union have entered into a conspiracy against Britain! And so on and so forth. Such evidence of fellow-thinkers never really carries the weight we want it to. And let me add that from the contents point of view there was nothing in those three sketches that couldn't have been written by you yourself, and I don't just mean "jigged up", my dear Verity, or by any member of your team, even the somewhat 'non-Entertainment' quotation from Traherne. (I have a feeling, I may be wrong, that you've used that poem before, in your *Parkers' Bedside Book* perhaps?) I'm not saying, Heaven forbid, that you – or one of your gang – actually did write the three proposals you submitted, but, to tell you the truth, Verity my love, I wouldn't be all that comfortable putting money that you *didn't*...

I don't think it took a very subtle ear to detect in the episode of *The Parkers* for Feb 18th, and in the related subsequent ones in which Newstead was discussed, that emotionally the load was stacked against departure from Greenfield End, but at this stage this doesn't matter too much. Good marks, good girl, you did what you were asked, clearly and efficiently, and so now the possibility of a move to Newstead – however conducted and whoever of the cast it entails – is already an established fact with your audience. I use the word 'fact' advisedly. Let us make no bones about it. Newstead is indeed a fact of life.

Verity – and I realise, for all the business-style heading at the top of the page that this is going to be a personal rather than an official departmental letter – we all know you were the 'onlie begetter' of *The Parkers*, we all know you not only battled for it to be put on the air but heroically wrote it single-handedly for a year or more, and have been unsparing in your guidance of the script team (as well as in your own writing of it) ever since. And no-one could admire what you've done more than I. In addition to *The Parkers* there's been so much we've worked on together: that programme's delightful predecessor, *The Robertson Family*, for which I often can wax nostalgic (and do); that series of programmes on the childhoods of famous English writers; your Sunday night adaptation of Mrs Gaskell's *Wives and Daughters*, that Victorian masterpiece which only you, myself and Lord David Cecil at Oxford seem to know about. So take it in the right spirit when I say now: 'Beware of entertaining a wrong idea of your standing!' (It's something I often have to tell myself, if that makes the remark any more palatable.)

If, to use the old angelology (I used to be rather up in such subjects, but have got a bit rusty of late), if *you* belong to the Seraphim and Cherubim of writers for the Beeb, and *I*, with my big important desk in Broadcasting House, to the Thrones, then let's be honest and realistic enough to admit that we are members of only the First Circle. (There are three circles, just in case you'd forgotten.) Beyond us lie the Dominions, Virtues and (how apt in this particular case!) the Powers – and it is to them and their decrees that the Third and ultimate circle listens, those whose light is so great my eyes dazzle even as I contemplate it: those Principalities, Archangels and Angels who stretch up to the very pinnacles of the British Establishment: the House of Lords, All Souls, the Royal Household, and goodness knows where else. Well, The Dominions, Virtues and Powers have decided that Greenfield End and all that therein lies doesn't belong to the age of rock'n'roll, coffee-bars, the Campaign for Nuclear Disarmament and ambitious New Towns. (Nor does it; little point in debating *that*!) In its huge benignity this Second Circle has recognised the meaning that Elizabeth and Derek Parker *et al* (or some of 'al') have for the British public and has granted them a continued rather than an axed life. *The Parkers* has not been given the death sentence – which is what has happened to many another apparently much-loved programme. On the contrary, in *your* case, a rebirth that would delight any self-respecting Hindu has been arranged. So be grateful for this, my dear, be grateful and be sensible. Otherwise, whatever the intimate depth of your relationship to the programme, it is you, and not Newstead, who will be consigned to that outer darkness with which the Ultimate Angelic Orders will have nothing to do.

I may have written brutally, but I have written as honestly as I can, and, my good Verity, you can perhaps read further brutality and honesty between the lines of this rather long but wholly necessary, good-intentioned but decidedly cautionary missive.

Believe me to be

Your old friend, colleague and well-wisher,

Julian

(xv)
Sunday, March 16

Dear Bruno,

Further to your telephone call last night – isn't that how a secretary, particularly a Perfect Secretary would begin? Yes, Verity's got so tired recently, poor lambkin (or poor kid, as I would say, of course, only people wouldn't get the point!) that she's asked old Nesta Coolidge to act as secretary for her, and this I'm only too pleased to do so.

Do you know a rhyme rather popular down here in Dorset (pity you can't hear the tune!):

"Funny Nesta,

Who can best her,

When it comes to eccentricitee?

Mistress Coolidge,

Very foolidge
But full of a curious sanitee!;

Well, I'm going to show my sanity right now. We haven't – that is, Verity hasn't, and I, as her Almost Perfect Secretary haven't either – the time to bother with pleading wheedling scheming boys (for I refuse to call you a MAN), who ring up saying: 'Please, Verity, did you like my ickle ideas? Will I be rewarded for being such a clever diddums-widdums and have my name spoken out loud on the wireless, for the whole world to hear goggle-eyed with admiration? Please, Verity, say what a good little boy am I?'

Well, pull out your thumb, and get on with whatever you're able to get on with. (Can't think what it could be – selling a few mouldy antiques, I suppose.)

And so from the household of The Puzzle (a writer's household) I say (and I mean it): Be off with your bother!

I lead a busy life, Bruno. Busy: Know the word? B.U.S.Y. Goats, hardy as they are, *do* have their troubles from time to time, and a responsible owner and breeder *does* have to deal with them. How would *you* like to be 'drenching' a goat, the technical term for giving them fluid medicine to stave off infectious parasites? I snort with laughter at the very notion! How would you cope with 'scour', the poor goats' form of diarrhoea? Why, you'd quiver from nausea the moment you saw any of the runny stuff slopping out of their bums, and would never get round to whipping up the curative white of egg in water.

So you just leave a busy household alone.

I always said you were more nuisance than you were worth, and now Verity – *at last!* – is beginning to see my point.

'Funny Nesta,
Who can best her,
When it comes to eccentricitee?
Mistress Coolidge
May be foolidge,
But she's rich in perspicacitee.'

(xvii)
New Statesman Competition Page – issue Friday, March 21 1958

Readers were asked to celebrate or lament the fortunes of any popular radio or TV programme using the form of any equally popular traditional British song. Given the dramatic news of the likely departure of the Reverend Derek and his brood from the begardened snugness of Greenfield End, to Newstead (is that Crawley? Hemel Hempstead? Harlow?), it's not surprising that *The Parkers* was the favoured subject. We had, for example, 'In Greenfield End baht t'script' ('On Ilkla Moor baht'at') and 'What shall we do with redundant Parkers?' ('What shall we do with a drunken Sailor?')

But we have to admit preferring the following, printed below:

(To the tune of 'Early One Morning')

'In the weekday gloaming, just as the pot was boiling,
    I heard a Vicar singing to Cornish and Co:
    "Oh, never leave me, oh, don't deceive me,
How could you u–use a poor Parker so?"

'Remember the vows you made to my listeners,
    Remember old *Radio Times* which promised to be true,
    "Oh, never leave me, oh, don't deceive me,
Don't send me to an Overspill so "common" and so "new.""
    (Etc etc.)

(Five further entries follow.)

Saturday, March 22

Dear Neil,

Ever since that drink we had together at the Bag o' Nails – drinks rather, it wasn't just a half, and not swift either – I've felt I've got a new friend. I hope I'm not wrong about this, because I feel I have need for one right now. We seemed to talk so easily. I was a bit taken aback by your opening gambit (!) but before long we were talking as if we'd known each other years instead of hours.

I think we have a lot in common: an important father, a good public-school behind us where neither of us did ourselves full justice, a taste for fun and novelty – and an ambition to succeed in the media. I was interested by what you said about your wanting to do radio acting only for so long, while building up knowledge of TV filming and camera-work in your spare time. In other words you've embarked on stepping-stones. Same here. I've always seen *The Parkers* as a useful road to establishing myself in the world of radio (and more particularly) TV drama. I intend to keep the sharpest weather eye open for opportunities in these fields.

But that isn't what I'm writing about. I want to tell you something, Neil. Which is – what you said to me as we sat down with our pints at the Bag o'Nails is true (as I'm sure you knew). It wouldn't be how I'd put it myself, of course, but that'd be splitting hairs. As you'll appreciate, I've got myself into a situation I loathe, and which I'd like more than anything to extricate myself from. It isn't the real me at all, and I don't even *need* the "particular friendship" any more. I'd be really glad of help and advice here, and I can't think of anybody else I could discuss such a business with. I can hardly try an Agony Aunt, can I? with those fucking stupid laws of ours. If you could ring up and propose a time and place for a drink (or two or three) I'll be your friend for life.

Saluti,

Bruno

(xix)
Article in *New Statesman* – issue Friday, March 28, 1958
by Peter Cuthbertson, Head of English Department,
Aireside Polytechnic, Leeds

It has become axiomatic among those seriously concerned with cultural health that hard scrutiny should be applied to artifacts intended for the recreation of important sections of the mass-public. A radio serial or television series, however limited its range, will reveal abundantly and often inadvertently the debates that animate, on one level of general awareness or another, our whole society.

That NS readers have taken an interest in those debates as waged in the BBC about the direction of one of its most popular weekday programmes, *The Parkers*, is evident from last week's competition. But their cultural significance (not to mention consequence) has, in my view, gone largely unremarked. This is a pity because what has happened – off and on air – is surely an index of national health, and therefore deeply deservant of the closest attention.

There has been a good deal of 'shall we? shan't we?' in the programme these past weeks. Shall we stay in our suburban community – the very lack of geographical precision concerning its location is interesting and indicative in itself – or shall we go to one of the New Towns, somewhat over-emphatically called Newstead (but then was Dickens any more "subtle" in his greatest novel, *Hard Times* with his Coketown?). For those of us for whom an organic society remains a constant desideratum (Raymond Williams' masterly *Culture and Society* will, it is hoped, give us no excuse for not being able to provide cogent definition of this key term), the conflict between the alternatives posed in *The Parkers* contains some disturbing ambivalences, all the more disturbing, dare one say, because not fully seen by the programme-makers themselves (either Verity Orchard, creator of *The Parkers* and still its principal script-writer, or Home Service apparatchik, Julian Cornish). Possibly a few reminders of what is involved are necessary here.

Derek Parker is the Vicar of St Luke's, the parish church of a Metroland community of (it would seem) a fair degree of prosperity, called Greenfield End. We may pause briefly to note that, though unequivocally Anglican, both church and vicar are without any detectable attachment to any faction or 'party' within the church. The incumbent of St Luke's would seem to have a fondness for the divines and devotionals of the seventeenth century, indeed we have been hearing him of late quoting Traherne with some fervour, but on the whole his is a social rather than a spiritual or (overtly) political position: providing that shoulder to cry on in which modern life is so strikingly deficient. (The shoulder, it should be noted in passing, is today a doctor's as a rule – see a novel as distant from us in time but as contemporary in preoccupations as Dickens' *Bleak House* for accurate intimation that this would be the case.) Derek Parker keeps, his wife tells us, 'open house' for the parish, but just how 'open' is it? A question hard to answer because we know so little about Greenfield End itself – but then perhaps there is not so much to learn.

It has no manufacturing base (at least none we have heard mentioned): presumably most male members of the Reverend Derek's congregation go up to London to work and earn money at the offices of unspecified firms. That leaves in the town as we experience it a largely non-working population of middle-class women, married or otherwise, some of whom have enough money and leisure to become the eccentric 'useful in the parish' characters which have always abounded in British fiction, Miss Venables, whom the public 'loves to hate' having in truth a pedigree extending back to the 18th century. It also leaves a few people in service professions, and of these we have various somewhat arbitrary specimens: two vets and one aspiring one, a keeper of a private hotel, a writer (of again a largely unspecified nature: who could say what kind of books Kevin O'Flynn produces?). As for the working-class of Greenfield End (for it must exist!), you could listen to the programme for many hours, and probably months, without any awareness of the lives of those who constitute it. We do however regularly encounter certain individuals, sociologically classifiable as working class, who are virtually retainers of the Parkers themselves, the ludicrously named Mrs Bobbington (a name even a *Punch* humorist like F. Anstey might well have baulked at) and Verges (whose name the more literary listeners will recognise as originating in *Much Ado About Nothing*).

142

Now there is little doubt in my mind that if one were to visit the vicarage of such a parish as Greenfield End (and one could easily enough find approximations to it in Kent, Surrey, outer Middlesex, south-eastern Buckinghamshire, Hertfordshire, and that part of Essex adjacent to Hertfordshire), one would indeed find such inclusions and exclusions as pervade the Parkers' ménage – and for that matter their entire mental *Weltanschauung*. In that sense *The Parkers* is not precisely unrealistic. What should concern NS readers is the line of defence about the retention of Greenfield End that has been recently passionately employed.

In contrast to the dismal prospect of a New Town (for that, in a phrase, is how Elizabeth Parker views any move to Newstead) we have Greenfield End presented to us, lingeringly and lovingly, as the very pattern of the organic community (though it would be more incongruous even than a quotation from Thomas Traherne to hear cited in the programme any proper adult definition of this, – Greenfield End would appear innocent of even F.R. Leavis and Denys Thompson, never mind Raymond Williams). Here, in a community where most of the men with whom we are likely socially to consort go away to work, and where women draw Brahministic lines between their ranks, *here* we are told is true neighbourliness, togetherness, the kind of ease and freedom and permission to be individualistic and eccentric that is – somehow – *truly* and inherently British, loosely linked to Home Front sentimentality (in both wars but in particular of course the Second; the shades of ITMA can sometimes be felt in *The Parkers*, ecclesiastical though the context may be). Opposed to this is the technocratic socialist dystopia of Newstead where men stay in the vicinity to earn their bread-and-butter, and most women will also be working, where those Brahministic divisions will have less architectural definition than in Metroland, where there will be perhaps less room for capitalist lackeys as at home in The Vicarage as Kevin O'Flynn – who has the freedom to write his superfluous books in padded idleness with everyone he knows approving and cluckingly admiring. And yet it is Newstead – not Greenfield End – that has been found wanting by a large proportion of the *dramatis personae*, and ticked off for being inorganic, while the amorphous money- and class-centred subtopian

143

society which the programme has made us familiars of for almost a decade receives all moral encomia going.

All one can ever do is bear witness to what seems morally right and promotes the spirit of growth and democratic reverence for life. It therefore seems to me that the BBC's decision to move *The Parkers* from Greenfield End to Newstead is wholly to be applauded. No doubt the clichés will go on, but at least the milieu will be growing, expanding, inclusive, not the closed self-referential affair where nothing is real that can't be confined behind high well-trimmed hedges, and where Mrs Bobbington comes in every weekday to clean and talk about her corns.

(xx)
Sunday, March 30

Dear Bruno,

I've been pondering ever since I left you yesterday (well, today, to be more accurate, considering the hour), and I'm not one to ponder as a rule. But then I don't think anyone's been rash enough to ask for my advice before, at least not on such a weighty issue.

I got no impression yesterday that the relationship with CC (call it what you want) means a bloody thing to you, at any rate not now (and I for one doubt that it ever did). So do what we agreed yesterday: get the hell out of it by any means you can, and don't budge one inch in your resolve until you've made the old queen (who's behaved thoroughly selfishly, in my book) understand absolutely, unequivocally, your intention of being free from him. And until you've completely kicked the dust of that Fulham Road prison from off the soles of your feet.

Be ruthless, be a MAN.

Talking of which I feel quite honoured to have been the one to take you to Your First Ever Soho Strip-Joint. Talk about old Virgil and Dante. (Not that I do talk about them much. I only scraped through in "0" Level Latin.) I also know a club if you're interested any time that specialises in films of Swedish girls – stunning films, you'll be sitting through them fully extended, I can promise you. And turning to

Swedish films which get beyond the X certificate, I *insist* that you come with me – perhaps even next week – to Bergman's *Wild Strawberries*, it'll be the fourth time I'll have seen it. Bibi Andersson and Ingrid Thulin must be two of the most beautiful women in existence – or who have *ever* existed. And the photography's out of this world. Bergman, I've noticed, often uses this man Gunnar Fischer, and one of these days I'll get round to writing to him and see if he can't do anything to help me in my own career.

Anyway chin up, Bruno, and I won't give you any peace till you're brought Things to an End. (And I don't mean CC's poxy arsehole either!) It'll be far easier and more painless than you imagine, believe you me.

All the best,
Neil

(xxi)
Wednesday, April 2

Dear Verity,

I'm sorry to be bothering you – and Nesta – when you obviously need peace and quiet right now, and richly deserve them too, but I've got something to tell you which I think you should know.

On Monday, in the early evening, I had a visit – well, more accurately *you* had a visit, but I was the one there to take it – from Enid Berridge, accompanied by her daughter, Cassie. She was in a highly distressed state.

"Oh," said Enid, whom I took a moment to place so great was my surprise at her presence, "it's that boy who turned up to our rehearsal not so long back! The one who nearly put me off my lines because of the colour of his hair." She was speaking extremely loudly (in fact some passers-by turned round – maybe they'd identified her!) but not all that clearly, in fact in very slurred fashion. The reason? – Verity, she was greatly the worse for wear. She'd got it into her head you'd said you were coming up to London this week, and even though she admitted she knew you hardly ever stayed in Fulham but were put up

145

by friends elsewhere (she'd tried all of them, she said), she was determined 'to leave no stone unturned' – and so, ignoring the advice of Cassie, who was pretty worried by the whole business but trying her hardest not to show it, she'd absolutely *insisted* on coming round to P. Dickinson, Antiques! A headstrong lady!

The thing is – I hope I'm not acting officiously, but honestly, Verity, her visit has really shaken me – she is convinced you think she's betrayed you by agreeing to stay on with the Newstead *Parkers*. She says she owes all her 'fame and fortune' to you, that you were the one who gave her a break and a part that 'would be anyone's envy', and that the last person on earth she'd want to hurt was you. But she says that her husband's work as picture-restorer hasn't been going too well of late, and the family needs money, they having no private income to fall back on – Cassie looked away at this point, I noticed – and so really she has *no alternative* to continuing with the programme in its new form. She desires nothing more fervently (she kept on repeating these words) than to be on the best possible terms with one of the people she respects most 'in the entire universe' (her very phrase!). So I know she'd value it enormously if you could assure her that all is well.

I couldn't help liking her, I have to confess, just as I liked her at the rehearsal. Yes, she was being theatrical and unselfcontrolled but she's also warm and genuine, I believe. (I wonder why she makes herself up so heavily and in that erratic way, eye-shadow going way beyond the eyelids, and lipstick beyond the mouth.) Her distress struck me, I have to say, as entirely sincere. Her daughter Cassie kept looking from her mother to me, and back again, as if she could enter the feelings and reactions of both of us in turn, and wanted neither of us to be embarrassed by the other but to realise, however we might seem outwardly, that we were equally nice and worth-while people. Most girls, I think, would have tried to apologise for a drunken mother, most girls would make out to a boy their own age that they were distant from the situation, but not she, not Cassie Berridge. She didn't dissociate herself from it at all, but was anxious to improve it as best she could, which meant trying to track *you* down, Verity, and putting the relationship between the two of you on a good footing again. Cassie struck me, in the short time we had to talk more generally, as very

146

responsive and imaginative. She is particularly fond of the Pre-Raphaelites, she told me, which is funny because I'm just starting to be fond of them myself.

I sincerely hope, Verity, that you yourself are not feeling too got down by everything. I'm sure, after you've given yourself space and time to think things over, you could return refreshed and do really lively, altogether WONDERFUL Newstead scripts. Everyone else thinks so too, Enid especially, who says 'PLEASE let Verity re-consider things, and make the move with us all! We're all lonely and lost sheep without our Good Shepherdess.' And I must say that I can hear in my own head as I write this letter scenes in a new town that show your intimitable touch at its most dazzling and inspiring – all kinds of people meeting up by the civic fountain in the town-centre, interesting talk in the public library or recreation centre.

As for me you must know that I will always be on hand to give you any help you require. Right now I very much like looking after the shop, and it isn't going at all badly though I say it myself. Tell Charles that, please. Fenders, five in all, and the set of High Wycombe balloon-backed chairs, are all in place and looking splendid – and very tempting to any potential buyer, so there's no call for him to come up here at all. Much better, now it's spring-turning-summer, for him to stay down in Dorset in your beautiful Puzzle, which I would like to visit again some day soon, if I may.

Have a very good Easter,

Bruno

[Whatever happens to me – even, I increasingly think, after I'm dead – I'll be able to see, as in a still from a film, Cassie Berridge on that fragrant blossomy spring evening which proved the watershed in my life. She was wearing a sage-green corduroy skirt and above that a man's shirt, green-and-white striped, over a thin fawn polo-neck. Her light-brown hair had a coltish quality about it, and came down low on her forehead, to emphasize her large, slightly apprehensive brown eyes. Had she not been so charming in movement and gesture, I would have wanted to magic her into stillness, into a statue, and keep her my captive for ever.

As it was, I did far, far better.]

(xxii)
Tuesday, April 8

My dear Bruno,

I've just seen your long letter to Verity. So glad all's well, but am I to take it you don't WANT me to come up, or are you just thinking about what's best in the face of all the Great To-do we're having at present? (Curse *Parkers*, curse Newstead!) Can't wait to see High Wycombe chairs, but, even more important, can't wait to see (and be with) YOU. And make my regard for you flesh as well as word.

I longed for you all through Easter,
C C

(xxiii)
Wednesday, April 9

Dear Bruno,

Thank you for your letter. (I concede that it had to be written; we couldn't go on fending you off by phone indefinitely, more's the pity!) It made me very cross. No, I lie: it made me furious. Who DO you think you are? Well, I probably could answer that question all too easily, and most likely will have had a stab at doing so before I've signed off. And I don't need *your* good Easter wishes!

Fact: I am NOT writing any more *Parkers* scripts. I have had a major difference of opinion with the powers-that-be at the BBC, and, even though there has been a good deal of acrimony (know that word, Bruno? or will you need a dictionary to look it up?), I have emerged from the wretched business with the respect that's due one of the country's leading and most influential script-writers. (I already feature in several major histories of the still comparatively new and innovative art of radio, in case you didn't know.) My position over the move to Newstead has been made public and reported widely – and news of my official and entirely voluntary resignation will be broadcast to the world very shortly. I most certainly am *not* going to change this situation to appease Enid's (rightly) uneasy conscience. Nor to indulge your own misplaced notion of yourself as some gifted diplomatist, a sort of Universal Uncle with a special mission for distressed Berridges.

Fact: As I have retired, so to speak, from *The Parkers*, I am hardly likely to be asking for *your* help (whatever that means) over scripts, let alone to be 'requiring' it. (But then exactness with language has never been a strong point of yours, something I would conjecture motivated your examiners into giving you the grades they did.) Perhaps you should be more clearly in the picture than would seem the case.

Being the age you are, one of the Younger Generation, and with a declared enthusiasm for my programme (the declaration itself could get decidedly tedious at times, but we'll let that pass), you were of use to me. I could take those ideas of yours, of which you were so inordinately proud (neither good nor bad, neither intelligent nor unintelligent, just average, to quote my actual words to Julian Cornish Himself), as ammunition in the battle with the BBC that had (unbeknown to you, so plainly lacking in any information about our institution) already started – long, long before little you came on the scene. True, I went on to employ some of the stories you proposed – to whit, the somewhat piffling and routine business of Tom Cavan's missing weekend – *but*, my dear Bruno, to no greater extent than I have been using ideas sent in by countless listeners over a whole decade. (See that *Everywoman* interview that so took your fancy.) I do so hope you haven't been nurturing childish little vanities on this subject; I rather fear you have.

Fact: You are at present living rent-free in a property belonging jointly to Charles and myself. For services rendered. At the moment – Charles being so utterly devoted to the Dorset countryside – it rather suits us to have you minding the shop while we're both down here, and probably enough old queens pop in from time to time and respond to your winning ways for the odd mother-of-pearl jug or ormolu snuff-box to be sold, or even, thrill of thrills, High Wycombe chairs with balloon backs. There are of course *other* services you've rendered. You *know* that I *know*, don't you? You know that I've always known, don't you? Or did you take me for a complete fool? Did you *really* believe that I thought you dragged out that uncomfortable camp-bed and slept downstairs every time Charles came up to London? Did it really not occur to you that you've had, during the years of my marriage, about a hundred predecessors, and God knows how many before Charles and I trotted up the aisle? And this present *folie* of his with you (for so I see it) doesn't take a Sigmund Freud to perceive; it would be amusing to know what the Berridges *mère et fille* made of your presence in Fulham.

Nesta got you right first time, Bruno. You dismissed her in your mind as a cracked old thing with a mania for goats, little knowing that, in her farouche way, she is, quite simply, a genius, a seer, a moral intelligence who can distinguish the false from the genuine in less time than it takes a billy-goat to toss his head.

After this letter, I doubt you'll want to come down to The Puzzle again, and anyway I shouldn't think I'd get Nesta's blessing for the invitation. But you can stay on at P. Dickinson for as long as you care to. It seems an arrangement to the benefit of all parties.

Yours faithfully,
Verity

(xxiv)
Wednesday, April 9

Dear Bruno,

I hope you won't mind me writing to you (though how will I ever know whether you've minded or not, because the next time we meet, you may have got over minding and be all nice and polite to me so I'll never have been aware of the annoyance or embarrassment that came over you on getting this?). But I want to thank you for how you were to Mum and myself when we called round at your place in so odd a fashion on Monday last week. Even your initial surprise (perhaps 'shock' is the better word) didn't last long. The moment you'd digested the situation you tried your best (successfully) to put us at ease and appreciated the dilemma we were in (particularly Mum, obviously) and showed no kind of disapproval whatever of tears or talk about money (the lack of it, and Dad's fecklessness) or – being frank – the deleterious effects on a highly-strung middle-aged woman of booze. (What is it about the BBC that makes so many of its best-known employees drink? Verity Orchard's pretty fond of the bottle herself – *I* know, I've been a witness.)

In fact I got the definite impression that all these kinds of things you are able to take in your stride by your very nature, and that it isn't in you to make so-called *moral* objections or judgements. You see people as people first, a whole mass of often contradictory qualities, some good, some not, some, for the moment, very trying, others more appealing. (That's how I see them myself.)

Anyway, Bruno, this – and no kidding – is the impression you made (and not only on me, I may add, but on an afterwards very repentant Enid too). Of course – see above! – I shan't ever know whether I'm right or not, shall I? Perhaps I've been altogether wrong, and you were busy all during our visit moralising like fury inside and later getting out your psychology or theology manuals, and writing furiously in their margins whenever you came across a particularly stern observation: 'Enid and Cassie Berridge precisely!' But somehow I doubt it.

I'm writing this after finishing a holiday project (of my own choice) on 'Who is the greatest of the Pre-Raphaelites?' I had to go for a walk all round Ravenscourt Park before deciding on what my answer was going to be. Much as I love them all, I knew I wouldn't decide on Millais (his big things are just too big for my taste and seem somehow to show the rest of him up – a little bit inflated and over-ambitious), and I knew it wouldn't be Dante Gabriel Rossetti (too mushy; I don't much care for him as a man either). Then I thought: 'Ah, I've got it now, Holman Hunt! so grandly mystical, so mysterious in his colours, so real an heir to the great Italian Christian painters.' And then – I was by this time communing and communicating with a couple of the park's mandarin ducks, by means of some pieces of bread concealed on my person – a rather shameful thought came to me: 'All the others are going to say H.H. I want to be original (for once!)' So do you know who I chose, Bruno? Arthur Hughes, a marvellous illustrator, as everybody knows, but also a marvellous painter. Do you know a work of his called *April Love*? (Not to be confused with the frightful Pat Boone hit-song of the moment!!) The almost daring vividness and moisture of his greens (I refer to hues not to vegetables) says so much, gives a context to the human beauty of his subject in such a compelling fashion. It's a painting one feels one could (and would like to) *inhabit*.

So the essay is completed now, and so (very nearly) is this letter to you. (I wonder if I will be bold enough to post it?) Mum is reading through the latest *Parkers* script, a harmless but strong-brewed pot of tea by her side, brother Adam – who can survive any crisis, big or small, simply by not noticing that it's arrived – is passing the time with Hemingway's *Fiesta* and imagining himself one of the Twenties sophisticated set drinking and fornicating their way through Europe. And Dad is in the kitchen confronting a table completely covered in bills he hasn't paid, some of which have had to be rescued, scrumpled up, from jacket pockets and waste-paper baskets. C'est la vie.

I hope we meet again, and thanks again, even if we don't,

Cassie Berridge

(xxv)
Excerpt from *The Parkers* (Thursday, April 10, 1958)

KEVIN O'FLYNN *(with justifiable irritation)*: Tom, will you kindly not come into the house in that manner. It's like a herd of hobnailed elephants you sound – and just when it's quiet and peace I'm wanting.

TOM *(not too apologetically)*: Sorry, Uncle Kevin, I wasn't thinking.

KEVIN: Wasn't thinking! That's the truth you're telling for once.

TOM *(a touch insolently)*: In the middle of writing something, were you?

KEVIN: Something that is merely the most beautiful chapter of my whole novel. The one in which I express all the melancholy –

TOM: Of your boyhood in Limerick. I know!

KEVIN: No, you do *not* know, Tom. And there's many a thing in heaven and earth that you're not knowing. The melancholy *not* of my boyhood in Limerick but of a brief but tragic period of my youth in Dublin. It was at my grandfather's deathbed I was then, and him the most virtuous man who ever drew breath, and the disease crushing his lungs like a steam-roller.

TOM: I'm very sorry, I wasn't aware...

152

KEVIN: Wasn't thinking, don't know, wasn't aware – is it not a story that suggests itself behind all those words, Tom? That you're turning into a young man who doesn't think the way he should, doesn't know the things he ought to, and goes around unaware of the effect he's having on others.

TOM: I'm not sure I get you, Uncle Kevin.

KEVIN: No, I don't suppose you do. Or, shall we say, choose not to. It's been a lot of dashing up to town you've been doing lately, quite the city dandy, amusing yourself with extravagance and foolishness.

TOM: Has it?

KEVIN: Was it not at a smart Soho restaurant you were on Tuesday night, and you with only a few pounds of your wages left?

TOM: It may have been.

KEVIN: And wasn't it that beautiful and innocent creature, Minty Macdonald, you were trying to impress so? Showing yourself quite the gentleman as you ordered the fine dishes and the costly wine for the pair of yous?

TOM: It was just once in a while, Uncle Kevin. I was feeling happy I'd helped with that op. so successfully on the Rentons' old black tom, and felt like celebrating... I wanted to show Minty...

KEVIN: And I suppose it was the Rentons' old black tom who paid the bill?

TOM *(clearly ill at ease)*: How could it be?

KEVIN: How could it be indeed, Tom? Old black toms don't have money. But someone nearer to hand *does*. It was your hapless Uncle Kevin who paid, wasn't it? with those pounds he'd left out, in his foolishness, on top of the sideboard, meaning them for the succour of the poor Miss Venables who's suffered the Good Lord's own troubles this month.

TOM *(trying to stand on his dignity)*: I was going to put them back. You can hardly doubt that, Uncle Kevin. I'm not a thief.

KEVIN: And there's me thinking a thief is someone who takes money or objects that don't belong to him. It's clearly stupid I've been all these years.

TOM: I'm so sorry. But in other respects....

KEVIN: In other respects, eh, Tom? And here's Davey Parker, his

153

good self, the most truthful young man who ever walked this planet, writing me the saddest letter I've ever received.

TOM *(horrified, fearful)*: A *letter*, Uncle Tom?

KEVIN: Yes, a letter, Tom:

"Dear Kevin, It's hard to write a letter to a famous writer, and harder still when you have something painful and difficult to communicate. But the fact is your nephew Tom's work has been this last month consistently below standard – and has given concern to all at the Practice and to not a few of our longest-standing patients. His love of animals is not in question, but his attention to any form of detail – accounts, filling in forms, keeping a tidy register – most definitely is. Nor is his time-keeping what is expected of an employee here. The list of mistakes and oversights that have been an embarrassment for us, is, I fear a long one...

(xxvi)
Thursday, April 10

Dear Bruno,

Well, would you believe it? would you sodding believe it? That nationally beloved character, that darling of the housewives' motherly hearts – yes, it's TOM CAVAN of the winning ways I'm speaking of – is, to coin a phrase, out on his ear. From having been a lovable youth who only put a foot wrong in the *sweetest* sort of way, he's all in a trice become a bad lot, Public Enemy Number One (at least as far as Greenfield End is concerned). The Veterinary Practice doesn't like him, and his uncle's discovered him to be (with trumped-up proof) shiftless and dishonest.

You could have knocked me down with the fucking proverbial feather when we were confronted at rehearsal/recording with a scene in which it was established that I'd nicked my uncle's money for a costly night on the town with Minty Macdonald, and that my work as a budding vet wasn't passing muster either. Just a spot of the usual ham problem-dramatics, thought I, which will be spun out at tedious length, not for the first time, before being happily resolved in Tom's (my) favour. But not a bloody bit of it! Betty Reed took me aside today and

154

told me that in the light of all the enormous changes ahead, *Newstead* in a word, I'm to be written out of the script very shortly. There'll be a scene in which Kevin, having found me out in further deceit, boots me from the premises – and then curtains, finito. Character transplant isn't in it!! Even though the earlier scripts made it quite clear that, for all my nearness of kinship to Kevin O'Flynn, I came from *Leicester*, it's apparently been decided that I'm to go away (return?) to *Ireland*. Further off from Newstead, I suppose.

Well, I'm very tempted to follow in the script's directions, I can tell you. I've never been to the Emerald Isle. Time I went, I think, and spent some of the pretty reasonable handshake I'm to get after my *Parkers* exit. Feel like coming with me? But you're only coming along, of course, provided you've done the deed, and I haven't yet heard news from you that you have. I hope I've made my views 100% clear.

Hasta luego,

Neil

(xxvii)
Friday, April 11

Dear Bruno,

Alas and alack! I can't meet you on Monday after all. My well-bred and distinguished godmother (She Whom We Are All Proud of Knowing) has turned up from Italy (where she lives), and the wicked idea of Dad and Mum (thoroughly shared by brother Adam and myself) is that – She May Well (if we're nice and hospitable enough) Save the Economic Day. (And I hope a little bit more than just the day – the Berridge household is badly in need of some Five Year Plan, I can tell you, meanwhile what *would* we be doing without the *Parkers* off to Newstead?) 'Aunt' Cora (what a name!) will be staying with us till Saturday. I go around with a permanently sweet obliging smile on my face, and have mugged up Italian names and phrases etc to show her that I'm always thinking about her and pining to go again to the rather dreadful house near Amalfi where she lives in battered splendour.

Please ask me again. I would suggest a time and a place myself, but would that be *comme il faut*? So many things turn out not to be, don't they? Most things, in fact, including I expect this very letter. Perhaps I should talk this thorny etiquette problem over with Aunt Cora?

Yours,

Cassie

(xxviii)
Tuesday, April 15, 1958

Dear Charles,

This is an exceedingly difficult letter to write. But I expect you can guess what I want to say. I'm nervous of putting things down on paper – it mustn't get into the wrong hands, must it? for either of our sakes. On the other hand I know only too well I couldn't speak these words to your face, and even worse would be trying to get them out over the telephone.

I want the situation I'm in with you to terminate – and at once. Why? Because I resent it, because I have no feelings for you – at any rate suitable for expression *that* way – because (as you've guessed, judging by your last card to me) I've come to dread your visits to London. I find I have to force myself to stay in the shop to endure them. My natural inclination would be to disappear into the big city for just as long as you're in town. I often do my best (as in my last letter to Verity) to dissuade you from coming up. If that isn't a sign of something having gone wrong with a relationship, I don't know what is. And it's not a wrong that's ever going to get put right. In fact it *simply* can't be put right. Particularly as other people know about us, have known for some time, and that in itself oppresses and alarms me. It also kills off any idea I could possibly have entertained of even the briefest future.

Besides I've met someone else, a girl in case your suspicions suggest otherwise. I would prefer to say nothing about her here, however. Maybe that's superstition.

I'm sorry to write like this. I'm pleased I met you, and I'm grateful for (and have enjoyed) my time at P. Dickinson, Antiques. But enough is enough. There can be no changing my mind.

Bruno

156

Thursday, April 17

Dear Bruno,

Your letter has utterly devastated me. In fact I'm still reeling from its impact. I went for a walk up on the hill behind The Puzzle and I have to tell you I could hardly see the countryside for tears. Then I returned to the house and shut myself in my bedroom and cried for a full hour. I knew then how true Keats' phrase is, how grounded in physical experience: 'My heart *aches*...' It does indeed.

Of *course* I respect your changed feelings, of *course* I respect your interest in this girl you've met. I would never, never want to do anything to upset your chances of happiness. After all I myself married.

But don't cast me aside without at least a proper goodbye. Your present wish to dismiss somebody from your life, to airbrush him out, will do harm to *you*, Bruno, though you may not believe that. Not yet. I'm coming up to London on Monday, and I shall use no powers of persuasion on you at all. I shall merely want to wish you *bonne chance* in person, and part with you on the good, kind, mutually caring terms on which our friendship has proceeded.

Yours in sorrow, but not anger,

(and with love still, interpret it how you may)

Charles

(xxx)
Saturday, April 19

Dear Daddy,

I wonder if it'd be possible for me to live at home, at least for a while. If you wish to charge me rent, I'll willingly accept that condition, though you will have to give me time to find the means of doing that.

You will appreciate it takes some swallowing of pride for me to be writing to you like this, and I hope you will bear that in mind. All my life I have been aware that I am not the kind of son you would have liked to have had, something that has not always made life easy for me. I know my brains aren't up to the standard of yours, perhaps they are more like those of my poor mother – from whom, by the way, I've recently had an extraordinarily silly and unhelpful letter. As much use to anybody as a sick headache – no wonder you couldn't put up with her.

I realise too that I was lazy and feckless throughout my school career, I don't always understand why. I still think – though I have become somewhat pacifistic of late – that I would have enjoyed the Royal Navy, and would have been rather good at things there. Sometimes I'm a bit resentful at Fate that it wasn't possible for me to be a sailor just for a while, but there it is. I went for a medical check-up recently, by the way, and they all seem pretty pleased with me. I have to go again in another three months.

So what is poor Bruno to do, eh? Give him time, and by all means let's have a serious man-to-man chat. We surely should be able to come up with some respectable occupation I could do reasonably well at. Recently I've built up quite a bit of knowledge of antiques (masses yet to learn, of course). I think I've got something of an eye – and you might be surprised to hear that already in this short time there are dealers and buyers who've come to trust that young Mr Armitage and think he has a firm business head on his shoulders.

There's something else I want to tell you. I'm starting to see a girl, and I think it could be serious. I'm sure you will like her and approve of her when you meet her. The only thing that will give you food for thought is how someone as nice and sensible could see anything in an idiot like me. I'm busy wondering the same. Her name is Cassie Berridge.

Obviously I expect you to weigh the pros and cons of having me back, and so I don't expect an answer by return of post or anything like that, but I do hope you can manage to let me know fairly soon whether my request is at all acceptable to you.

Love,
Bruno

Monday, April 21

Dear Bruno,

I *am* replying by return of post! I would indeed have telephoned had I got your number, but you never saw fit to give it me.

Your letter only added to the bad conscience I have about you. You must never say again such a dreadful thing as your not being the son I wanted to have. As for your request, of course you can, and should, come back home to live – gratis, it goes without saying. I hope that will help you to see things in a different light.

I suppose I have to confess – what must, sadly, be obvious enough to you already – that I wasn't cut out to be a family man, neither husband nor father. Like poor old departed Leslie I have always been happiest in a world of work: only with a pile of papers before me (a few gritty reports; a few testing balance sheets) am I really content. It's always been like that, for as long as I can remember. My brother Brian, Ian's father, inherited all the family's share of warmth and personal interests as well as charm, but of course he had weaknesses in other directions, as poor Eileen came to find out only too thoroughly.

You refer rather slightingly to your mother. She was – indeed is – a sensitive woman full of feeling, who didn't know what she was doing marrying a man like me. For a brief while I was crazy about her; then I let her go, emotionally and even as a companion. No wonder she sought solace elsewhere – time and again at that, I'm afraid. You perhaps shouldn't let Eileen – a good person but a conventional one – prejudice you against her as I'm afraid she might already have done; it'd be odd if Eileen did appreciate her. As I see things now, it's only right that she rebelled and went on to build up a totally new life for herself in the US. I've little doubt her letter was a pretty silly one (as we see things), but it probably tells of heights and depths that we, in our less spiritual way, have never been able to attain.

I am extremely glad to hear that you're seeing a nice girl. (It doesn't matter, by the way, whether I personally like her or not, nor should you think that it does). Good luck! Maybe it'll be what you call 'serious', maybe it won't. But please, Bruno, remember that she is a person too, a whole complex world in herself of feelings, thoughts, desires etc. and don't treat her, as I fear (indeed, as I *know*) I did your mother, as if she's a part in some drama of which you're the hero and only significant character. Mark those words well! I haven't offered you much in the way of advice during your life, so take it from me that I have my reasons for offering you this.

As for the move back home, please notify me by phone (I'm working in London till at least mid-summer, when I shall go to Brussels) as to when you want to make it. Hadn't you better take a taxi over to Primrose Hill? You must have accumulated quite a load of stuff by now. I'll foot the bill for that; it's the least I can do.

Love,
Daddy

(xxxii)
Monday, April 21

Dear Neil,

I *have* done the deed. That is, Charles Compson did me the favour (so to speak) of coming round here in person to beg me take back some of the harshness of the letter that (true to my word to you) I wrote him. So I in person was able to make my position 200% clear. He pleaded, I wasn't having any, I stuck to my guns. But Neil, it was all very pitiable and awful – and I didn't like myself as I said and did what I had to, not one little bit. Be a good mucker, and don't refer to it all when next we meet. It's something I'll want to expunge (that is the right word, isn't it?) from my memory, and not talking about it is the best way of doing this I can think of.

Thanks for your help, and see you soon,
Your friend,
Bruno.

["Did what I had to", eh? No, I can't accept that now. For, of course, I didn't expunge the scene from my mind – though I have to confess, and it surprises and troubles me, that in the years immediately following I didn't revisit it very often. My account to Neil (or outline substitute for account) is not a truthful one. Charles' behaviour was dignified, (not pleading really at all, not even pitiable in the external sense of the term) – he was restrained, thoughtful, understanding. He said he was happy I'd got a girl-friend, he was so genuinely fond of me and as a *friend* etc he wished me nothing but fulfilment. He was in fact (unusually) far more convincing in the flesh than on paper.

The trouble was – he *wasn't* at the other end of a sheet of paper, he was standing right there before me, a man I'd been intimate with, had had my first sustained sexual experiences with, whose most secret crannies and crevices I knew, and most private tastes and responses too. And that unnerved me.

And at one point, as if to prove the sincere and disinterested nature of his feeling for me, he threw his arms round me and kissed me – on the cheek, chastely but slobberingly, and with evident emotion.

That tensed me up, infuriated me, disgusted me. I pushed him away from me so viciously that he fell sprawlingly against one of the antique chairs. How ridiculous, how pathetic and contemptible he looked then, with injury on his face and held-back reproach in his bloodshot eyes. "I want you out of my life, you repellant old man!" I shouted, "you make me want to puke! And puke's all you're good for."

Then it was he began to cry. More like a little girl than an adult man, as I lost no time in telling him.

"For fuck's sake, shut up, can't you?" I said. "Why don't you take your weeping carcase somewhere else. I'll be out of this house day after tomorrow at latest."

[It was only later that day that I realised what the whole hideous set-to had naggingly reminded me of. Wasn't it a sort of reverse play of what I'd had with Nina Cardew at *The Pig and Whistle* in Tanbury – when I had flung myself on a girl who hadn't wanted my advances and hadn't spared her my pent-up violence. This didn't make for comfortable reflections. So why reflect?]

(xxxiii)
April 23

Dear Charles,

I've arranged with the Post Office about the forwarding of mail etc and have contacted those dealers and customers who would expect to find me at the other end of a phone – or letter. *Thanks again* for letting me live and work here, and I hope you think the place – both in its living and business aspects – is in good trim. I've certainly put time and thought into it, I realise that now as I look my last round it. In fact I'm pretty fond and proud of it.

Don't think too badly of me. That wasn't a nice scene between us, not worthy of either of us. And if I lost my rag it was more than I meant to do, but I did have to find a way of making you realise that my word is my word. When I say something has ended for me, it has ended. And ended completely.

Bruno

(xxxiv)
Excerpt from *The Parkers* Friday, May 21, 1958

ELIZABETH: Goodness, how time goes by! I now feel I've been living in Newstead for years instead of a few weeks. But that, I suppose, is the result of the extraordinary spirit of *togetherness* we all have found here. The community here accepts you as you are while giving you the impression that all this time it's been waiting for you. Suddenly there's so much to think about and do that you haven't time for those little problems, let alone regrets, that once seemed of such importance.

Of course I'm missing my beloved Vicarage garden, and often wonder how the plants that Verges and I cared so much for are faring there, and how that dear old man is coping with the new incumbents. (I do hope they'll respect his vast stores of knowledge.) But really there are gardens a-plenty here in Newstead even if the private ones aren't the size we got accustomed to in Greenfield End. Really I can't help feeling that it's perhaps the *public* gardens that really count, and here in Newstead they extend right into the very heart of the town, right up to Founders' Fountain itself. Every time I go to the Newstead Stores I admire the Solomon's Seals just as I used to back in the Vicarage, only now I know that a hundred, a thousand eyes are enjoying the spectacle of those lovely delicate green-hued flowers at the same time as my own are.

This morning Mark Bywater called round. Already Derek and I feel rather fond of Mark; he makes us think of what Tom Cavan could have been like in a few years' time if he'd only chosen to mature instead of to gadabout. We all admire Mark's mural for the church so much. At first I have to admit I was a bit 'square' in my attitude to it. Were such bright poster colours right for a church interior? Shouldn't the Biblical figures be a bit more subdued and solemn? But after a few visits I saw how wrong my thinking was. There's real joy in Mark's work, and it makes the old familiar stories come bang up to date, or *(with a little laugh)* "with it", as I should say.

MARK: Morning, Elizabeth.

ELIZABETH: Oh, Mark, how nice to see you! But aren't you teaching?

MARK: Of course, but I've sent my Sixth-Form class out to do sketches at the local bus station, and thought I could drop in for a few minutes without being unduly irresponsible...

ELIZABETH: I'm so glad you did, I always enjoy our chats. That's what I like about Newstead, the Vicarage being just an ordinary house like any other right in the middle of things, where everybody can drop in at any time. You *will* have a cup of coffee with me, won't you?

MARK: Don't mind if I do, Elizabeth.

ELIZABETH: It's such a beautiful day for your class to be out drawing, isn't it?

MARK: Yes, but they shouldn't have to bother too much about that. I've told them: the flowers and blossoms are all very well, just as the birds and bees are all very well, but what I want you to be paying attention to is that pair of concrete-mixers over there, where the new bus station annexe is going to be. Notice the way they're going round, the terrific shapes they make as they cut the air, and the visible vibrations they cause. And – they're useful objects into the bargain. And I want the kids to take in the forms and the individual details of the buses themselves.

ELIZABETH: It all sounds very exciting, Mark.

MARK: There was something I was going to ask you, Elizabeth. *(A touch shyly, self-confident though he is.)* That nice girl who moved from Greenfield End with you – Minty Macdonald, isn't she called? – do you know if she is interested in sketching...

ELIZABETH *(significantly)*: Ah, Minty is interested in so many things, Mark. And yet she's something of a mystery to us all...

MARK *(betraying his attraction to her)*: A mystery, eh? Well, we'll soon find out about that!

(xxxv)
Saturday, May 22

Dear Bruno,

Well, I hope you're satisfied! I knew it was a dark day when you wormed your way down to The Puzzle back in the autumn, and old Nesta has been proved right yet again.

You may have read the papers, and you may not. I do hope you've not turned squeamish, young man, and refuse to hear spades called spades. Because you're going to face a whole lot of spade-calling in this 'ere letter of mine. One thing that looking after goats does is make you a realist, with no times for frills and furbelows. All those udders, all that mounting, all that shit and piss – we 'goat-ladies' haven't much time to be ever-so-refined or ever-so-romantic-and-rosy, like certain so-called 'young gentlemen' I could name without much difficulty.

Charles will almost certainly go to jug. There, that's made you sit up, hasn't it? Just in case you haven't recently been buying *The News of the World* or *The People* – both of which have had a high old time with the story, paying him the compliment he's been wanting for years of calling him '*Well-known* English Stage Designer' – Charles has been had up for importuning.

[How could I have failed to have seen the newspaper headlines – and the furious, histrionic, trashy, inaccurate, blood-baying articles that followed, often accompanied by a photograph of a Charles Compson at some long-ago Chelsea Arts Ball, effete, flamboyantly-dressed and unrecognisable? *The Parkers* connection seemed to give the journalists particular pleasure – in fact some, with strange, perverted logic, used it as a justification for the programme's move from Greenfield End to Newstead (without guilty Charles' wife writing its scripts any more). It was a horrible business, and I refused to keep any of the newspapers. Two that I did buy I used quite literally to wipe my bum with – before chucking them into a neighbour's dustbin.]

Nesta continues....

'Cottaging', I believe, is the charming word by which the 'offence' goes. I put that last word in inverted commas because it makes me laugh like a flipping drain that this dear country of ours, which thinks nothing of women's bums being pinched black and blue in buses, on tubes, and in queues, and permits any boy or man to wolf-whistle after and generally harrass any passing female, finds it so appalling that one man dares, in a public place, without so much as laying a finger on him, to proposition another – generally a chunky lad who could well look after himself (and in this case a young attractive copper in disguise) – that it claps him in prison. Which seems the most likely fate of your former friend, lover and benefactor. Apparently there's a bit of clampdown on That Sort of Thing going on in official circles right now (when *hasn't* there been a clampdown, I'd like to know!) as Those Who Know Best think that society's been getting a little lax about its morals recently. And our Yankee friends, in their wisdom, have apparently been getting scared of queers in high places in Britain (to say nothing of those in low ones) and have ordered our Elders and Betters to get tough and cracking. So Charles is likely to be in for the high jump – which means being locked up somewhere where he'll hardly be able to turn round to fart, pardon my French.

'Oh, but I had nothing to do with anything so vulgar as an episode in a public *lavatory*!' I can hear your Lordship saying in that la-di-da voice you obviously fancy as sophisticated and mellow. 'I never went

165

further than the safety of a bed above an *antique* shop!' (Oh, we've known all about it for a long time, Verity and myself. It's made us positively cackle that you probably thought we were two innocent ignorant women to whom such a gross idea would never occur!) Well, Charles has told all, has spilled the beans. We know that after availing yourself of his stupid susceptibility, you then ditched him. And it really upset him returning to his own house, to find nothing but a cruel little note from someone he loved (heaven knows why!) so he went out into the evening to get himself a bit of sexual solace. And got caught in the act, the chump. And he'll pay for it. But what does that matter compared with the Important Subject of the Emotional History of Mr Bruno Armitage. Mr Bruno Armitage had got a bit bored with things, Mr Bruno Armitage was ready for something (or someone) new, Mr Bruno Armitage had better be moving on, Mr Bruno Armitage believes himself to be in love with a girl, Mr Bruno Armitage believes that girl to be keen on him. Mr Bruno Armitage is poised to become affianced to one of the *Parkers*, no less.

Well, Mr Bruno Armitage, she's welcome to you, that's all I can say. Not one of my goats took to you when you infested The Puzzle with your presence, not a one. And that's as good a sign as any of your essential worthlessness. As for the girl you've chosen, (yes, the grapevine stretches its tentacles even into the Purbeck region of Dorset), not only is she the daughter of that old gin-soak and double-dyed traitor, Enid Berridge, she shares your own (I've gathered) rather erratic educational and intellectual credentials. Couldn't face exams, the poor wee creature! Didn't like it when nasty schoolmarms got cross with the sweet little girlie-wirlie! Had to moon about at home instead, hadn't she? the pitiful bairn, as if she were some sort of sister to the Lady of Shalott. I will have you know that, in contrast to the pathetic pair of you, Charles was Head of House at Rugby, and a Cambridge graduate who then passed out of RADA (speciality, theatre design) with particularly flying colours, while *Verity* was one of the best pupils St Paul's School for Girls ever had, and was given a BBC script-writing contract at an unusually early age, when these were bloody hard to obtain. And funny old Nesta herself won two (no, three) prizes, no less, at the posh Convent she was sent to (one was for Setting a Moral

166

Example, so you'd better mark these words, hadn't you?).

As if to contemplate Charles' fate isn't horrible enough, I'm having to worry about Verity, aren't I? And who have I to blame? Why, Mr Bruno Armitage again. He used his charms (I suppose I have to concede that he has them, even if not for me and my herd!) to convince Verity that he could come up with good ideas for her programme. Could he? Could he heck! Simply hadn't the brains. There you were, needed by Auntie Beeb, to make interesting fresh proposals in favour of Greenfield End RIP), and what did you come up with – NOWT! (Or nowt of any merit.) I suppose it isn't *your* fault you've got such an extensive vacancy in the upper storey. A pity you and others weren't quicker and more honest about recognising this sad fact... So poor Verity has had to undergo two reverses of fortune; she's lost out on *The Parkers* and, having a silly weak husband (whose brains, as the saying goes, are too often, in fact *chiefly*, in his trousers), she's had to face the glare of publicity which exposes every wretched antic of her stupid, thoughtless mate. It's been too much for her. She is the most remarkably sensitive being, my poor Verity; only once in my lifetime have I met her equal, and that was Lady Bountiful, a goat still alive and well and living in Pembrokeshire, a British Saanen (if that name means anything to you!) with a quite remarkable pedigree who won three prizes at the Bath and West Show, and features most impressively in the annals of the British Goat Society.

Of course a soul as sensitive as hers has to have its solaces: Enid Berridge is not the only one to whom the bottle can and does beckon. Had you been more observant and less of a flatulent-headed egotist, you'd have appreciated that Verity had had more than her fair share of "mother's ruin" that first supper you had at The Puzzle. But I think it went unnoticed.

So, to make our cup of happiness complete, Verity too has had to make an appearance before the magistrates (who admittedly let her off with a caution) – for being 'drunk and disorderly' in a Dorchester shop. Poor love, the fact that they hadn't got the coffee she wanted in stock was just the last straw for her, after all she's gone through. Being half-seas over as a result, she just sat right down on the shop-floor and sobbed like a baby, and said she *knew* they had the coffee and were

167

trying to deny it her, like she'd been denied everything this year. A sad exhibition. Old Nesta wasn't there to stop her, unfortunately. Absolutely criminal of the stupid shop to call in the police and have the poor darling charged! But they did!

So The Puzzle depends on Nesta Coolidge now. It just couldn't function without her. Whatever the gravity of the problems ahead, Nesta'll be the one who sees that the place continues, and that Verity and Charles survive their ordeals:

> 'Funny Nesta,
> Who can best her
> When it comes to eccentricitiee?
> Mistress Coolidge,
> Very foolidge,
> But full of a wondrous jollitee!'

Now they'll have to write a new version, won't they?

> 'Funny Nesta,
> Who can best her
> When it comes to dependabilitee,
> Mistress Coolidge,
> *Far* from foolidge,
> A pillar of a communitee!'

So thank you very much, Bruno Armitage, Esq. for having played your part in two good people's misfortunes? *Thank you* for contributing to unhappiness and for seeing that their creative gifts are blocked? *Thank you* for casting a shadow over the marvellous, unique place that is The Puzzle. An alleged explanation of the curious name of our house (the explanation not usually mentioned in polite company) is that it refers to female pudenda, and was originally a place, like nearby Maiden Castle, sacred to womanhood.

May every woman reject you!

Nesta the Wise.

(xxxvi)
May 26, 1958

Dear Ian Armitage,

Thank you very much for your kind inquiries about our Outward Bound Academy. And apologies for the extreme lateness in answering you, but secretarial assistance isn't always easy to come by up here, where Cape Wrath is nearer than any fair-sized town. I have pleasure in enclosing literature, which also includes details of fees. It would seem that the courses of most interest to yourself would be those open to Sixth Formers (and not to those below this level) – see our brochure *Striking Out*. It may be that Oxfordshire could give you some help here, though this state-aid is not usual, except of course in certain of our Inner City Aid projects.

May we venture to recommend a somewhat more integrationist approach to your own school in Tanbury. It's not necessarily a sign of independence to level complaints against your educators, and at the Academy here, while we certainly encourage hardihood and freedom, we also revere the sense of belonging and team-membership.

Yours,

Jim Cholmondley (Deputy Head)

P.S. If you would care to take part in our various nationwide fund-raising schemes, please write to us and I will be glad to suggest some ways in which you could help us.

[*Ian's note*: I'm certainly not going to fucking fund-raise for you. All your letter shows is that teachers who have special missions and special subjects are just as much prigs and pricks as the more conventional ones.]

(xxxvii)
The Age We Live In by Ian Armitage 3A

This is a big subject, and I think, Mr Daley M.A. B.Ed (Oxon), that you're getting too fond of setting big subjects someone of my age cannot possibly write about with any proper knowledge. Last week we had *My Ideas about the After-Life* when I've only just had my thirteenth birthday, and am far more interested in the Raleigh Lenten Sports bicycle (a very handsome Lenten green colour, by the way) that I was given then as a present than I am in what may or may not await me in (I hope) – even by the old Biblical reckoning – fifty-seven years at the least, and probably more. But, as I am in a subordinate position, I'll write you an essay on the subject, but will make it shorter than I used to do (following your instructions) so that it's a bit of a practice for the 'O' Level examination I shall have to sit. There, I've already written you 153 words, and you could make the number bigger according to whether you think 'I'll' etc is one word or two, and how many words you think your qualifications when written down add up to, and some other problems. Anyway it isn't *less* than 153, and I've just offered you 54 more, with similar possibilities of re-calculation.

Do you want me to give you my views on last month's Aldermaston March, and tell you whether, if I'd been there, I'd have cheered the CND lot on *(Comment: slangy! you know my view on 'lot' and 'lots'!)* as they went off to make their protest to the tune of *When the Saints Go Marchin' In?* Probably, but then my knowledge of what making weapons is worth in terms of international peace-keeping or of maintaining people in employment isn't very great, and anyway I wasn't there! Perhaps you're expecting to hear my opinions on the King, by whom I mean Elvis the Pelvis, of course. I bet most of the other blokes *(Comment in margin: that word is absolutely forbidden)* are writing about him, but though I like his music, like it a lot, I don't think I have anything to say about him that anybody else hasn't said. I'm sorry he has to do his military service after all, though he says he doesn't mind, and I've enjoyed all the fuss there has been about *Jailhouse Rock*, and, no, I don't think either Tommy Steele or Cliff Richard are anything like as good as Presley, even at his least good.

170

(Comment: This is getting too chatty in style.) And I could go on to mention what I think of what the British Government thinks about the Communists in Malta and the Nationalists in South Africa, but what I think even more strongly is that it's best for me to stick to something I know about, like radio programmes, because they are a sign of the times, aren't they? *(Comment: Are you asking me, or are you using what is known as a "rhetorical question", a device which has to be handled very sparingly? Anyway we're coming, at last, to what you were supposed to be addressing.)*

I haven't done a word-count of the last part, but I think I will keep on for another page or two of this exercise-book.

The producers at the BBC must have given a great deal of thought to *The Parkers* and whether or not it represents the Age We Live In, because they have gone to the trouble of moving the main characters of the serial from Greenfield End, a comfortable town near London which did not seem to have too many problems, to a New Town called Newstead (and that is a very, very, very boring name for the place, don't you agree?) which seems to have heaps of them, although it is also meant to be somewhere very good to live. My mother and my cousin, Bruno, when he lived with us, were very fond indeed of the programme in its old Greenfield End form, and I know that I wrote an essay on this subject in the autumn (*A Favourite Radio Programme*) which is to be found in my English-Composition-exercise-book-before-last. In that essay I said that I was a fan of the programme, and that's what I suppose I was back then, but by the beginning of this year I had decided it was a lot of pretty soppy mush, and I only went on listening out of habit and to be kind to my Mum. (I still do listen for that reason, by the way.) Personally I'd come to think Elizabeth and Derek Parker quite thunderingly uninteresting people, and I am an atheist anyway, so I wouldn't be in the least interested in going near the Vicar's stupid old church. I thought it quite extraordinary that the young men of the programme, Tom Cavan and Davey Parker, were content to live such flat, unexciting lives, and that the girls showed no kind of initiative at all. Kevin O'Flynn I imagined as an even duller writer than Sir Walter Scott (whose *Ivanhoe* must be the dullest book ever written), and Miss Venables, who made so many listeners laugh with her interferingness,

171

struck me as simply the kind of person it's sensible to cross the road to avoid.

So when I heard *The Parkers* were going to leave Greenfield End, I was really quite pleased. An astonishing number of the characters have all gone to Newstead with them. I mean, I shouldn't think when the Vicar of Tanbury (whoever he may be) leaves our town, that his charwoman, the local vet (together with his chief assistant), and the doctor's daughter will all decide to move to the same place, would you? Perhaps it *would* be better to live at Newstead than Greenfield End, less snobby *(Comment: not a proper word)* and with more for young people to do. At the same time it doesn't appear so very fascinating there either. Instead of Kevin O'Flynn saying that melancholy it was for him to think about his boyhood in Limerick, you have various people calling on the Vicar – who has stopped being absent-minded all of a sudden (something to do with a change in air, I suppose) – and yakking on to him *(Comment: Ugh!)* about maternity clinics and crêches and youth clubs, and whether there are enough books in the public library with big print so that people with bad eyesight can read them, and whether there should be a sandpit for little children in the park in the town centre. Electrifying, huh!

So I think moving to Newstead from Greenfield End is a *real* sign of the age we live in, because it is meant to be a move from an old-fashioned community to a new-style one. Verity Orchard no longer writes any of the scripts, and her husband's been locked up in jug for being an old homo *(Comment: word, especially in this vulgar form, and topic also, forbidden)* – my mum says "Bruno" (cousin, who knew and part-worked for him) "has had a narrow escape, hasn't he?" – and the signature-tune isn't 'Sellinger's Round' any more but a sort of skiffle-type tune (but not a proper one like 'Tom Dooley'). I don't know which I'd honestly prefer to live in, the truth is I wouldn't want to live in either.

What I want – and I'd want the same, even if the characters had stayed in Greenfield End – is for more exciting things to happen, and for the people, particularly the young men and boys, to be more enterprising and daring. I'd like them to insult one another and have more rows generally, and even sometimes fights, and do altogether mad

172

things, like climbing up a church-steeple and putting a pair of soiled underpants on the top, or carving interesting grafitti on a bus shelter (having decided not to burn it down). Even better would be to go to some wilderness country – of mountains and forest and wild seas, where animals and birds live and roam about free, without too much bother from man, and you attend to the elements and their meaning, provided of course that priggish fuss-pot schoolmasters with names like Cholmondley don't get there first *(Comment: I don't understand this!)* but I don't suppose they would make the best setting for a soap-opera (or would they?). Anyway with that thought I'll sign off.

Some lively points made, and I wholly agree with you that the change in The Parkers, *about which there has been so much publicity, is a sign of our age indeed. I choose to ignore the facetious, coat-trailing opening to this essay, though I would prefer there to be no repetition of it in subsequent compositions. Various other sentences later on with gratuitous subsidiary clauses – rather in the nature of would-be humorous asides – could be removed to the piece's improvement. Here also I've preferred to add no comment. It is a sad truth that the harder a young person strives to sound sophisticated or blasé, the more childish he invariably ends up sounding.*

(xxxviii)
Monday, June 2, 1958

Dear Bruno,
　　I'm committed as the phrase is. No use now in bemoaning my fate – or for anyone else to bemoan it, for that matter.
　　I'm writing because I would like you to be in charge of P. Dickinson, Antiques during my period of absence. This would be a proper business arrangement. I've left matters not in the hands of Verity and Nesta, you'll be pleased to hear, but in those of my trusted solicitor, whose card I enclose.
　　With best wishes,
　　Charles

June 5

Dear Charles,

There's nothing I can say about what's happened to you that would sound at all right. But about the antique shop there is. I will be extremely happy to manage the antique shop while you're away, which I do not expect will be for so very long, and I am writing to your solicitor, Howard Henshaw, accepting your offer and suggesting that I go up to meet him in Southampton Row as soon as possible.

With all good wishes,
Bruno

(xl)
NOTES FROM PRISON

For the first month or two, possibly more, disbelief at being where I was – address, The Scrubs – was so overwhelming it all but prevented my having any proper reactions to my surroundings and definitely blocked systematic thoughts about my life, my personality, or society and justice. Perhaps as well. Incredulity must be the best weapon against bitterness that exists – though I don't think it's in my nature to be very bitter, too uncomfortable, too demanding, perhaps rather too serious. But "For *me*, Charles Compson to be here! It just can't be true!" – no mantra could be more powerful than that.

Never once here have I found myself regretting my proclivities (as they're often archly called); in fact, boredom being the great promoter of memories, I've rarely had intenser or more frequent erotic recollections. Gino, Franco, Ernesto, Paco, Jean-Louis, Ed, Mike, Paco (the other one), Nikos – every detail of our intercourse – and its preliminaries and aftermaths – has hallucinatory exactness and sharpness for me, like Holman Hunt's in *The Scapegoat* or Millais' in *Christ in the house of His Father*, to be looked at, inspected and found satisfactory (and more) over and over again: Gino putting his arms round my neck as we slipped behind that wall in the Sicilian villa garden; Paco kissing the shell of my ear in the bedroom darkness; my running my tongue over Ed's long and crooked penis – well, I don't need to go on, and I feel excited (yet again) as I write these lines. But it was not only a matter of excitement (sexual need, lust). Nor of the heart (love, affection). It was a more a question – it now strikes me – of having made something beautiful, an aesthetic object (the experience itself), which can be used, when required, as an instrument against the passing of time (or, in the present melancholy case, as assistance in the passing of time). Paco, say, and myself – we formed a moving human object that will last as long as I last, (and who knows? – maybe longer) and which can be enjoyed repeatedly because of its completeness – the fact that once it was animated and demanding, and now has come to an end...

One lover I never recapture in all this over-abundant time I have is Bruno Armitage. Hardly surprising. But there have been times when I have felt on the brink of unveiling particular tableaux with him. What held me back, though, was not any feelings of anger at him, or the thought (incorrect surely) that the distress he brought me is responsible for me being here, but my realisation that really there was never a real dialogue of the flesh (and therefore of the spirit either) between us, such as there was (however briefly) with all those on the above list (and many another besides). If I take a *Parkers* analogy, it's as if the actors (for I don't exculpate myself) had failed to quite identify with their parts – or were substitutes brought in because the real actors were elsewhere, in some grander production of the BBC Repertory Company, for example.

The colourlessness of Wormwoods Scrubs – part of the punishment, I suppose, though I doubt if the authorities would be aware that it had played any part in their penitential programmes. I who have always delighted in colour – my plum-hued velvet jacket, the shirts and ties of boys I was lucky enough to engage with, the paintings of Bonnard and Vuillard and Dufy, the fuzzy skins of peaches, the smoother skins of apricots, and the whole flower-world – mimosa, daffodils, flag-irises, morning-glories. When I go out into the Exercise Yard, I find compensations if I try hard enough to look for them: sun on roof or on puddles, the brilliant glare of windows receiving light, sparrows and

175

starlings who often have the aspect for us prisoners (and most of the men here delight – really delight – in the birds) of the most exotic parakeets or humming-birds. But too often I think it's as if Nature has entered into a conspiracy with the prison governor, and has banished as many of its colours from sight as possible, has decided that we deserve only the dullest and most restrained of her faces.

Unbearable to imagine The Puzzle now. How it looks, how it feels, the fragrances of the land in which it's set. Perhaps I loved that house too much? Soon the year will have come round again to the month in which, fool that I was, I took Bruno down to meet Verity and Nesta. Ah well! I see in my mind's eye (and half-wish I couldn't) the Dorset heathland, the reddy-brown of dying ferns everywhere, and the green, green wall of the Purbecks rising above the scarred sweep, and glimpses here and there of a sea with its blue darkening as the year moves slowly (and with sombre but vivid colours) towards its end. Verity – who knows so much poetry by heart – has a whole stock of autumn verse she can recite at will. She often used to speculate on *why* autumn was such a constant inspiration to English poets – because it was the fusion of full beauty and transitoriness, she supposed:

> "My very heart faints and my whole soul grieves
>   At the moist rich smell of the rotting leaves,
>   And the breath
>   Of the fading edges of box beneath,
>   And the last year's rose.
>   Heavily hangs the broad sunflower
>   Over its grave i'the earth so chilly;
>   Heavily hangs the hollyhock,
>   Heavily hangs the tiger-lily."

Tennyson! Will Verity ever say those lines for me again? I don't imagine so. We'll go our different ways henceforth as maybe we should have done soon after our first meeting. Oddly I feel no sort of guilt here about Verity. Even at the shame I brought her through all those newspaper accounts of my "fall" which after all were far worse for myself than for her (whose "side" the Press, in its obscene absurdity, pretended to take). The reason I feel no guilt is that Verity didn't mind very much, on any real level, what I did. It would have doubtless been better – as well as in some ways worse – had she minded just a mite more.

Though most of the day is silent and dull – dull, dull, dull – there's talk over the mailbag-sewing (at which I've got surprisingly adept – I didn't assist practically with scenery-making all those years for nothing!), talk in the Exercise Yard, talk over meal-tables – nine of us eating muck together within sight and sound (and smell) of the lavatories. (No erotic associations to be had with *them*!) I quite enjoy some of the conversations I have, gossip about the warders, about which "screw" is okay, which you could consider "bent". And boastings about what you've done in the outside world to get into this inside one. Tommy and Barry present their achievements as burglars (Barry's crime was stigmatised as "robbery with violence") in almost hilarious terms, as the biggest laughs out. And I laugh with them – and why not? Quite a few men here are "my kind": in fact Jim's offence was more or less identical to mine. "Can't say it'd of been my choice to end up here," he said yesterday, "but we had fun, didn't we?"

Did we?

Something other than fun, I think. We met needs. That's how I would put it.

You can listen to the radio at times, in public, under supervision. In case you're hamming into Radio Moscow, I conjecture. The other day *The Parkers* was on – many of the men here are very well-informed about the programme (I was going to say surprisingly so, but why should that be a surprise? especially as the majority have wives and children and old mothers). I did not own up to my personal connection with the serial – anyway, there'd be no point in doing so now that Verity's out of things. Goodness, even a quarter an hour of it was tedious! Of course I always found it so. And – as predicted – Newstead is twenty times more screamingly tedious even than the bland Greenfield End.

But it's against Greenfield End that I bear the largest grudges. When I think of all its multiple sweetness and the listeners in their hundred of thousands, their millions indeed, who rejoiced in all that

177

stuff every weekday (and often tuned in to the repeats as well), and how not a one of them was moved to do or say or write anything when I was arrested and tried and bunged into gaol for doing something pleasant and harmless with someone I thought wanted it – and how many of them, on the contrary, sided with the irate punitive hysterics the national dailies saw fit to orchestrate against me – then I feel like saying (surely with some truth) "It's Greenfield End, it's the Parker family and their friends and neighbours that've put me inside, that in its desire for ubiquitous niceness is perfectly prepared to see a good man (for I am that *au fond*) suffer humiliation and misery, fear and acute discomfort, for doing what in their heart of hearts doesn't shock them one little bit."

Enough!

I, who made Oscar Wilde into something of an idol (all the greater a one for having such heavily clay feet), remember how in gaol he wrote: "I tremble with pleasure when I think that on the very day of my leaving prison both the laburnum and the lilac will be blooming in the gardens." Last night a laburnum tree burned in the brightest golden-yellow throughout my dreams.

* * * * * *

Neil and I did go together to Ireland for a holiday, a short one in August. Neil borrowed an uncle's souped-up Aston Martin, though it took him two days to admit to me that the sports-car wasn't actually his. (I was beginning, sadly, to realise that almost everything Neil laid claim to was in fact borrowed, in one sense of the term or another.) It was in a spirit of release that I stood beside him on the boat deck watching Dublin, lighting up for the summer evening, present itself more and more fully, the sentinel-like headland of Howth beckoning us further and further in, and the Wicklows, pale blue forms against a sky of deepening blue, overseeing our arrival. "This is the life!" said Neil. He had spent two months without any work and had benefited from the experience.

178

We drove out to the West, to Sligo and the barrow-shaped hills in its vicinity, but spent most of our Irish time in Dublin itself, visiting pubs, frequenting scruffy cafés, trying to chat up girls (yes, despite Cassie) and finding two very nice and very blonde Swedish ones, Lena and Ulla, with whom we exchanged addresses. It was a really most unremarkable holiday, except for its sustained pleasantness, something I for my part wasn't used to – nor, I now learned, Neil either, who'd grown up amid severe marital discord. So perhaps its ordinariness – a few beers too many, a few snubs from ill-chosen females, a few smiles from others, beautiful walks along country lanes lined with flowering fuchsia, and girl-spying strolls along the banks of the Liffey – was important for both of us. We were never able to be quite so at ease with one another again.

As, on our return journey, we drove out of Holyhead, the Welsh mountains darkly ahead of us, I said: 'Neil, I'd like to see my aunt and cousin on the way back. Perhaps tomorrow afternoon? Can I ring her up and say that we'll be calling?'

'Good thinking!' said Neil, 'a bit of peace-making in that quarter is called for, I'd say.'

We came down to Tanbury from the modest heights to the west of the town. The ribbon development along the Stratford Road – which I'd forgotten about – didn't obscure the view of the town below us and its surroundings as today's rash of adjoining harsh brick estates all but does. In the summer afternoon sun the Grand Union Canal, the elm-lined winding River Reedrush, the rail-track I'd travelled along so many times – these three roughly parallel lines gleamed and glinted, marking the eastern parameters of this somewhat geometric Middle Ages town, so very different from its Irish kin, once so rich on wool and livestock, with its two market-squares and its tree-lined Horse Fair, and its burgher houses built of the local honey-coloured stone. Sticking up above all this, and also picked out by sunshine, were the copper cupola of the classical 17th-century Parish Church (the older one having burned down in the Civil War) and the Market Cross, a Victorian replacement with swirling stone forms of the older one which had given rise to the nursery rhyme:

'Ride a cock horse,
To Tanbury Cross,
To see a fine lady
Upon a white horse,
Rings on her fingers,
And bells on her toes,
She shall have music wherever she goes.'

'Nice place!' observed Neil, as we descended into the the town proper, 'you really feel you're back in England now. So this is where your *Parkers* mania started. Now you'd better start giving me directions.'

Auntie Eileen's house in Church Terrace was such a drab little affair (but then I was a snob, wasn't I?). Neil, who'd visited me a good number of times in Primrose Hill, had clearly not been expecting anything as 'common' as this. Perhaps he was a bit of a snob himself? Auntie Eileen, in a cheap floral-patterned cotton frock, and sweating under her unshaved armpits, looked on the whole pretty much as she had when last I saw her, but Ian had changed extraordinarily in so short a period. How was it possible? He was a lot taller (could he *really* be as much so, or had I during my stay in Tanbury psychologically chosen to see him as essentially a small boy?) and there were small blotches of acne ('shag-spots' as we called them at Riverbury) on his once so fresh-complexioned face. He was clearly not unimpressed by the Aston Martin, but was determined not to show this.

Auntie Eileen didn't really know what to say to me, there being no delight in our reunion palpable – or, I suspect, actually felt. "Neil Micklewright!" she said, "I never thought to be giving tea to such a household name. And we *Parkers* fans miss Tom Cavan, I can tell you that straight."

Neil grinned boyishly, but already Tom Cavan was receding into the not-so-important past, and perhaps my aunt guessed this. She now began to twitter on disconnectedly about a visit to Dublin she'd once made herself, while Ian sat there sullenly and pointedly skimming through the pages of a cycling magazine. The topic of *The Parkers* caught no further fire.

We had tea in the pocket-sized back-garden, so small compared to Neil's family's Putney one, and Auntie Eilen was a little too vocal for anyone's interest about her roses – but a very good tea it was, I have to say, with one of the best feather-light jam-sponges she'd ever made.

Neil showed a side of himself I wouldn't have guessed at; he was appreciative of flowers and food, and asked all the right questions, seeking information.

Eventually, thinking that I should break what for me was dullness, I turned to my younger cousin, and said: 'I'm sorry I forgot to send you a birthday card, Ian. Back in May! I've been hearing you got that bike you wanted as a present.'

'Yeah! 'Course I did!'

'The very make you were so keen on?'

'Yeah. Raleigh Lenten Sports. Want to see it, Bruno? It's in the shed.'

This being the first friendly remark Ian had addressed to me so far, I said: 'That'd be great, Ian!'

So I followed him to the end of the garden; the shed stood close to the back gate which gave onto an alley-way lined by fencing.

The prized machine glowed at us in the shadows of the shed, an elegant clean-lined creation, the basic colour of which was a shiny Lenten Green, the colour of leaves and grasses at their newest and freshest.

'Smart!' I said, 'very smart indeed!'

Ian gave me one of his quizzical smiles which took me back to the better days of my Tanbury sojourn. He hadn't, I thought, been a bad lad at all. In fact I'd *actually* liked him. Why had hostility grown up between us? Through my own foolishness and deceit. In later years the gap in our ages would close. Wouldn't it be a sensible, as well as a virtuous, thing to cultivate a friendship with him, the only relation I had of my own generation?

'I feel quite envious,' I said.

Ian grinned: 'Want to see how it goes?'

'You bet!'

Ian, suffused with pleasure, wheeled the bike out through the wooden gate and into the alley. He mounted it with careless ease,

181

revealing just how long his legs had got in the months since I'd last seen him. He mounted the bike and rode off, with a curious deliberation, without turning round.

We hung around, Neil and I, for at least an hour, half-expecting him to return, half-realising that he'd do no such thing. Auntie Eileen showed herself as neither worried nor surprised. In the end it could scarcely be doubted that Ian had no intention of coming back to the house so long as we were in it. Gauchely but thankfully we took our leave. 'Thanks for the tea,' said Neil, 'it was great. Please say good-bye to Ian for me.'

That was something it was impossible for me to say.

I fell asleep, though it was only early evening, almost as soon as I got back to Primrose Hill. To have a short and terrible dream. I was wandering through the dark, dank vastness of a prison, and came across an old inmate, a starved stubbly bloodshot-eyed man who was nevertheless quite unmistakably the once debonair dandyish Charles Compson. But shout as I did, to get his attention, he never heard me. The tears were running down his dirty tired face.

I must forget him, I told myself.

When fully awake I went over to the telephone; my fingers dialled the Berridges' number automatically. 'Cassie,' I said, 'Cassie, I can't tell you how pleased I am to hear you. Can't we meet tonight?'

'Of course!' she said, 'there's nothing I'd want to do more.'

PART FOUR

Bruno Writes

Friday, February 12, 1999, 5.40 a.m. – date and time of my arrival by train in Östersund, northern Sweden.

I was jolted awake by the guard ringing his bell and announcing the next station (mine) – what a solemn sing-song sound Swedish has! Only a few minutes later the great express was slowly pulling in. I hadn't slept well; my throat was now sore, I had a bad headache and a crick in my neck. Night had fallen as far back as mid-afternoon yesterday, and it was still completely in charge of the land. I'd surfaced into consciousness many times during my long northbound journey and peered out of the window, to see – nothing, nothingness. That is, I saw, every time I looked out, motionless uninterrupted forest, a million firtrees at a glance stretching away and back on either side of the railway, all of them growing out of snow, laden with snow, topped with snow, and eerily identical. Villages – mere handfuls of lights that for a few moments assaulted the eyes then disappeared utterly – happened only very occasionally, and even then you saw the blackness of forest behind them. After Gävle, there were no towns, not that I noticed anyway. A huge, lonely country!

And yet I was where I wanted to be, where I had long fantasized about being!

That calls for explanation, I know.

I'd like to record first, though, that among my short-lived dreams on the way to Östersund, I had one in which I was arriving anew, the unfortunate youth who hadn't been accepted for National Service because of a health-problem, at Auntie Eileen's terrace-house in

Tanbury. 'It'll be *so* nice for Ian to have a young man in the house,' she told me, just as I was thinking – odd how you *can* think in dreams, can stand back from their scenes and people, and reflect! – 'I'd never realised relations of *mine* lived anywhere as *common* as this!" I'm not even wholly sure I didn't say these dreadful words aloud.... I hadn't often visited Tanbury before for all that my father and his brother had grown up there, I was a stranger in the place. 'What ghastly wall-paper!' I went on thinking, and possibly saying, 'and what dreadful fitted carpets for your hall and staircase! Horrible pattern, horrible colours.' And then I'd been jerked awake, to catch another glimpse of great, changeless forest-land.

Whoever said the unconscious is a realm of riches? Mine has such petty things stored inside it.

I don't care for early rising, though don't recall any occasion when I've actually not made a flight or train. The chambers of my head always feel empty after short sleep, and its bones too light, too brittle. This was so this particular morning as I stumbled out of the train onto a bleak platform. Östersund, capital of the northern province of Jämtland – well, here I was, after so many miles and hours, and all it could manage by way of greeting was a stinging snow-carrying wind that made me gasp and choke.

Still I repeated to myself: I'm pleased to be here!

Quite a number of people for such a godforsaken hour were hastening to the parking area outside the station. Here the harrying flakes made it hard to hold one's head up to look around one properly. Car-lights were picked up by the falling snow and, it seemed, smeared across one's moving line of vision. I was looking out for someone: *Northlands Enterprises* who had arranged, with help from my credit-card, this day in Jämtland, had been most insistent there'd be someone to drive me from the station to their location headquarters. These – I'd been informed more than once, with something like pride – were at quite some distance from Östersund, and there was no public transport, so a driver was really necessary. I had the *Enterprises'* fax on me, and now, reeling back from the fierce wind, I put my hand into my coat pocket to touch it (as if to prove the whole expedition wasn't an invention of the imagination). The fax had arrived in my luxurious waterfront Stockholm hotel, a place that all at once had turned hard to believe in:

DEAR MR ARMITAGE, A TAXIDRIVER FROM SJÖBYN, CARL-GUNNAR, WILL WAIT FOR YOU AT THE STATION IN ÖSTERSUND TOMORROW MORNING. HE IS SPENDING THE NIGHT IN ÖSTERSUND TO BE THERE IN TIME, SO PLEASE DON'T GO WITH ANYONE ELSE! HE IS NOT VERY TALL, SLENDER, DARK AND HAS A THIN MOUSTACHE. HE IS THE SHOP-KEEPER'S SON AND VERY NICE, AND HAS BEEN INVALUABLE TO *NORTHLANDS* – YOU MAY EVEN RECOGNISE HIM FROM THE ODD EPISODE OR TWO. SO GOOD LUCK, AND WELCOME TO SJÖBYN. ANNA AND AGNETA

Well, if I'd been bold enough as a youth to go down to The Puzzle and beard the maker of *The Parkers* in her strange den without ever having so much as set eyes on her before, then the middle-aged man he'd become – who was a *Northlands* devotee – who most weekday nights went vicarious snowmobile journeys, encountering Sami (Lapps), bears, drug-smugglers and skiers of miraculous dexterity, who made (virtual) love to lithe and savvy Nordic girls or teamed up with their glinting-eyed, taciturn, muscular brothers – he just had to rise to the challenge now being offered him, didn't he?

So where *was* this 'very nice' shop-keeper's son and taxi-driver? But again, wouldn't it have been a bit of a let-down to have been straightway ushered into a warm car by a waiting chauffeur?

To explain why I was there expecting Carl-Gunnar to appear, I have to pass quickly through almost four decades.

* * * * * *

After three years of going out together and never seriously wanting to go out with anyone else, Cassie and I got married. It was quite unusual in those days for a couple actually to live together before the wedding, and in this respect, as in so many others, we showed ourselves conventional enough. After all we had already found out our sexual and emotional compatibility. Our wedding-day was one of the few unsulliedly happy occasions of my life; it might have happened at Greenfield End itself.

The ceremony took place at a North London church, on a September Saturday of ripe apples and snapdragons and nasturtiums in all the Highgate gardens. In the Chiltern countryside, where we spent our honeymoon, the corn-stooks glowed against banks of beech-woods where brown was just touching, but no more than that, the still unfallen leaves. Enid (whom I could now call 'Mum' if I wanted to) had become sufficiently famous – a national symbol, believe it or not, of new, classless, English community living – for no fewer than *four* photographers from wide-circulation dailies to be sent to cover her only daughter's wedding. 'Elizabeth Parker's Daughter Marries – But NOT in Newstead' read one head-line. 'Parkers Girl Weds – But Where's The Rev. Derek?' said another.

We still have our wedding album, of course.

Here are photos of my father, his natural aloofness emphasized rather than reduced by morning-dress, rose in button-hole and self-conscious smile. Here are ones of Auntie Eileen (poor Auntie Eileen – not long left for her to live!) and Ian, Ian now a style-minded teenager of the times, in black leather jacket, tight dove-grey trousers and snazzy dark glasses – easy to see that Marlon Brando and Zbigniew Cybulski (hero of Wajda's "in" success, *Ashes and Diamonds*) were *his* heroes. And here – for he came to both church service and reception – is Charles Compson. Who could suppose, looking at his bland manicured elegance, that this was a gaol-bird? No Verity Orchard, however, and – scarcely astonishing – no Nesta Coolidge either. Enid had of course asked Verity, asked her *twice*! – 'for the sake of auld lang syne, darling!' – but she'd never replied. (She was no longer living at The Puzzle, but, with just Nesta for company, in a smaller house somewhere in Somerset.) I'd asked Neil Micklewright to be best man, even though, for

186

some reason that eluded me, our friendship had considerably contracted since our Irish holiday and the visit to Tanbury that had rounded it off. 'Sorry – no can do. Don't like weddings!' was his reply scribbled on the back of a postcard of Tower Bridge. (His dislike didn't apply to his *own* wedding apparently which took place two and a half years after mine, and to which I was not invited.) So the important rôle was played by Alexander Gifford, an old 'mucker' of mine from Riverbury, who'd turned up in the antique-shop one afternoon looking for a snuff-box for his great-uncle – to disproportionate pleasure on both our parts. In his too long and too facetious speech he twice or thrice referred to me simply as Armitage (as of course he always had at school); that's how close our friendship was!

Cassie and I waited thirteen years to have children, and then had our three in close succession, Roderick, Amy and Lucas, all born into – and brought up in – the Buckinghamshire converted farmhouse which is our home. All three have partners now, and nice ones at that, though only Rod so far has offspring. Perhaps because of our comparative maturity as parents but more probably because of features of our own early lives, we quite consciously took a worldly, an orthodox middle-class approach to our children's development. Neither Cassie nor I (it hardly needs saying) had enjoyed academic success, but we were keen that Rod, Amy and Lucas should go to good schools and acquit themselves well there. Cassie felt her parents' fecklessness had got in the way of her doing herself intellectual justice, I for my part was anxious to show my father (the figure who represented society to me) that I was something more than the airhead he'd always considered me. ("Just you look at the children Bruno's produced! They just couldn't be the children of a *dunce*, could they?")

Rod was a model pupil endearing himself at an early age to Daddy who soon saw him as his true heir; he is now a financial analyst for a Japanese bank. Amy has inherited Cassie's interest in art history, and, though fully qualified for a lecturing post, has preferred to free-lance as critic and historian; she's written a coffee-table book on Max Ernst. Only Lucas has received from his genetic fairy god-mother something of his dad's indecisiveness and need for guidance. But after a ragged school career – with useless grades and a prolonged drugs episode –

187

he has trained as a silver-smith, and I have taken him into my business, where he's already proving competent, and often a lot *more* than competent. Lucas, with his groundless boasts and apprehensive smile and eagerness to be cool, is, I have to say, the child with whom I have always identified the most closely, often cherishing his pathetic failures more than his brother and sister's triumphs. Cassie says that's perverse of me. Well, I suppose it is.

My business, my life's work which had got well under way before marriage and to which I devoted so much time and thought in those thirteen childless years – what to say about it, what to say about 'Treasure-Trove' that isn't really rather widely known? It's been the subject of not a few articles in newspapers and magazines, but always I have – for reasons this book will have made obvious – withheld key aspects of its history.

While Charles was in prison (The Scrubs), I looked after P. Dickinson, Antiques, with a thoroughness, a dedication, a passion for detail, that no-one who'd known me at school or at home would have suspected. I re-decorated the whole ground-floor; stepping inside the shop became an aesthetic pleasure in itself, and many a person said so. More frequently even than I recall my wedding-day do I bring back to mind, when tired, the Fulham establishment as it looked after I'd got to work on it. I see my own acquisitions of those months: the corner cupboards, the dressers (bang in fashion at that time) with their arrays of decorated mugs and plates, most of them bought by me from two old farmers up in Lincolnshire, the Victorian armchairs, backs draped with fringed shawls, the child's rocking-horse, the *papier mâché* table, black, inlaid with mother-of-pearl – each of these items for me had its own beauty, charm, quiddity.

Certainly when, after just over eight months, Charles came out of gaol, he found his little concern patently flourishing and, in the right circles, enjoying a reputation. It was then I carried out one of the few actions which, even at my darkest times, I am morally proud of.

Borrowing from my father, and with his permission for what I was about to do, (it was only a few months away from my twenty-first birthday), I bought Charles out of the business, and set him up, with a manager's salary, in P. Dickinson, Antiques itself. This became Branch

188

No 1 of 'Treasure-Trove', the now renowned chain. Next I applied myself to establishing Branch No 2, up in Kentish Town. By the end of the Sixties I had branches in King's Lynn and Thame, by the end of the Seventies in Taunton, Bury St Edmunds, Beverley and Lancaster. In the Eighties all did extremely well and expanded, and Bodmin, Ripon and Ludlow joined their ranks. By this time 'Treasure-Trove' dealt in pictures as well as furniture, china, *objets d'art*, rugs. We have also created a reputation for ourselves as consultants, valuers, and – my errant, charming, unreliable father-in-law to the fore here, of course – restorers.

About two years into our marriage Cassie and I came to a decision about where to make our home. In London, so Cassie felt, we couldn't, when we wanted to, escape from the demands of her parents – her father begging for an introduction to someone-or-other who owned a picture *hopefully* in need of treatment, or simply (and more frequently) for 'a little loan, you know, just to tide me over until...', her mother demanding an audience for her problems with her husband or with other members of *The Parkers of Newstead* cast, (always hinting she might hit the bottle again were this audience to prove insufficiently sympathetic). For hours, so it seems in memory, Cassie and I would lie side by side in bed with either a real or an imaginary map of Britain in front of us. We thought of Cornwall, we thought of Northumberland – 'Right opposite Holy Island might be *exactly* the place for us!' Cassie once enthused – but clearly we had to live far nearer London than either of these, and in the end we settled on the countryside of our honeymoon, the Chilterns. Here we were lucky enough to find a farmhouse, cheapish, in need of alteration and doing up but structurally sound, about five miles from Prince's Risborough: Walnut Tree House, and it's a near-impossibility to imagine existence itself not forever containing it. (Not that I don't, quite regularly, try to do this. What about my journey into the Swedish north?)

If I were asked to write, Elizabeth Parker-style, a *Round and About Our Vicarage* about Walnut Tree House, I could, I think, produce a convincing and attractive book. Thanks to the business having done so well, the interior of the house is, every room of it, both pleasing to the eye and comfortable, and the exterior, with its pantiled roof and creeper-covered mellowed brick walls, is inviting enough to appeal to many passing photographers. The garden (more Cassie's creation than mine) extends over four acres to a beechen Chiltern flank. We have a herb-garden and a rose-garden, which, on summer weekends, we open to the public. There's an orchard that's home to our Chinese geese and our bee-hives. Perhaps, if one can make such a division, Cassie is more interested in the flora of Walnut Tree, and I in the fauna. The dogs have always been a particular concern of mine – right now, I have a Red Setter and a Tibetan Terrier, Rufus and Dalai – and they have always provided a bond between myself and Lucas. But wild creatures too mean a great deal to me; I know intimately a badger-sett just to the back of us, I make our walled kitchen-garden a winter sanctum for hedgehogs – and then there's our constant visitor, the (now) elderly dog-fox who, I like to think, knows what a friend to him I am; I'd protect him from any number of hunters.

So why, then, am I *not* the author of *Round and About Walnut Tree House*? That's a serious question.

Answer: Because the place can never be my (or our) all. Perhaps our chief mistake – my mistake mostly, but Cassie's also – has been to think otherwise.

Is Cassie happy? She and I have never loved – or, for that matter, ever fallen in love with – anyone apart from each other. Our marriage is still – we would both, I'm sure, agree – a living entity. For the last ten years or so, however, Cassie has indulged in what I think of as obsessional preoccupations with the marginals of our life. If it isn't her brother Adam's sister-in-law with her problems with men, it is (I'm not joking) our elder son, Rod's ex-girl-friend's brother, who can't, poor lad, hold down a job. Selfless of Cassie (I suppose) to be so intimately engaged with so many others, selfish of me to summon up such slender interest in them... This large cast of persons (to use soap-opera phraseology) has provided enough dramas to deliver my wife from any feelings of monotony that prosperity, security and neighbourhood stability might have brought about. For example – Adam's sister-in-law took up, briefly, with a Jamaican revivalist preacher who staged a Holy

190

Roller-style prayer-meeting in Kennington which Cassie just *had* to attend. Rod's ex-girl-friend's brother was accused of 'dipping a hand' into the petty-cash of some small magazine outfit unwise enough to employ him, and Cassie, needless to say, felt obliged to go to its manager to plead Will's innocence and get the charge dropped. (I myself never doubted his guilt.)

And me, Bruno Armitage? what have been the dramas of *my* last ten or so years, those leading me from one century, one millennium to another? It won't take me long to answer this question. They have been first and foremost, depression, later to be sometimes relieved and sometimes actually increased by *Northlands*.

Depression struck late afternoon October 19, 1995, a date without any anniversarial significance that I could see, and now an anniversary in its own right. I've been asked many times – and by many (differently) qualified people – what this occurrence felt like. Favourite similes have been offered me. Was it as though a curtain had suddenly descended? (But onto what? And was I player or spectator?) Could it be likened to a huge dark bird flying across the sun? (Well, yes, in a way, but a bird, when its passage has been made, leaves the sun intact. My sun, for the most part, has withdrawn. No wonder I wasn't really fazed by the nether-Polar winter when I travelled through it, but had an odd sense of homecoming.)

One indisputable fact about my life was, I realised, that most of it was now over. The future didn't frighten me; Cassie and I had together applied our minds to it, we'd be materially comfortable at the very least. Death, if anything, had become less real than it'd seemed in the fearful nights all of us know in adolescence, when you realise beyond all assurance that it's not to be avoided, not by you, not by anybody. But the past – that was another matter, its shapeless size, its dreadful length, the mass of days and nights which made it up but which couldn't be distinguished, even by the keenest mind, one from another – it was more than bewildering, it was unmanageable, tracts of territory as vast and untameable as – yes, as the great forest that was Sweden. And how about the figure looking for something in it all, Bruno

Lawrence Armitage? He was scarcely easier to define than any old nameless day or tree.

Insofar as I *was* able to get a hold on him, what a jerk he seemed. And the Bruno who'd got involved with *The Parkers* was the biggest jerk of them all. That fatuous delusion of his that he was going to be a nationally-known scriptwriter would make you laugh were he not so seriously unfunny, a real study in egotism and conceit. As for *The Parkers* itself – it had been complete codswallop, hadn't it? out-and-out tripe, a load of old cobblers.

All the popular dismissive expressions of the past decades I'd lived through couldn't do justice to its vacuousness.

But no sooner had I dared to articulate this to myself than I was overcome by a nostalgia for the part it had played in my life, and by a corresponding and almost painful desire for a serial in my life now, for a soap-opera – or *soap* as most people said *tout court* these days. A regular weekday rendez-vous, an omnibus edition at weekends – what could be better?

In fact I first watched *Northlands* by accident, fiddling around one evening to see what was on which channel in a mood of greater than usual despondency. Not that I didn't know about the programme and its sizeable following; ignorance, it will be agreed, would have scarcely been possible so constant was the media interest in it. "*Northlands* star in sex scandal" a tabloid headline would shriek, "Is there life beyond *Northlands*?" asked another, after the grizzly demise (on screen) of one of its major characters.

My search that day rewarded me with an image of deep winter shimmering on the screen, of fir-trees zooming past credit titles from a variety of angles. Now these were sombre giants towering over you, now you floated over their tops, saw them from above standing in close rows to resemble waves of a measureless sea. Imposed over these were lozenge-shaped cameos of the programme's cast, swathed in protective clothing of deep blues and deeper reds, but no mere stock Nordics – some short rather than tall, some dark rather than fair, and one as red-headed as myself. But all, without exception,

192

giving off instant charisma and a sense of secrets.

To lead you into the evening's action a few beguiling bars of music sounded, these bars being repeated and then again repeated till fade-out, the music of the kind the profession knows as 'techno-folk' – in this case (as I learned later) strains of an electric key-harp (an traditional old Swedish instrument, the *nyckelharpa*).

And then the episode proper began. Of course at first I had the greatest difficulty in sorting out who was who; it brought back to me those first charmed tea-times in Tanbury when Auntie Eileen and Ian had had to explain *Parkers* characters as they came on air, explain how they stood in relation to each other, the habits and favourite sayings and little dramas that accrued to them. With *Northlands* the difficulty was compounded by every scene being of a tantalising brevity, telescoping into the next in a way that I – less of a TV-watcher than my wife and children (and grandchildren) – found confusing to the point of challenge. Tanbury days again, though the real similarity between then and now lay not so much in the programme as in my own need for an absorbing transforming feature in my own increasingly empty-seeming life.....

I'd already (I'd better confess) tried out other soaps. *EastEnders* was lively and fast-paced, all the inhabitants of Albert Square having an attractive, enviably perky self-confidence about them. But they lived too cheek-by-jowl for my tastes, I'd never been a one for pub conviviality, was simply not gregarious enough. *Emmerdale* carried you to a very different milieu, and I took at once to the bare hills and dry stone walls of the Yorkshire Dales landscape of its setting; I felt, though, that it had nothing to offer me which my own Chilterns background – my charming pastoral prison – couldn't, if properly attended to. The characters of *Hollyoaks* were too young, too bland and too cocky – it had been hard enough for me in the recent past to be agreeable to Amy and Lucas' friends (harder than to the more serious Rod's) but these smug smirking youths of Chester were more than I could take... *Brookside* (*Hollyoaks'* older *Mersey TV* brother) was decidedly more promising, and bodies under patios, a would-be-priest giving up his vows because of his hots for a nanny, these and other similar story-lines really had me interested. But if I compared it, as I couldn't help doing, with *The Parkers*, it never made me anxious to be among the people it featured, to inhabit it as a complement or refreshing contrast to my own life. Who in their right minds could want to live in that dismal cul-de-sac, Brookside Close? Walnut Tree House was in all ways superior.

But *Northlands* among the spruce and snows (most of its action took place in winter, but then winter lasted so much longer 'up there', didn't it?) – *that* was quite another matter. Life in those parts had – how shall I put it? – a certain (maybe a necessary) magic about it. Mine, at Walnut Tree House, had, quite simply, none whatever. In Jämtland (as I found out the region of Sweden in which it took place was called) there were thrills, there was seductive danger.

After half a dozen episodes things were beginning to make sense for me. I now knew the episodes' questions, and could make a stab at answers, while knowing that they were still a pleasing long way off, and might indeed never be given at all. Why had that obviously libidinous middle-aged couple enticed a hysterical black girl (so distraught in so alien a locality) into their car only to drive her in the opposite direction from that they'd offered to take her? Who was the cunning-eyed young man explaining an old Sami way of bringing on an abortion, and what was his motive for doing this?

It was not at all a nice world these folk frequented; just one single episode of *Northlands* told you that. That was just its charm - and, in fact, there was a lot in it about charms and enchanters and spells in the episodes, though the characters were also all extremely physical people, skilled with guns and knives, capable of felling trees, dealing with a savage bear, or re-roofing a house, and, most of them, adepts too at using the snowmobile, a machine which had become, as far as viewers and promoters were concerned, all but synonymous with the programme. To give its dictionary definition this is 'a small vehicle used for travelling over snow. It has runners at the front and a caterpillar track underneath'. In *Northlands* you saw it again and again, being driven over semi-Arctic terrain on missions of love (or fierce sex), of hate (or bloody violence), of profit (the realisation, or thwarting, of schemes for gaining money from the region's stupendous natural resources).

There was something else: the soap had beauty, and not only

because of its glamorous-faced, glamorous-limbed cast. What *was* it with the Nineties that led so many of us then (in our minds at any rate) ever northwards? Could it be that – as I read in a Sunday-papers article – the end (or top) of century, of millennium, sent us mentally to the end (or top) of globe. We were turned on as never before by Arctic (or sub-Arctic) territory, and yet that turning-on never took us far from murderous death. We admired *Miss Smilla's Feeling for Snow*, watched that 'feeling' of hers give a clue to a young Innuit boy's murder in Copenhagen and cause her to voyage dangerously to Greenland itself. In *Twin Peaks* we asked ourselves 'Who killed Laura Palmer?' up in the wilds of US' extreme north-western quarter, Washington State, and looked to a cop with a head full of Chinese wisdom to help us out up there. On a wintry north Pacific island, with *Snow Falling on Cedars* we tried to solve another murder, while in *Blackwater* – set in the very Northern Sweden I later saw for myself – we dealt with another murder puzzle, of two hikers hacked to bits in a tent put up beside a lonely lake. I wasn't the greatest of readers, as has been made clear, but, like so many others, I read my way through all these, but was even more pleased to see such scenes – with their magic, their beauty, their violence – on the screen.

In my Chilterns sitting-room watching *Northlands* I could positively feel the snow coming down on me, on hair and shoulders, while sex took its charged, compulsive, wrestling course, and, in the savage outside, inexplicable people waited in solitude or in speechless collusion to deal smilingly vicious blows and then make orgasm-like get-aways on snowmobiles. Cassie didn't like me watching *Northlands*. Not from the first. Later – for I am speaking not of months but of years – she came positively to resent me doing so.

Cassie is very practical; she always was, I believe, but the quality has become more and more conspicuous in her (to me at any rate) with the years. Not that I myself am *im*practical, in fact the history of 'Treasure Trove' would suggest the reverse, but clearly it is in this direction that my priorities and tastes differ from hers. Cassie thinks the 'real reason' for my depression (wouldn't *any* reason be 'real' after a fashion?) is that, outside my work, I don't have enough activities, social engagements or hobbies. She doesn't, I need hardly say, regard watching soap-opera on TV as at all a proper pastime, and I suppose from the clinical point of view (of my depression) she's right; it *hasn't* gone away.

'You should *never* disparage soap,' I said to her, as I sat 'slumped in my chair' (as she unvaryingly puts it) watching a late Saturday afternoon *Northlands* omnibus (two episodes of which, as she knew, I'd already seen during the week), 'it held *your* home together after all.'

'Hm!' She cast her eyes upwards in a mocking moment as she often did when I mentioned the Berridges; her family life, looked back on, seemed to her to have been a cautionary muddle, no more.

'And it brought you a husband!'

Cassie smiled – a mite too deliberately perhaps, and not very broadly, 'Well, it served its purpose then years ago, didn't it? That husband doesn't need to go into his dotage watching a lot of silly stuff.'

'It isn't silly,' I replied, not by any means for the first time, 'it's very clever and compelling.'

'Certainly compelling, I could hardly disagree, with you sitting there like that, slumped in your chair... But *clever*? who are you trying to convince?'

She enlisted the children's help from time to time, my intensifying *Northlands* addiction galvanising her to do so more often than when I was just mooching by the hour about our beautiful garden or sitting in my study reading, a few pages at a time, some current best-selling book like *Snow Falling On Cedars*. I could sometimes hear her saying things like : 'Amy, why don't you ask Dad to look over your proofs. I know you've read them already, but it might make him feel important and occupied –and anything's better for him than all this solitary brooding and watching TV.' Or 'Rod, couldn't just you and Dad go out to drinks with the Bertrams this Saturday. Dad might come out of his shell without me, and you've always liked going to the Bertrams' place, and it would take him away from the television screen...'

Rod, that amazing all-rounder whom Cassie and I have so amazingly produced, said to me a day or so after his mother's proposal: 'It's boredom that's your great trouble, Dad!'

'Is it?' I said, 'well, I suppose you could look at it like that...'

'Other people have felt and expressed the problem of being bored, you know, it might be helpful for you to read what they've said,' my handsome, unbored, always profitably occupied son continued, 'remember I did a subsid. course at university on American literature.' I hadn't remembered this, I'm sorry to say, but didn't give the fact away (at least I don't *think* I did). 'There's some marvellous lines by John Berryman on the subject.'

'John Berryman?' I echoed dully. His was a quite unknown name. 'Who was he?'

'A poet,' Rod said evasively (I was later to look Berryman up and learn he'd killed himself by jumping off a bridge). 'I often think it's a good thing to find our own personal predicaments put into memorable words.' (And what were Rod's predicaments, I wanted to ask; the sun had smiled continuously on him since birth.) 'I'll look up the lines for you.'

He did. Here they are, and I can't deny they had an effect on me:

> 'Life, friends, is boring. We must not say so.
> After all, the sky flashes, the great sea yearns,
> we ourselves flash and yearn,
> and moreover my mother told me as a boy
> (repeatingly) 'Ever to confess you're bored
> means you have no
> inner resources.' I conclude now I have no
> inner resources, because I am heavy bored.'

It rang true, too much so for comfort – and yet I wasn't at all sure it was true. It wasn't *life* I thought boring so much as *my* life. Beyond that there were distinct possibilities – somewhere in the flashing sky, the yearning sea – for the absence of boredom. Over in *Northlands* for example.

And then something dreadful happened, to blight even further my unsatisfactory routine existence: *Northlands* episodes *did* start to bore me. One plot-line – about the paternity of a child, and whether the grandparents who suspected the worst should have DNA tests done on him or simply consult (yet again) a Sami wise-woman – went on and on, and really it wasn't all that fascinating even at the beginning. One of the most alluring characters, Ulla, for me the most beautiful of the actresses, didn't appear when you'd expected her to – even though she was said to be merely visiting relations down in Gothenburg. The dialogue, always a highly individual and much-imitated flat laconic English, became flatter and even more laconic than normal, to the point of tedium.

What would I do, if my prop failed me? I wasn't the type to drink myself drunk or go whoring in my middle age, just as I wasn't the type to sit on a Parish Council.

I contacted the *Northlands* website:

'I have been disappointed repeatedly by your programme this last two months,' I told it, 'something is going wrong. Possibly more than one thing –' I then detailed some particularly outstanding failures, but ended up; 'I am as great a fan of *Northlands* as can be imagined – an English professional man whose week is made by it, who deeply needs all the interesting things it has to offer. Please don't let someone like me down.'

The 1998 anniversary of my depression came round. I woke up to a dreadful if familiar feeling of heaviness, and all day, when not working on my computer, I found it an effort to drag my lugubrious but healthy body round house and garden. I was beset too – to my surprise and bemusement – by persistent images of Ian Armitage and Neil Micklewright, from such a distance in the past. In my mental visitations they'd heard of my low spirits and, smiling at me in boyish eagerness, said: 'Poor old guy! What can *we* do to cheer you up?' I'd not seen either of them for years, but – perhaps I should. Perhaps they, more than others, knowing as much about me as they did, could breathe the wanting optimism into me. Make me feel it was worth surviving my burdensome present.

'After all, the sky flashes, the great sea yearns,
we ourselves flash and yearn...'

And this October day was such a lovely one, the maple leaves, some still on trees but more on the ground, and the virginia creeper, all the vividest scarlet, scarlet too the cotoneaster berries – while the sky was a cloudless baked blue.

In the evening, fearing the worst, I switched on the TV, already tuned onto Channel Four. And – would you believe it? – *Northlands* was back to its old (gratitude-inducing) form – well, more or less: Ulla was still in Gothenburg. Interchanges were interesting and aroused the curiosity, there was a rumour of a rogue elk, old Lars-Anders had a strange and inexplicable look on his face when the word 'visitor' was mentioned – I watched, attention wholly captured again, nerves engaged and tingling, until the minimalist bars of the *nyckelharpa* signified the (as always cliff-hanging) end.

On this sad anniversary it had been proved – surely refuting John Berryman – that life *in toto* was not boring, not at all. I was back to being what the press in its media columns called a 'Northie'.

As I prepared for bed, it suddenly occurred to me what anniversary October 19 might be. When I checked in almanacs the following day, I proved myself right – and whyever hadn't I thought of it before, three years ago? On October 19 1957 I'd had my ill-starred date with Nina Cardew, had taken her to that skiffle evening at *The Pig and Whistle*, to be humiliated, to make a show of myself, to earn the disapproval of Tanbury society, and of my aunt and father? I'd been spurred to the occasion by that episode of *The Parkers* in which Elizabeth Parker encouraged young Tom Cavan to make clear to Minty Macdonald his interest in her. Without that débacle I might never have got involved with Charles or Verity.

This realisation brought those Tanbury days closer to me, and with them, of course, *The Parkers* itself.

You wouldn't think, would you? – some conventions of the *genre* apart, the juggling of plots and characters, the question-mark endings to episodes – that there could be any marked similarities between a soap about the Vicar of a prosperous London dormitory and his circle and one dealing with wild folk living up in northern wastes. But – soon after the perception I've just recorded above – *Northlands* episodes began to remind me of *Parkers* ones in a quite uncanny way. What tricks was my fatigued bored mind playing on me?

How about this for example? (It's not necessary to know about the people behind the names, though I'll concede for me they're more flesh-and-blood than my own Buckinghamshire neighbours.)

Pelle comes to stay with Lars-Anders, his uncle, who inhabits a remote cabin-like house on the slopes of a mountain. His uncle is a famous writer, whose novels of magic are known and loved the length of Sweden. Pelle – who at first endears himself to everyone – begins to take an interest (not returned) in a doctor's daughter, and decides that he will treat her to a restaurant in the nearest town. But how to do so, hard up as he is. His solution? – to steal money from the wallet his uncle had carelessly left on top of the dresser.

What *Parkers* listener from the Fifties couldn't have recognised the story of Kevin O'Flynn and Tom Cavan? Of course in *Northlands* the plot went on to wacky stuff way beyond the powers of Verity Orchard's imagination. Lars-Anders has a prophetic talking raven, while Pelle has a 'daily diet' of crack-cocaine, to the pleasures of which he wants to introduce that doctor's daughter. (And the doctor himself is naroleptic.) But still – the bare bones were unmistakeable, were they not?

There was worse to come – a month or so later, with Christmas looming, and my feeling every day that I simply could not cope with a houseful of folk at that season, no matter how near and dear. (Sooner or later I was going to have to go away somewhere.)

Another young man, the sly, self-serving, ever-ingratiating Erik, hearing of Lars-Anders' ejection of Pelle, decides to take his place in his affections. And wins them. They have a hectic gay relationship, the intimacies of which are shown with startling and by no means unerotic camera-shots. Lars-Anders proceeds to set Erik up in a small but lucrative folk-artifacts business (selling Sami crafts etc). But then along comes another opportunity for Erik, one he has in fact long been waiting for: to be apprenticed to a well-known sculptor now come to practise in the locality. He deserts Lars-Anders, leaving him and the business in the lurch. Lars-Anders, desolate, drives off to a household on the edge of a felled clearing, home to a group of young lumbermen, and throws himself on one of them, hoping for sexual, emotional release and compensation.

He has made an enormous mistake. The lumberman in question turns on him in outraged fury and proceeds to knife him to death. The talking raven guesses his owner's ghastly fate – and the snowmobile has to go out, over the benighted tracks to find the cruelly hacked body of the hapless writer.

That story remind you of anything?

It certainly did me.

My depression worsened – on mornings when I could, I delayed getting up, and most evenings I'd go to bed early. Christmas was horrible, very horrible. Cassie felt I let her down; up to this time I'd always put a good face on when I had to, now I couldn't. Rod, Amy and Lucas, and their consorts all took Cassie's side, and who could blame them? I took it myself.

I sent many messages – in varying tones – to the *Northlands* website. At first I didn't let on that I'd 'rumbled' them, as it seemed to me; I merely inquired about their plot-sources, to get evasive but polite replies. Together with thanks for the congratulations I never ceased to give the programme-makers. (These particular episodes deserved them too; they were the soap's best-ever.) But in the last e-mail that I dispatched before my Great Opportunity came, I was more unrestrained, more impassioned: 'I, Bruno Armitage, have secret knowledge of the reality behind your Lars-Anders story,' I wrote, 'I'm wiser even than the talking raven. Some day I'd like to share it with you.'

But I didn't really think I *would* like to share it. I wasn't as self-deceived as that. It was just a manner of speaking, to gain their attention over in Sweden. Which it didn't properly do. The producer and script-writer, said the PR officer's reply, were delighted that the story-line had made such a strong impression on me. They too considered it one of their very best.

I have probably been giving the impression that over the last year or so I've been doing little work: the truth is quite otherwise. I will admit, though, to having often felt that some inner commitment to it has left me. With so many competent and well-trained branch-managers of 'Treasure Trove' all over the country, I've been able to give time, however, to other aspects of my profession – of which, by the way, I'm thought a respect-worthy member – such as contributing to those bodies trying to establish European, indeed international standards for dating, evaluating and pricing antiques. One such body meets annually in a city of consequence somewhere in Europe. In 1998 the choice was Budapest – spring weather, terrific food and night-life, and Cassie and I in an almost honeymoon mood, a pleasant interlude indeed in my melancholia and her disengagement from me. For 1999 the choice was Stockholm, and the date, to suit various Swedish and Finnish group-members, was brought forward a little – to February. 'But how appropriate to visit a Scandinavian city in the notorious Scandinavian winter!' our coordinator said.

As soon as I knew I was going, I contacted the *Northlands* website. 'Will be in Sweden. Would really appreciate a visit to your northern location,' I informed them.

I was quite surprised, I have to confess, when an almost enthusiastic invitation came over the internet, asking me to specify ideal dates and times, and give contact addresses in Stockholm – 'and we will do the rest. Anna and Agneta.'

Who could resist that?

Cassie Armitage for one.

'Of course I haven't the *remotest* interest in going to see where *Northlands* is filmed,' she told me, 'as you know, I think the programme's quite ghastly – a lot of spurious sensationalist rubbish, whatever you say in its defence – and it's not had a good effect on either you or our household.... In fact I don't really feel like coming to Sweden with you at all. I mean, put it this way: if I *were* by your side in Stockholm, I wouldn't really be there as far as you're concerned.

You've gone so far away into your head that a lot of the time it's as if I don't exist.'

I stayed in Stockholm in a hotel in which from my bedroom I could see the (snow-decorated) copper roofs and spires of the Gamla Stan, its Old Town, that isthmus covered with medieval and renaissance buildings poised between an arm of the sea and the great lake, Mälaren. It was a visit of congenial meetings, interesting talks at which effective resolutions really *were* passed, and good meals, one of them in the famous *Gondolen* Restaurant suspended at the end of a permanent crane-like structure high above lakeside, city- and boat-lights shining away down below you as you ate. But all the time, and never more than that last evening, I was thinking about my visit to *Northlands* and how could I help comparing it with my trip down to Dorset and the creator of *The Parkers* – which had ended in sadness all round?

Except for meeting Cassie. Yes, except for meeting Cassie.

* * * * * *

Parting snow-curtains, a short slender high-cheekboned man, with a dark-coloured stocking-cap pulled down covering forehead and ears, made his way directly towards me, across the dark of the parking-square. The beams of our eyes met through the tumbles of flakes. 'Yes, *he's* the one!' we both said silently to ourselves, and 'Thank God for that!' He gave me a quick, half-interrogative salute with a fur-gloved hand. Not until he was all but upon me could I hear him so muffling was the weather. 'Bruno Armitage?' His voice was soft, throaty, clipped.

'Carl-Gunnar?'

'Carl-Gunnar, yes, I am Carl-Gunnar!' He smiled, and his smile had an odd sweetness, almost an ingenuousness, about it that didn't quite go with his weathered, experienced, hard-boned face, and yet also suited it, as surely many a woman must have told him.

'And I'm Bruno,' I told him unnecessarily, 'just like you said. It feels really *good* to be here.'

I spoke only the truth. Carl-Gunnar seemed pleased to hear this 'And I'm going to drive you all the way to Sjöbyn," he said. 'Great, great!' *Northlands* would, before so long, be materialised, reveal itself as a part of real life, but I was merging moment by moment into my pitiable earlier self who had been driven by poor old Charles Compson down to The Puzzle.... The Swede and I shook hands, his grip was almost painful in its firmness, that of someone (I tried to address myself facetiously) regularly cocking a gun, and even on occasions wrestling with a recalcitrant bear. Cassie, could she see us now, would laugh sarcastically at this encounter, but she had no right to. This was as much a part of existence as Walnut Tree House and its visitors. But perhaps she *wouldn't* laugh after all. She was kind enough.

Something else was bothering me. 'I've... I've seen you before, Carl-Gunnar!'

Earliness of hour never has done anything for my brains. What was it Anna and Agneta had faxed me? 'HE [CARL-GUNNAR] HAS BEEN INVALUABLE TO *NORTHLANDS*. YOU MAY EVEN RECOGNISE HIM FROM THE ODD EPISODE OR TWO.' Yes, I could have said to the young driver: 'Didn't we twice pass you on the mountain road into Norway when we were chasing those double-crossing coke-smugglers? And didn't you go spying on that old Lesbian when she was having a dangerous interview with the Mafia-type logging-company boss?'

I didn't, of course. But Carl-Gunnar's grin had broadened; no doubt he was only too used to being identified by *Northlands* watchers. 'Maybe, maybe!' he said, 'but I've got a *Volvo* with winter-tyres waiting for us, not a snowmobile.' But he was moved to chuckle disarmingly here as he nudged me towards that Volvo and told me: 'I *do* have a snowmobile, of course, and a very fine one!'

Nice to be in the warmth of the car after the painful cold of the car-park. Once we were off, memory (a viewer's memory, obviously, which is as potent as any other's) stirred. These snow-topped civic buildings presenting themselves to me, I knew them for what they were. Important meeting-places, essential to plot-lines. It was to Östersund that people in The Programme came when, in their remote lives, they needed anything at all civilised: restaurant, hotel, library, records office, and – rather more frequently, given their inclinations and hard habits – police station and law courts. The characters themselves might live according to their own moral laws, but from time to time authority stretched a keen and righteous hand into one of Europe's largest and most intact wildernesses and yanked egregious malefactors into its bastions.

For a short while Carl-Gunnar drove (as he informed me) along that E.75 motorway which connects Swedish Östersund with Norwegian Trondheim – but then he turned off it. And after he'd done so, I felt, even after the whole strangeness of the long night's journey that I was truly entering the world I'd come to find.

'We won't be reaching Sjöbyn itself for at least an hour and a half,' my driver said. *An hour and a half!* Carl-Gunnar wafted a map at me. Only *one* small township, I saw, would disturb the expanse ahead of us of quiet, dark, snow-floored forest through which this thin road was inching an unobtrusive way.

'There's one third of Sweden to go beyond this before you reach the end of our country,' Carl-Gunnar told me, 'think of that. Lots of folk don't understand how great is Norrland – our Northland.'

I perhaps had been one of these. I could, truth to tell, hardly think of what we were travelling through as a legal part of any country at all, as belonging to a proper earthly nation. Soap-opera characters apart, whoever could live here? Whoever – for I didn't know whether I liked what I was seeing, indeed suspected I didn't – whoever would *want* to?

'There are animals here?' I asked incredulously, despite my knowledge.

'Elk, lynx, bear,' Carl-Gunnar says. As follower of the soap I scarcely needed to be told this, I'd seen these creatures enough times on my screen, but then… that wasn't the same, this wasn't screen.

To dissipate a distinct rise of panic I cast my mind back to episodes of the past season. 'Elk,' I said, 'any chance of seeing an elk now?' I asked.

Carl-Gunnar turned his head to give me a quick appraising look, 'Well, not in the morning,' he answered, 'but – later, at night-time, when I drive you back to Östersund… yes. Then I could *guarantee* it.'

My hosts had been emphatic that I couldn't stay in Sjöbyn that night – their quarters not big enough, and there was nowhere for me in the village. I'd have to go back to Östersund for the evening; a hotel had been found and booked for me there. Not for the first time I wondered about the personnel I was to meet at my destination, and who had so far proved very efficient; Anna and Agneta, both in PR, would perhaps be more hostesses than staff proper and as such would be appropriate for showing me the real-life locations and answering my questions.

Fearful for some reason of inquiring about these unnamed others, I continued to Carl-Gunnar: 'It'd be terrific to see elk off-screen. Something to make me look forward to our journey back.'

And I re-applied myself to the country through which we were passing. Odd but true to think that just to walk off into the tree-dark territory on either hand could – and after not too long a while *would* – bring me death. The snow was now apparently between six and ten feet deep, and in some places considerably deeper. The whole land was possessed by silence; the Volvo's forward movement was a kind of gentle humming violation of this. Gentle because the quiet was so much more powerful than anything even so capable and strong a human as Carl-Gunnar could offer. Full daylight was still some hours away, but as we went on I was aware of a thin preparatory envelope to the east (our right) being, as it were, slowly pushed through a narrow slit between land and sky. Meanwhile the dark awning over much of the white road was being regularly relieved; breaking into the forest and opening us travellers up to light and space were – lakes (or was it different arms of but one lake?). Their frozen surfaces I could see were covered with snow pure and trackless and glowing up towards the sky.

'That's a whole chain of lakes that goes all the way up to the high mountains in Norway,' observed Carl-Gunnar.

The noiselessness, the loneliness, the stillness of the landscape all but overcame me. I tried to make conversation with Carl-Gunnar, asking him questions about his life. He grew up, he informed me, in Sjöbyn, a community of only 100 or so inhabitants. (Imagine that – out in this desert, a mere hundred people.) Before making a living as a driver, he'd worked in the forest, for a lumber-company (I shuddered to think of story-parallels here – would he have known those who'd hacked the Swedish equivalent of Kevin O'Flynn to death?), sleeping out night after night in a trailer. Experiences of his, and advice based on them, had been, he said with pride, very useful to the writers and producers of the programme I admired so much. He was, he told me, a man of the *North* rather than someone of any particular nationality, closer to 'neighbours' in Norway (his sister was married to a Norwegian) than to people in Stockholm. (He pronounced the name of that handsome city with something like contempt.)

'And that's Norway over there!' he remarked and pointed to a dramatic black line to the north-west.

I couldn't altogether stifle the feeling that this was a journey that admitted of no end. Not that we were going to cross that spine-like rise of mountains that was the Swedish-Norwegian border. It would be a permanent goal for a permanent quest; *Northlands* and its team were a chimera...

I tilted my head back – partly to ease that crick in the neck – and within seconds a light sleep fell on me. I awoke and fell asleep again repeatedly during the next half-hour, it reminded me of a child playing irritatingly with a window-blind. In one of the little sleeps I dreamed of Tanbury again, of that terrace-house there and of Ian and Auntie Eileen. This time she was not receiving me but lying in bed, dying of cancer which had spread from the lymphatic glands all over her body, including her liver, so her skin yellowed, her panting tongue virtually yellowed, her eyeballs shiningly yellowed, and beside her was Ian, kneeling at her side, weeping. This was a scene from life. But not one I had seen.

Of course Sjöbyn did appear at last, and even though it does have only one hundred inhabitants, it's a palpable place with an identity, and looked it. The timber house accommodating the *Northlands* staff was painted the traditional Swedish deep red and stood high, very high, above the road. You looked up and saw how the red glow of its walls and the shimmer from its lit-up windows illuminated the whole sheer bank of snow on which it appeared to be perched. Impossible even for Carl-Gunnar's winter-wheeled Volvo to make the ascent to the front door (a snowmobile could have managed it, however) so, bidding goodbye to the young man until the evening, I made a slow, extremely cold, unaided way, travelling-bag in hand, up the steep, icy, slippery track. But about half-way through this ascent the door ahead of me opened – to my great relief – and in the gap this created two figures appeared, and waved encouragingly at me. Further and needed light was now cast downwards towards me, and the climb became a little easier, but how piercing the below-freezing temperature! The two women – the one very tall, the other really quite short – stood there, very straight of posture, like angels before St Peter's Gate, but ones with amiably waving hands, and – as I could before long discern – smiles on their tanned faces. Here beyond doubt were Anna and Agneta.

'Welcome to Sjöbyn!' they were crying out, 'we are so very pleased that you have come successfully through your long, long journey!'

I felt the hero of some folk-tale who'd accomplished some set feat. Well, perhaps I was, and had.

'And we have a good breakfast waiting for you.'

'Wonderful!' I managed, breathless and resting a hand on the door-posts.

'A Swedish breakfast, and an English one rolled into one!'

'Wonderful!' I gasped again.

And the tall woman and the short one giggled archly in unison.

They shut the door on the still dark early morning. I had come into a capacious hall-cum-kitchen. A large tiled stove was giving out welcome heat – my face smarted after the exposure to the air – and near it, charmingly set out, was a table on which breakfast things were immaculately arranged. 'The plan is that you eat, taking your time, and then the men will be ready for you. The whole day has been organised most carefully.'

'Kind, really very kind!'

'So now – eat, Bruno, eat, drink and – be merry!'

This last was not really possible because in their slightly coy way Anna (from Östersund) and Agneta (from 'a long way from here, from our beautiful university city of Uppsala') were grave persons who clearly didn't care to waste words, and were besides almost pathologically deferential (so it seemed to me) to their bosses who awaited me on the other side of now closed doors. But as for the eating and drinking, the meal will rank as one of the most delicious I've ever been given – a bowl of soured cream sprinkled with cinnamon, a glass of freshly squeezed orange juice, a boiled egg with toast to cut into 'soldiers', and warm, light cardamom buns or *buller*, with, to accompany all this, marvellous coffee of the preferred Swedish kind, therefore very strong, very dark.

But the meal went on too long, much too long. I sat at the breakfast table in this pleasing, comfortable but lifeless kitchen for an hour and a quarter. After a while Anna and Agneta didn't concern themselves any more about making conversation, and every so often one of the pair would leave the room 'to see if the men were ready yet' and to return with an apologetic negative shake of the head. The feeling of unreality I'd had during the journey returned; for all the bodily well-being bestowed by breakfast I began to experience a definite disquiet. This was an odd way to treat a special guest, who'd been more than once assured of the pleasure his visit would give the company, was it not? And the term 'the men' acquired an ominous quality, as though it were some tribe, or band of hunters, I was soon (or not so soon) to confront.

Anna – or was it Agneta? – switched on a radio but this, far from alleviating it, only increased the eerie quality of my wait. The voices coming into the room now were, naturally enough, all Swedish ones, all, male or female, delivering their incomprehensible words in an up-and-down rhythm yet in tones that contrived, despite this, to sound expressionless. Never had I felt so far away from anywhere familiar, and indeed I had never been to a place so isolated from others.

I found myself longing for Cassie. As I hadn't for years.

Eventually Agneta, – or was it Anna? – seeing me glance pointedly at the brass-cased clock, left the room yet again. But this time when, after three or four minutes' absence, she came back, it was not to shake her head but to say: 'The men will see you now. I'm to show you in.'

Those 'men' again!

Good heavens, who *do* they think they are? I exclaimed to myself.

Yes, *Northlands* is a great programme, but is there any need for its makers to give themselves *quite* such airs. It isn't the Prime Minister of Sweden that I'm going to see.

I followed Agneta (I think it was her) as she flung open the most centrally-placed of the hall doors into a large room containing a large table.

And now it was all I could do not to stumble forward in a faint for there, sitting at the table's head, was my cousin, Ian Armitage, and on his left, with his back to the windows, was my old friend, Neil Micklewright.

'Well, how d'you rate *that* for an entrance, Neil?' Ian asked my friend (and therefore looking away from me) 'pretty hammy, huh?'

'Made by one of the cast, I'd say it'd have to be done *again*,' Neil said, and he wasn't smiling.

'So what are you saying then, Neil? That he should be asked to go out and then come back a second time? Like for a retake.'

'Nah!' said Neil, 'waste of fucking time. Might as well proceed with the job, man. Get it over and done with. We both know it's not going to be pleasant.'

I was asking myself: had I, somewhere in my being, *known* I would be facing my cousin (and even my old friend) up here? Surely not! How could I? Yet I was now possessed not so much by astonishment as by a sense of the grim inevitability of the situation.

Ian had put on weight since I'd last seen him. His face, now florid in complexion, was decidedly jowly, this feature emphasized by his rich morning crop of dark stubble; his stomach hung somewhat over his belted jeans – though to be fair to him I regularly saw many worse instances of such middle-age spread. He still had a good head of hair too, but his Murillo-like curly-top was more iron-grey than the black of the old days. And he was wearing gold-rimmed glasses which tempered his even now boyish appearance by endowing it with a disconcerting severity.

If Ian had expanded, Neil, in contrast, had shrunk, or so his slightly bent frame suggested. No flesh on his triangular face, and his cheeks had even hollowed a little, though this didn't give him the gaunt expression you might have expected, rather it heightened the brilliance of those only too familiar narrow light blue eyes.

On sudden fire with blushes, like a schoolboy caught cheating in an examination (as indeed at Riverbury I had been), I didn't know where to look – the saying being given an appalling literal truth – yet also the pair held my gaze magnetically, as if I were being presented with the stare of gone-by time itself. As, in a sense, of course, was the case.

Ian peered over his gold-rims at me. 'Your old mate's being magnanimous,' he said, 'more than *I'd* be, left to myself, I don't mind admitting – but I always respect Neil's opinion. As *you* did at one time, I gather. Especially over the matter of ditching poor old Charles Compson. *Matter*, please note, not *manner*. Anyway, to get to business... Take a pew, as you once said to me (you may remember), when about to confess to a peculiarly dirty weekend away from Tanbury.'

This was appalling beyond bad dreams. 'What *is* all this?' I protested wanly, helplessly, 'I don't get it at all.'

'You were always several apples short of a picnic,' Neil said, 'so your failure to understand's scarcely surprising.'

What could I do but pull out a chair to sit down on? The room, painted off-white all over with gilt edging where possible, was of generous proportions – far more generous than the house's exterior would at a casual glance promise. As for the table that virtually filled it, it must have been designed for board meetings of *Northlands Enterprises*; it seemed to me that I looked down an immense length to meet the gaze of these two from my past, of Anna and Agneta's 'men'.

'Why are you *treating* me like this?' I heard myself say, bewilderedly, piteously, 'I'm Bruno Armitage. Bruno Armitage, *Northlands* fan whom you've both known for... for yonks.'

The two, each turning his head towards the other, exchanged glances; they were having a joke at my expense, with their eyes. In the ensuing pause I was aware of much else in the room besides them – the large state-of-the-art computer on its own table by the windows; the windows themselves, three of them, ceiling-to-floor and double-glazed; the vivid red hangings patterned with animal designs (Sami?) on the wall opposite me; the mounted photos of *Northlands* characters, among whom I saw (well, how could they not be there?) Erik, Pelle, Lars-Anders – so many that I was surprised when from one of the pair words issued.

'Well, *fuck* me if that's who you aren't. And there was I thinking you were someone quite different,' jeered Neil, 'Bruno Armitage as I live or die! You know *us*, I take it? Neil Micklewright, drinking buddy from the good old days.' He turned his head again to my cousin, 'and Ian, *you'd* better introduce yourself too. You *are* his flesh-and-blood relation after all.'

I broke in, my voice both louder and higher-pitched than I'd intended (could Anna and Agneta in the hall-kitchen hear me, and how much had they known about this ordeal so obviously planned to take place?) 'Stop all this please. Of course I know who Ian is. I don't see why, or how, I've been lured all this way up here.....'

'To a godforsaken wilderness were you going to say?' Neil finished for me, smilingly, 'and there was I thinking you a real "Northie".'

'I've gone to quite a deal of trouble and paid quite a bit of money to visit the wilderness, so I don't think you can attack me *there*!' I replied, stung.

'Spoken like a true-blue Englishman,' said Neil, 'we're famous all over Europe for wanting our money's worth. But you must know that in the antiques business. Mr Bruno Armitage of 'Treasure Trove', entrepreneur.'

Ian leaned back in his chair and tilted it, in careless schoolboy manner. 'Come on, Neil,' he said, 'don't let's take the piss out of the poor bastard any more. I reckon we've got our effects now, made our point, haven't we?'

'Point?' I repeated. What was that? That – there could be no escaping the strange fact – that these guys hated me, yes, really *hated* me. How ironic that earlier fantasy of mine that Ian and Neil might take pity on me in my depression.

Neil was now saying, mockingly: 'Better put our minds at rest, Bruno, old bean, did you have a good breakfast?'

'Very!' I mumbled. I took a hold of myself; I was a man of some standing, and one of the pair in front of me was my junior: 'Had I known I was going to be the victim of some weird joke immediately afterwards, I don't suppose I'd have enjoyed the meal so much.'

'Not a joke, Bruno, not a joke at all...'

But my retort – or rather my ability to retort – had given me just a smidgen of strength:

'So why don't both of you come clean and tell me what the hell's going on?'

'Yes, it *is* time now!' said Ian, 'it is time. You see, Bruno, when we found out you were a fan of the programme and wanted to visit its location, it seemed too good a chance for us not to take. Fortune had played you into our hands.'

'We couldn't contain our pleasure,' Neil said, 'peeing in our pants at the very thought of your little trip up here, weren't we, Ian? At long last, we said to ourselves, the bastard can hear what we've been thinking of him all these years.'

'What *is* this, a kangaroo court?' I cried out.

'Something like that,' Neil agreed.

And outside the window it was still dark, and still snowing, but shapes were beginning to clarify over on what I knew to be the Norwegian border, and menacing shapes they seemed too; this had to be one of the most hostile corners of our entire continent, yet hadn't *Northlands* already told me that?

'We've both wanted for so long to make you realise what you are.'

'*What?*' I lowered my gaze, '*what* am I?'

'Devious!' Ian said.

'Selfish!' Neil said.

'Stuck up!' Ian added.

'And much worse!' said Neil.

I now had nothing to lose in finding a voice: 'But you haven't told me how I come to be here listening to you both saying these – these horrible things,' I was able to protest.

'You've taken so little interest in my affairs over the years,' Ian said, 'I don't expect you've a fucking clue what it is I do, what,' he corrected himself with a mirthless little smile, 'what it is *Neil and I* do. But it's important for you to take it in now if you're to understand how you're up here. Undergoing a trial.'

'You'd better tell me,' I said.

It was true, of course: I hadn't followed Ian's life at all keenly, not since Auntie Eileen's tragically early death (she'd died before I'd been able to visit her) and the end of his Tanbury home. Ian hadn't gone to university but had joined a Birmingham newspaper as what used to be called a 'cub-reporter'; his work had always, my mind went vague here, been connected with the media, if not on a paper than in some sort of other way. He'd married at age thirty, a languid-looking Spanish girl with large moist near-black eyes, but the marriage hadn't been a success, and the two of them had parted, without children, after seven years. (I remembered the length of time, because, unusually, Ian had visited us in Walnut Tree House to tell us his news. 'It's sad, and it isn't sad!' he'd said, 'know what I mean, Bruno. I wasn't cut out to be a Rev. Derek Parker, but I'd have liked some of *those...*' he'd gestured here to our children – well, to Rod and Amy, Lucas wasn't yet born. 'Oh, well,' I'd replied, not wanting an emotional familial conversation, 'there's still a lot of time ahead.' His counteracting look had disconcerted me. 'Not for me there isn't!' he'd said, 'not for me!' He'd turned out right.')

As for Neil, I knew – or, more accurately, now remembered –that he had become a friend of my cousin's; in fact it was I who'd introduced them at one of the rough-and-ready family-style buffets Cassie and I'd given during the early years of our marriage, when we were still living in London. Neil gave up acting soon after the Tom Cavan débacle, but, true to his background, did a BBC training course in camera-work, and, after that, was for years a member of staff associated particularly with travel programmes. I hadn't been interested to find out more. (And why should I have been, after all? *He* had never inquired after the fortunes of 'Treasure Trove', let alone bought any of the items it deals in.) Personally (as I recalled) Neil's life had been successful enough (and mine *hadn't* been?) – a wife, Annie, and more kids than most people had nowadays, five, was it? or six.....

'Tell me,' I repeated, 'I can hardly acquire the information through osmosis.'

'We're media consultants,' Ian said, 'Neil, myself, and a third guy, Charles, who's in London; he didn't come with us here this time. When I was a full-time journalist, I spent most of my time covering media events – particularly radio, TV, and films and the personalities connected with them. So I became something of an expert. Then came the period when I wanted to set up on my own, and – as good luck would have it – this coincided with the time when old Neil here wanted to branch out from the Beeb into something new. He felt he'd done his full stint behind the cameras himself in strange quarters of the globe.'

'You could say we're in one now!' I couldn't help saying. For what could be stranger than that gaunt line of mountains preparing for the sun on the opposite side of the valley to this house, or than the huge snowbanks surrounding it?

'You could, but we're in it on our own terms, aren't we? we don't stay up here so very long, do we, Neil? we don't *live* here.' They both chuckled at the very idea of this, and I had a swift, unpleasant, not to say alarming vision of their announcing by-and-by, when this 'court' was over, that they were off – back to our own England – leaving me here, to fend for myself up in sub-Arctic Sjöbyn as best I could. But no, Carl-Gunnar had been adamant that he would drive me back to Östersund this evening.

'Neil and I formed a company, and we get called in when a programme, or even just a project, needs outside advice, has gone stale on itself, requires assessment of its personnel, or just an injection of fresh ideas...'

Having launched himself into it, Ian proceeded to go on in this style for a surprising while, Neil chipping in (not always too shortly) every so often. Talking about their work, increasingly in the idiom and tone of voice they would have used to potential clients, relaxed the two of them – so it seemed to me – as if the very thought of their history of success temporarily checked their anger towards me. I can't say I listened to all the details they were now pleased to give me, but I did grasp the essentials of what they were telling me, and saw quickly enough how I fitted into it. *Northlands* had called in *GoodIdeas.com* (Armitage, Micklewright and Clapton) because – just as I, the programme's addict, had realised only too clearly – it'd got into 'a bad patch'. Ingrid, one of the principal script-writers, had broken off an affair with another of them, Ingvar, a talented up-and-coming young man, who in his distress

215

at rejection had let his work suffer, before undergoing a clinical break-down. The actress who played Ulla (that wonderful Ulla) had had to drop everything to look after a dying father. There'd been difficulty too with an important sponsor, something which had affected the whole team's morale and creativity. So, it had been felt, outsiders should be consulted, and, for objectivity's sake, better outsiders from England than from Sweden. Now, of course, everything made sense. The suggestions that Neil and Ian had made for story-lines had to come from somewhere; it just happened that in this case (apparently, though, never before) they'd decided to draw on *The Parkers* which, obviously, they both knew well. So I hadn't been a neurotic paranoid, I'd just recognised situations with personal significance when that radio programme had been part of my emotional life... 'Of course,' said Ian, 'we'd no idea that one Mr Bruno Armitage would be a "Northie".'

'Not that we gave the matter much thought,' said Neil characteristically.

'Well, it did cross my mind, Neil,' said Ian – they'd clearly had this talk before, 'but then I thought: so Bruno might recognise a *Parkers* situation in disguise. So what? So fucking what? So we pressed ahead.'

'But when you e-mailed our website,' it was Neil who was tilting back in his chair now, 'what a laugh! fuck, what a laugh! And then when you made your little proposal to come up to Sjöbyn....' And laughter appeared to be still the order of the day.

For him. Not for Ian. He took off his gold-rims and, leaning forward, elbows on the table, said: 'Let's get to the nitty-gritty. Bruno, you *did* something to me that I've never got over: you *betrayed* me, and my mother too, in such a way that it's scarred me for life. Mum took you in when it was felt that was what you needed, and I for my part was really pleased at having an older male about the place. I admired you, Christ knows why, even wrote an essay for my English teacher saying so. But you – you looked down on us, for the way we lived, the way we spoke, our tastes, but we pretended not to notice; you could be charming as well. We introduced you to *The Parkers*, and it filled an empty place in your life. And then things took off....'

'Thanks to a coincidence!' I interrupted, 'thanks to a coincidence over which I had no control.' And I gave them the details of it, smarting though I was from these sentences of Ian's 'judgement', but what I said had, I could tell, little impact: presumably they knew it all already.

'A coincidence you made ruthless use of. You went behind our backs, Mum's and mine, lied to us, and then – it can still hurt even today – you tried to use me, *me* in all my then innocence, to cover up your furtive sordid little indiscretions. *Shit*, even giving all this back to you makes me want to spew up.'

'I'm sorry,' I found myself whispering, 'I'm sorry, Ian.'

'You're so ignorant, Bruno, so fucking ignorant!' Neil told me, 'let's move to myself for a moment. You never asked yourself questions about me, about what had got me so important a part on *The Parkers*, what had led to my being Tom Cavan. Let me give you some overdue information. Dad was in the BBC, wasn't he? He *knew* Verity and Charles. They both "took to" me, strange as that might seem. I was your sodding *predecessor* in their smoochy affections, Bruno, and it never so much as crossed your mind.'

'I'm sorry!' I said again. It must have been hard to hear me, so low was my voice. But it *had* once crossed my mind, I recalled.

'Sorry, my arse! I wonder if you've ever been sorry for *any*thing you've done to *any*body. I tell you, my friend – and I was no saint in those days myself – when the two of us called on our way back from Ireland on Ian and his mother in Tanbury, and I saw your disgusting misplaced condescension, why, it was all I could do not to kick you hard in the gorbals on the spot. It wasn't as if –' He stopped.

'As if?' I asked. I could, after all, hear nothing worse than I had already.

'*You* put him in the picture, Ian,' said Neil, 'it's *your* business more than mine.'

'Yes, you tell me, Ian,' I said, 'Ian, I was probably all you say I was – but there *were* times when we got on together, weren't there? You'd refer to me as "my cousin the writer".'

Unexpectedly, at this point, the two men burst into laughter. It was the harsh, uncomfortable laughter of some *Northlands* animal, wolf or lynx, I thought.

'What's up?' I inquired, with a stab of fear, 'is it something I've just said?'

'Ian, it's now or never!' directed Neil.

Ian gulped before speaking: ' "My cousin the writer",' he echoed, 'well, the fact is, you're *not* my cousin, Bruno. I must confess I didn't know this until that horrible day of the Great Row about your visit to Dorset; Mum told me that very night, in my bedroom in confidence. You're not my cousin, you're my brother. Or to be properly accurate, my *half*-brother. My dad and your mum – my foolish dad and your foolish mum – had an off-and-on affair for years, and *you* were the result. Uncle Raymond knew the truth, of course. In fact the only key person in the drama who didn't was yourself.'

I put my head in my hands. 'Cassie,' I said, 'Cassie, I want you here so much.'

'Kangaroo court over,' Ian was saying, 'and we do have a programme planned for you as a *Northlands* admirer, Bruno, believe it or not. I think you'll be interested: you'll meet cast and some members of the camera-crew. Weather always permitting.'

It was still snowing, but dawn was visible.

Of course I was interested in the day's meetings, and of course treasured moments of *Northlands* acquired a new reality for me. I even saw – and rode in – a snowmobile. After the arranged kangaroo court, here (I supposed) was the arranged forgiveness. But I couldn't feel it. I was consumed with guilt and a feeling that I myself had been betrayed – and that I'd been stripped of the greater part of my identity. Not perhaps that it was worth all that much......

I was glad when it was time to leave. I was glad to see Carl-Gunnar again and then to embark on our long journey back to Östersund. The silence, repose and darkness of the forest were, if anything, even more overpowering than on our way out, but now I almost welcomed them. No slit of incoming light to herald the relief of daybreak but instead an austerely beautiful moon, which seemed to have drawn to itself the cold of this land below it. If I could extend a hand to touch it, I thought, my palm would come back filmed with ice.

So full of emotion was I, so shattered by Neil's and Ian's vision of me and their revelations, that I felt robbed of thoughts – none anyway that I could cope with. I was a travelling creature, little more – and probably my only course for the time being was to try, with difficulty, to accept this. But when I got back to England, I would try, for my own peace of mind, to write the story down of my sad doomed involvement with *The Parkers*. That would be my occupation for the century, the millennium ahead......

Every now and again Carl-Gunnar would say: 'You wanted to see elk. *Here* might be a place. *Here's* where elk often are.'

But tonight it wasn't so. At intervals, though, we saw prints, large two-toe prints – elk were in the vicinity.

Elk are solitary animals, herbivorous, feeding (in winter) off shoots of trees which their great height enables them to reach, and (in summer) off water-plants in the forest marshes and ponds. Their life-span is twenty years, quite often more. During the mating season (September/October) the males will fight for the cows, but it's a ritual fight with antlers; usually no damage is inflicted. At such times the males give bellowing calls which the females will answer from deeper in the forest.

Because I sensed Carl-Gunnar's increasing disappointment at my possible disappointment (there, I *was/am* capable of kindly appreciation of others), I kept a conversation going. What did he do these winter evenings? Well, obviously, most evenings he was out with his snowmobile!! He spoke too of his own relationship to the moon, so bright tonight; when the moon was full, he couldn't sleep, felt possessed of strange unconquerable energy, just as he was when the Northern Lights were bright in the sky.

So many worlds, one no more or less real than another, Greenfield End, Tanbury, The Puzzle, Walnut Tree House, Sjöbyn. But they interlocked.

And then – we were into our second hour of travel – Carl-Gunnar took one hand off the steering-wheel and briefly touched my arm. He'd caught sight of an elk, and drew my attention to him. 'He's quite a young one. Look at him up there on the bank.' I now had no difficulty in descrying him; high above the thin frozen road to which he now began slowly but gracefully to descend. And in our direction. Carl-Gunnar slowed the car down. The elk jumped. He landed on the

219

roadway. For our part we drove on for a few yards, and then stopped.

The night in all its great quietness was all at once intensely a presence, more, a personality in itself. Splashed by moonlight the elk was walking away from us down the white road with a lovely dignity of gait. Carl-Gunnar, a real *Northlands* man, got out of the car.

The cold struck at one cruelly; it was hard to stand up against it. Carl-Gunnar was moving in the direction of the elk with a stealth that revealed how, ever since boyhood, he'd been developing his kinship with the denizens of his region. He halted, and cupped his mouth with his hands to deliver himself of hallooing calls which in truth sounded more animal than human.

And now it was the elk himself who halted. He turned round. Muscular, tall, potentially dangerous, he was already a formidable creature. But I – I felt no threat at all. I had been threatened all day, tomorrow I would return to Stockholm, then to England, and – maybe my work on *The Parkers* would, bit by bit, take some of the pain of this dreadful northern day away from me. But maybe not.

Meanwhile there was only this encounter with a wild animal to assert reality. I had an instant but deep sense of rightness and peace. The face the elk presented to Carl-Gunnar and me in this forest night was one of the most tremendous gentleness.

For a full list of our publications please write to

Dewi Lewis Publishing
8 Broomfield Road
Heaton Moor
Stockport SK4 4ND

You can also visit our web site at

www.dewilewispublishing.com

Other titles available from Dewi Lewis Publishing

Longlisted for the Booker Prize

WOLFY AND THE STRUDELBAKERS
Zvi Jagendorf
£8.99, ISBN:1-899235-38-8

'Rightly included among the Naipauls and the McEwans on the Booker Long List; it would be a small travesty if Wolfy did not inveigle his way at least into the final six.' – The Observer

'A most impressive novel full of narrative power and unforgettable description.' – Jewish Chronicle

'Astonishing finesse.' – The Guardian

'A quiet gem... good humour and high quality writing.'
– The Daily Telegraph

'The delight is in the comic detail, even when the matter is serious.'
– The Times

Set in wartime and post-war England Wolfy and the Strudelbakers is a comic take on the disaster zone of displacement and exile. Wolfy lives with the 'strudelbakers' – his super-critical aunt and melancholy uncle – in the surrealistic world of refugees granted shelter from persecution. He is an expert at living in two cultures – the chaotic, dark world of uprooted people desperately hanging on to their Jewish religion – and the vitality, variety and temptation he finds in London's streets.

Wolfy observes it all with a sharp eye; the bafflement of his English neighbours at the odd, secretive nature of his Jewish family and their comical habits as they reluctantly learn to stop being 'aliens' and discover England through blitz, evacuation, menial work, school reports, team sports and Christmas. For Wolfy everything is new and exciting. He is a success as a budding Englishman. He lives near Arsenal Football Club, practises ballroom dancing with the help of the BBC and, of course, he is getting ready for girls.

❖ ❖ ❖

Shortlisted for the Booker Prize

THE INDUSTRY OF SOULS
Martin Booth
£6.99, ISBN:1-899235-51-5

Arrested for spying in the early 1950s and presumed dead by the British Government, Alexander Bayliss survives 20 years in a Soviet labour camp. Eventually freed, he has no reason to return to the West. Now, on his 80th birthday Russia is changed. Communism has evaporated and he must now make a choice, perhaps for the first time in his life...

> *'Beg, steal, borrow or buy this book. I'm not exaggerating, he really is that good.'* – Sunday Star-Times, New Zealand

> *'His description of the death-trap mine is genuinely scary... a good read.'* – Ian Thomson, The Daily Telegraph

> *'Booth's spare, unexaggerated style makes his description of Sosnogorsklag 32, the camp in which (Bayliss) is incarcerated, powerful and stark.'* – Erica Wagner, The Times

From the Winner of the 1999 London Writers' Award

DEPTH OF FIELD
Sue Hubbard
£8.99, ISBN:1-899235-82-5

> *'A very remarkable first novel.'* – John Berger
> *'Lyrical, highly visual, beautifully observed.'* – John Burnside

Depth of Field is an acute observation of the nature of memory and identity. Having grown up with her Jewish identity submerged, Hannah experiences a deep sense of alienation. After her marriage falls apart she returns to London's East End in search of her roots and to work as a photographer. A failed affair, a breakdown, and a lost custody battle for her children, leave her alone to discover her own way to reconstruct her life.

A FUNNY OLD YEAR
Alan Brownjohn
£8.99, ISBN:1-899235-38-8

'A fast moving, dryly amusing tale…Brownjohn's latest effort comes highly recommended' – Time Out

'An adroit comedy of manners… it is a lovely piece of characterisation full of sharp insights.' – The Daily Telegraph

Mike Barron is not as young as he was – though he's not quite ready to accept it. Fifty eight years old, in early retirement, and showing all the signs of late middle age, he still manages to deceive himself into believing that he can attract women.

But when the husband of his long-term lover Rosie dies he finds himself having to decide whether the affair should end and marriage begin. His answer is escape – a trial separation in a seemingly quiet seaside town.

And so he begins a very strange and eventful year; a year in which to decide whether he really is grown up enough to face responsibility.

This is poet Alan Brownjohn's third novel. *The Way You Tell Them* won the Authors' Club Award for best first novel of its year. His second, *The Long Shadows*, was hailed as the best fiction to come out of the 1989-90 changes in Eastern Europe and described as 'a consummate literary thriller'.